The Swansea Marina Murders

Stephen Puleston

ABOUT THE AUTHOR

Stephen Puleston was born and educated in Ynys Môn, North Wales. He graduated in theology before training as a lawyer. The Swansea Marina Murders is the first novel in the Inspector Caren Waits series.

www.stephenpuleston.co.uk
Facebook:stephenpulestoncrimewriter

OTHER NOVELS
Inspector Drake Mysteries

There are twelve novels and a prequel novella in this series. Full details are available on Stephen Puleston's website below.
https://www.stephenpuleston.co.uk/ian-drake/

Inspector Marco Novels

There are five novels and a prequel novella in this series. Full details are available on Stephen Puleston's website below.
https://www.stephenpuleston.co.uk/john-marco/

Copyright © 2025 Highgate Publishing Limited
All rights reserved.

ISBN: 9798294677244

In memory of my mother
Gwenno Puleston

Chapter 1

Emily Hughes convinced herself that nothing bad ever happened in Swansea Marina. But she couldn't shake off a sense of foreboding as she made her way along the quayside. There had been an argument in the bar earlier that evening and now she regretted intervening between the two men involved. Had one of them followed her?

She glanced over her shoulder. But nobody was pursuing her, so the niggling sense of unease dissipated slightly. Perhaps it was the chilly night air that was unsettling her. There had been a recent newspaper report about attacks on young women in the city centre at night. She was convinced she could take care of herself and believed she would be safe in a well-lit public area once she left the marina. She toyed with the idea of paying for a taxi to take her home – just in case.

Both the local press and radio station had made a lot of the attacks. One programme had included a discussion between one of their broadcasters and a woman police officer who reassured the listeners that the Wales Police Service was doing everything it could. Emily walked on and skirted around the base of a block of flats, passing closed shop units. Since it was dark, she felt tempted to retrieve her mobile from her jacket pocket and use the torch function. As the way out of the marina and back to her flat was one that she had done many times, she didn't bother.

Even so, she picked up her pace slightly.

When she reached the corner of one building on her route, a person ran towards her. Her heart raced and her body tensed. He dodged past her, apologising for giving her a fright. He bustled on towards the marina and she looked towards the direction he had come from and saw the car park. Nobody runs along the marina quayside at this time at night, she said to herself, so she stood for a few moments looking at the man as he disappeared into the distance. She had never seen him before and perhaps he didn't know his way or was delayed for a yacht taking advantage of the tide to get out of the harbour. She had heard lots of sailors making comments about catching the tide.

Her body relaxed when she realised he had vanished from sight, so she resumed her journey. Ahead of her was another block of apartments. Well-off owners of expensive yachts in the marina had purchased most of them. She envied any family rich enough to afford a second home like that.

She didn't think she'd ever be able to afford such a luxury. Even though she knew it was probably foolish to think that anybody would hear her if she were attacked, the lights in the upper floors provided her with a feeling of safety.

She pressed on to the edge of the far side of the marina. It was a sheer drop to the water below, so she edged away from the quayside and pondered whether there was a shortcut that she could take towards the road into the middle of town.

The shadows were deep while she navigated around a commercial building used at the marina. She didn't have time to see the barest movement behind her before it was too late. Something cold and metallic curled around her neck and immediately she reached her hand towards it. She made an effort to yank and pull at it but it was no good. Her fingers tugged at the wire and her nails scratched her skin.

It was being pulled ever more tightly; she couldn't understand what was happening. She struggled to grasp at whatever it was. But the person was strong, too strong for Emily.

She tried to move to glimpse her attacker. Then she felt her knees being kicked from behind and she fell to the ground. She wanted to scream, but no words came out. There was just pain, a tight searing pain.

And then nothing.

Chapter 2

Caren Waits woke to the sound of her young son, Aled, sleeping by her side. Leaving his own bed in the early hours and snuggling up with his mother was something he was an expert at. She hoped that once he was a little older – he'd be five in a couple of months' time – this would be a habit he'd grow out of. But for now she watched her son sleeping. She ran a hand over his hair, moving it away from his temple, and he stirred slightly.

It reminded Caren of Alun, Aled's father. It brought back fond memories of when they had been a family before his premature death in a car accident. But the more recent events came crowding into her mind. At the coroner's inquest, she knew she would have to face the woman who was alleging she had had a relationship with Alun. Once it was over, Caren could move on from Miss Hale's disruptive presence and focus on her own life.

Her late husband's involvement with this woman was unresolved in Caren's mind. The discovery that Alun had a child with Miss Hale had been startling, and one that Caren had found hard to deal with. She hadn't wanted to believe that Alun had been unfaithful to her, but the DNA evidence that he was the father of Miss Hales' daughter had been conclusive proof.

It had meant that Miss Hale and Alun's child – it was still painful for her to think of the situation in those terms – had a claim against his estate. The solicitors could handle it. Once settled, she'd be free from Miss Hale.

After her promotion to detective inspector, Caren had been determined that Alun would be proud of her, and that resolve continued after his death. Now she wanted to ensure that her son would be equally proud of her. Running her own team in Western Division of the Wales Police Service gave her an immense sense of pride and achievement.

She had carefully filed the letter the solicitors had written to her, confirming the prison sentence for the driver of the vehicle that caused her husband's death, with the other paperwork that was part of her life. She hadn't expected for one moment that things would become so complicated after his death. 'Why did he get involved with another woman?'

Would she trust another man ever again?

At least the driver who had caused Alun's death was safely locked up for several years. She had read the prosecution papers – sent to her as a courtesy to her professional status – but trying to read them as a detached detective had been impossible. Only a few pages in, her emotions took over and she had teared up.

Looking at her son sleeping quietly by her side, she knew she would never share with him the details of what had happened to his father. It was bad enough that Aled wouldn't know Alun. She was determined to make sure that her son knew she loved him and that his father had done so too. And now she had to face explaining to Aled that he had a sister – she had no idea how or when she would do that.

The remaining matter was the coroner's inquest. She had already notified Superintendent Brooks, her immediate superior, that she would have to attend the hearing in a little over a week's time in Cardiff.

Caren had decided she would instruct solicitors in Carmarthen to deal with any claim against Alun's estate from Miss Hale. She was fed up with having to consider travelling to North Wales for meetings with lawyers. And the smallholding she and Alun owned jointly was on the market. The estate agents had already told her she could expect viewings and offers reasonably quickly now that Easter was imminent.

The sound of the old malfunctioning boiler in the utility room downstairs firing up reminded her that the house where she was living wasn't hers. She resolved to speak to the estate agents again, to ask whether a further reduction in the asking price of the smallholding might be sensible. She really wanted to have her own place, preferably with a reliable boiler and heating system.

Once she had showered and dressed Aled in his school uniform they sat at the kitchen table eating breakfast. It was always a hurried affair. Caren indulged her son with his favourite orange-coloured cereal, and she was pleased he enjoyed the healthy snacks and pieces of fruit she packed into his school bag.

'Is Mamgu collecting me today?' Aled said, enquiring if his grandmother would be at the school gate.

'I should be there,' Caren said. She smiled at her son, knowing he enjoyed his time with her mother.

Kitchen table cleared of breakfast debris and the worktops given a cursory wipe, Caren bundled Aled into her car. It was a short drive through the town of Carmarthen and she drew up and parked a little distance from the school gate. She walked the short distance to the gate and watched as Aled joined his friends. As she turned to leave, she spotted her friend Susan Howard, a senior crime scene manager at Western Division headquarters, who was dropping her son Ieuan. Caren had struck up a close friendship with Susan since she had moved to Carmarthen and often relied on her to collect Aled if her mother wasn't able to do so.

It meant a lot to Caren to know he had some good friends among the boys in school. And she also valued her friendship with Susan, who knew all about the demands of working for the Wales Police Service. Their conversation was about the activities of their sons at school and their plans for the impending Easter holidays.

Once Caren was back in her car she drove to Western Division headquarters on the outskirts of the town. She parked and made her way into reception and then through the corridors to the open-plan offices her team used.

Detective Constables Rhys Davies and Alice Sharp acknowledged her presence with a simple 'Morning, boss' as she made her way towards her room. The sergeant in her team,

Huw Margam, hadn't yet arrived. Her superintendent had assigned her to take charge of an inquiry into a string of domestic burglaries where the officers had made little progress. It meant a pile of paperwork on her desk. Superintendent Brooks' comments about having a fresh pair of eyes had raised the bar of his expectation that she could achieve something where another team had failed.

After two high-powered investigations in the first few weeks of her appointment, she hadn't had the chance to get her office looking just so until recently. She had strategically positioned two pot plants on top of her small cupboard. They required very little attention other than occasional watering. She had carefully positioned three landscape paintings she and Alun had bought so that they could be seen from her desk.

The presence of her predecessor had been well and truly expunged from the room. She doubted it would be that easy to expel the shadow that he cast over her team. She heard Huw Margam arrive and moments later he appeared at the door to her office.

Since she had started working with Huw she had found him to be a solid and reliable sergeant. Although he was a university graduate and she was not, he had never made her feel inadequate. She hadn't found that to be the case with other officers she felt were jealous of her success.

She waved him into the room and pointed at one of the chairs by her desk.

He sat down and unbuttoned his jacket. He dressed sharply and the powder-blue shirt contrasted perfectly with the deep navy suit. He was in his early thirties, a few years younger than Caren. His thin lips and close-cropped curly hair gave him an intense appearance.

'Later this afternoon, the superintendent wants to review the progress we've been making with his outstanding burglary enquiries,' Caren said.

Huw nodded his understanding. 'I'll chase the forensic laboratories for an update.'

'Have we contacted all the witnesses from the initial investigation?'

'Rhys and Alice are working on finalising that today.'

The telephone on Caren's desk rang and she scooped up the handset while continuing to question Huw about progress.

'DI Caren Waits.'

'Morning, Caren.' She recognised the voice of Superintendent Brooks. She was about to tell him she would have an update of their progress in time for their meeting later, but he continued: 'I need you down in Swansea Marina. A body has been found floating in the water.'

Caren glanced at the folders on her desk. 'Could it be someone who accidentally fell in?'

'No chance – there are reports that the body has signs of ligature marks. So I need you and your team down there immediately. Reviewing those burglaries will have to wait.'

Caren stood up abruptly and her office chair crashed against the radiator behind her. She sensed her eyes widening and her eyebrows lifting as the excitement of a new inquiry burst into her mind.

Huw looked surprised, his brow furrowing.

The immediate priorities for the start of an inquiry buzzed through Caren's head. Has the scene been secured? Were there officers present? Were the CSIs en route?

Brooks went on: 'I want you down there as soon as you can. I'll make certain operational support send you all relevant information. So far as I'm aware there are two uniformed officers who have secured the scene. Don't delay, Caren.' He finished the call.

Caren turned to look at Huw and then shouted for Rhys Davies and Alice Sharp who arrived at her door seconds later.

'We need to get out to Swansea Marina – they've pulled a body out of the water.'

Chapter 3

Caren accelerated out of the car park at headquarters and then joined the A48. After a roundabout she negotiated her way onto the A40, a stretch of dual carriageway leading to the Pont Abraham roundabout where she'd join the M4.

Huw, sitting alongside her, had been busy on his mobile, relaying the information operational support had provided. Once he had tapped in the postcode for the Swansea Marina into the sat nav he announced, 'It should take us fifty minutes, boss.'

It was a warm spring morning, and luckily the traffic was light. Caren pressed on, flashing the car's headlights at vehicles dawdling in front of her. She knew that reaching the crime scene was her priority. The initial hours post-discovery of a body were crucial. They were vital for securing the scene, identifying possible suspects and persons of interest.

'Find out the CSI's status,' Caren said, avoiding eye contact with Huw. The dominating question in her mind was the length of time the body had spent in the water. Several hours may allow for recovery of relevant information, but days made establishing a time of death difficult.

'CSI team is right behind us,' Huw said. 'Apparently, Susan Howard's in charge.'

'Good.' Huw knew she and Susan were good friends, but more than that, they were effective colleagues. Susan Howard was just as dedicated as she was. She was thorough and committed.

'I'll try to find out if the pathologist is on his way too.'

Caren kept the vehicle in the outside lane of the M4 motorway, glancing occasionally at the speedometer keeping her speed under the limit. She didn't bother looking at the sat nav and relied on Huw to announce when they were likely to arrive at the marina.

'Making good time, boss,' Huw said.

'Tell Rhys and Alice to direct the uniformed officers at

the scene. And for them to find out who is in charge of the marina. There must be a manager or a harbour master.'

Caren paid little attention to Huw as he made the calls. She was more intent on driving safely. Their progress slowed once they had left the M4 motorway and Caren's frustration bubbled to the surface - she flashed the car's headlights to clear cars in her path. Occasionally, she had to resort to using the car horn.

When they arrived Caren spotted a uniformed officer standing by a marked police vehicle, its hazard lights flashing, making certain that members of the public were kept well away. She parked nearby and when the officer gave her a quizzical look, she produced her warrant card, as did Huw. The officer pointed towards two other officers at the top of a ramp that led from the quayside down onto pontoons.

As they walked over, Caren spotted another uniformed officer on the opposite side of the quay, ushering away onlookers.

Huw joined Caren as she flashed her warrant card at them.

'Two officers at the scene, ma'am,' the older constable stated. 'And you need a code for the security gate.'

Caren nodded. She tapped the number the officer had given her into the keypad, and the gate swung open on its pneumatic hinges.

Their footsteps clattered on the pontoon as they followed the route towards the location of both officers.

'There are lots of swanky yachts and motor boats here,' Huw said.

'Have you ever done any sailing?'

'It's a rich man's sport and you need deep pockets for this sort of hobby.'

Caren scanned the various yachts and motorboats moored up at the pontoons, but she could see no sign of activity. Perhaps it was too early in the morning and she guessed the sailing season wouldn't properly start until after

Easter.

Both police officers standing there looked pleased when they saw Caren and Huw arriving.

'Where is the body?' Caren said.

One officer tipped his head towards a section of the pontoon. 'She's over there.'

Caren followed the officer and stopped when she spotted the body of a woman, her clothes caught in the pontoon's construction itself.

'Who found the body?' Caren looked up at the quayside above her.

'It was one of the boat owners. He was coming to prepare his yacht for the season.'

Caren turned to look at the body, and after she knelt she could see a deep wound around the neck. 'Where is he now?'

'He is on his boat. We've got the details and we've told him not to leave until he's spoken to you.'

Caren got back to her feet. 'We'll need the CSI to get her body onto the pontoons urgently.'

Then she spotted Susan Howard hurrying towards the ramp down onto the pontoons with a team of crime scene investigators in tow.

'Perfect timing, boss,' Huw said.

'Once they've arrived, we'll talk to the man who found the body.'

Susan Howard was slightly out of breath when she arrived. 'Hi Caren. I didn't expect to see you so soon again.'

Caren nodded her head at the body in the water. 'The body was spotted first thing.'

Susan turned to the investigators alongside her. 'Disturb nothing, we want to preserve as much evidence as we can. You know the routine.'

Caren and Huw left the CSIs to their work and followed the instructions the uniformed officer had given them to the yacht nearby. Caren called out the name she had been given. 'Mr Wolf, it's Detective Inspector Caren Waits, Wales Police

Service.'

Moments later a face appeared from under the canopy covering the wheelhouse. A man in his fifties appeared, balding slightly with long curls to his shoulders. 'That's me.' He scrambled off his yacht and jumped onto the pontoon, offering Caren and Huw his hand, which they shook.

'What can you tell me about the discovery of the body this morning?' Caren said.

'Not a great deal. I arrived early to get my boat ready as we're going on a long cruise down to Brittany. There's a lot of preparation to be done. I needed to check some kit. While walking down the pontoon, I noticed the body bobbing up and down, suggesting the clothes had become entangled in part of the pontoon structure.'

'Did you touch the body at all or try to pull her from the water?' Caren stared at the man, trying to judge his response.

'No, of course not. I saw a ligature mark when I looked down at her. I'm a surgeon at a hospital in Cardiff and I realised quickly she was dead – but I was still shocked to see the body. I dialled 999 without delay. I waited until some officers arrived so that nobody else could get anywhere near her.'

'That was very sensible.'

Huw made his first contribution. 'Did you see anybody else on the pontoons when you arrived this morning?'

'No, the place was quiet.'

'Did you notice anything unusual on the quayside or around the marina?'

'No, but I wasn't paying much attention.'

'We may need to speak to you again,' Caren said.

Wolf nodded and after Huw had taken down his contact details, they retraced their steps to where Susan Howard was examining the body.

A sodden leather bag sat on the pontoon alongside the body. Green streaks of algae clung to her saturated hair. She wore a pair of black denim jeans and a short, waist-length jacket of the same colour. It was difficult to make out whether her clothes were expensive or cheap throwaway versions designed to be worn for one season only.

Susan Howard was flicking through a purse and Caren hoped that soon they'd have an identification. She would be somebody's daughter, perhaps even a wife or mother. Caren peered at the young woman's face. Her best guess was that she seemed to be in her twenties.

Behind her the sound of footsteps clanking along the pontoons took her attention and she spotted Nigel Langmore.

'Morning, Caren,' Nigel said, once he stood by her side.

'Nigel,' Caren acknowledged.

The pathologist peered down at the body on the pontoon. 'I don't think I'll have any difficulty pronouncing that life is extinct.'

'We need a time of death and a preliminary cause of death.' Caren tried to hide the impatience from her voice. 'Anything that can help us in the next few crucial hours.'

Nigel didn't respond, and shooed Susan Howard out of the way. He knelt over the body. He found a thermometer in his case and took readings from various parts of the corpse.

'I'll get the post-mortem done tomorrow afternoon.'

The pathologist got to his feet.

'It's difficult to be certain about the cause of death. But the wound on her neck suggests a ligature of some sort. And as for a time of death' – the pathologist pitched his head up and scanned the quayside around the marina – 'I'll give you a better indication tomorrow afternoon at the post-mortem.'

Then Nigel left the scene.

'I've got a name for you,' Susan said. She held up a plastic evidence wallet with a student identification card from the university in the city. 'It's an Emily Hughes.'

Susan knelt, comparing the photo ID to the dead woman's face. Then she looked up at Caren and nodded.

'Any bank cards with an address?' Susan said.

'No, and I can't find a mobile.'

'It's probably at the bottom of the marina,' Huw said. 'Along with whatever caused those ligature marks. It might be worth getting some divers to do a search.'

'You'll never get authorisation for that cost,' Susan said. 'Even if you could find a wire or cable or something similar, the chances of it having any evidential value is practically non-existent. And I found a receipt from a tattoo shop in Swansea and a lot of jewellery.'

'Thanks, Susan.' Caren took a photograph of the student ID card before leaving the crime scene manager and her team to finish their work.

'She looked so young with all her life in front of her, boss,' Huw said as they walked away from the scene along the pontoons.'

'Young and vulnerable and someone killed her. And we need to find the killer.'

At the quayside they met Rhys Davies and Alice Sharp.

'We've spoken with the harbour master and also the marina manager,' Alice said. 'And there are lots of CCTV cameras around the place.'

Rhys added, 'We've asked for the footage to be sent to us from the marina building and there are a couple of bars and restaurants we need to contact.'

Caren never wanted to get over that feeling of utter loss and sadness when a person had been murdered. A young girl had been murdered, and her family and friends would grieve. Caren couldn't share the depth of the family's anguish even though she knew full well what it was like to lose a loved one.

Caren nodded at Rhys. 'Get that done. Whether she was thrown in from the quayside or from one of the pontoons doesn't matter. And after you've spoken to the bars and restaurants I need you to get over to this tattoo shop in Swansea. We only have a name – Emily Hughes. We urgently need to find her family.'

Caren jerked her head at Huw. 'Let's go and talk to the University authorities.'

Chapter 4

'This is a crime scene,' Caren said as she led Huw around the marina. Emily Hughes had potentially been killed near the quayside, and her body dumped into the water, most likely the previous night. So Caren wanted to picture the scene.

Susan Howard had extended the crime scene perimeter to include the quayside and adjacent areas for the CSI team's search. Caren was certain that even the most careful killer would leave a trace. It was only a matter of discovering what that was.

Even the minutest scrap of evidence might lead them to a person of interest and, in due course, a suspect. For a moment, she paused while they gazed at the marina. Susan Howard had insisted that Mr Wolf had to leave the pontoons and Caren spotted him arguing with one of the crime scene investigators who was ushering him back towards the ramp up to the marina. The cruise to Brittany would have to wait.

'If she was killed on the quayside, we might find no evidence of that,' Huw said.

'But there'd be blood,' Caren said. 'It would be all over the killer. The CSIs might find some trace.'

'We'll need to do house-to-house' – Huw pointed towards the blocks of flats on either side of the marina – 'and let's hope Rhys and Alice will get some CCTV from the bars and restaurants.'

'Let's go,' Caren said.

As they returned to Caren's vehicle, her mobile rang and she recognised Susan Howard's number. 'This will be a lengthy process for us,' Susan said, 'I'm going to insist all the homeowners in the flats surrounding the marina leave their homes, at least for one night, so that we can complete a full search of the outer perimeter.'

'They won't like that,' Caren said

'I don't see any alternative.'

Caren paused and saw groups of people gathered in the distance, some gesturing toward the marina, others deep in conversation. 'I agree. Get it done.'

After thanking her, Susan Howard rang off and Caren could imagine the complaints from the homeowners about having to leave their properties as a search took place. Taking one last look at the marina, she knew she'd be back before the inquiry ended.

For now, they needed to know everything about Emily Hughes. What was she like? Who were the people she loved? Caren thought about Alun. And how little she had really known about him. It made her even more determined to provide an answer to Emily Hughes' family. To give them closure.

Caren and Huw returned to their car and Huw called his partner, Christopher, who worked at the University. She listened to the one-sided conversation where Huw asked about the student services office and her sergeant nodded his understanding of the directions Christopher had given him.

'It's not far,' Huw sounded positive.

It wasn't as easy as Huw had believed and he cursed as he found it difficult to give directions for Caren to find the building. Eventually down a side street as part of the main university buildings, Huw pointed a finger at an entrance. 'That's it, that's how Christopher described it.'

Caren made an effort to find a suitable parking spot but eventually abandoned her search and opted to park on double yellow lines. She displayed the *On Police Business/Heddlu Swyddogol* sign on her car dashboard. No traffic warden, no matter how enthusiastic, would give her a ticket.

After leaving the vehicle, they walked towards the building. It took them a few moments to become accustomed to the signage. It led them to the second floor, where there was a suite of offices reserved for student services.

Caren entered and approached a counter where two students were complaining about their room in one of the halls of residence.

'Did you have this trouble when you were at university?'

Caren said to Huw.

'First world problems, I'd say.'

Caren wasn't going to wait around, so she produced her warrant card and interrupted the person at the counter. 'Police, I want to speak to somebody in charge as soon as possible.'

Caren was frowned at by a woman in her fifties sporting a ponytail, oversized glasses, and unsightly earrings. 'I'll call the manager.' There was anger in her voice, as though it was Caren who was at fault. She left, then returned with a man younger than her. He looked at Caren intensely.

'How can I help?'

'We need some details about a student,' Caren said.

'All our records are confidential.'

'Is there somewhere we can talk privately? I am Detective Inspector Caren Waits of the Wales Police Service and this is my colleague Detective Sergeant Huw Margam. This is an important matter.'

Her official tone had the desired effect of silencing the conversation between the students standing at Caren's side as they gaped over silently at her.

'Yes, of course,' the manager sounded nonplussed.

He took them to his office, where Caren showed him the photograph of Emily's student identity card.

'I'm in charge of a murder inquiry. We require all available information on Emily Hughes.'

'My God, has someone killed her?' His eyes opened wide.

'We need the details, please.'

The man sat down at his desk, navigated into his computer, and stared at the screen.

'Emily Hughes is a second-year student studying Psychology. The home address we have for her is in the Gorseinon area of the city. Should we be warning the students to be wary? We have a duty to look after them, after all.' The man sounded shaken now.

Despite the man's request for information, Caren wasn't

going to discuss anything until they had spoken to the family.
'And do you have the name of a next of kin, mother or father?'

After Caren and Huw had all the information the student services had about Emily Hughes, they retraced their steps to the car and at the same time Rhys Davies rang Caren's mobile.

'Have you made any progress, Rhys?'

'We've spoken with the tattoo shop and they confirmed that Emily Hughes and some of her friends had been in recently. They didn't have any other details, but they gave us details of her bank card.'

'We've got an address for her parents in Gorseinon. We're heading there now.'

Chapter 5

Caren slowed at traffic lights, allowing pedestrians to cross.

'At least we've got her bank details. We'll need to do a full financial search on her.'

Once it was safe to proceed, Caren accelerated away from the crossing.

The sat nav told them they were nearing their destination. After a few minutes, Caren pulled up at the kerb near the address she had been given. Before leaving the student services offices, she had arranged for a family liaison officer to be present to support the family. It was standard procedure for an FLO to notify a grieving family of the loss of a loved one. But Caren didn't have time to wait – she would have to break the bad news herself.

Early in her career she had accepted it was part of the job. The family needed to know and the early stages of a murder investigation required gathering information about the victim quickly. Seeing the property, she felt the same anguish she had felt when officers had come to her door to inform her of Alun's death. She had felt utterly devastated, as though a heavy object had collided with her. She hadn't comprehended all the officers had told her. The family she was going to speak to would feel lost, unable to take in what had happened.

Huw took a call on his mobile and, once he had finished, he relayed to Caren that the family liaison officer would be with them in half an hour. They couldn't spare that time.

Caren reached for the door handle. 'Let's break the bad news.'

They walked over to the property at the end of the terrace. Caren wondered what sort of lives Mr and Mrs Hughes had and how they would deal with the loss of their daughter. Is it possible for anyone to truly recover from the death of a loved one? Caren had certainly found it difficult, and the disclosure of Alun's secret life had reopened old wounds.

A small silver-coloured family saloon stood parked on a

section of the neatly paved area, occupying what must have been the front garden at one time. Caren took a few moments to compose herself as she stood in front of the fading white UPVC front door. When she pressed the bell, a cheerful noise rang out inside. She glanced at Huw, his face serious and expressionless. He gave her a curt nod, as though he knew what they were facing would be difficult.

A man in his mid-fifties opened the front door. He kept his short greying hair neatly trimmed and his deep-set eyes reminded Caren of Emily's on her student ID card. He wore a flannel shirt and work trousers, and he held a shoulder bag in his right hand.

'Mr Hughes?' Caren said.

'Yes, who are you?'

'I'm Detective Inspector Caren Waits of the Wales Police Service and this is my colleague Detective Sergeant Huw Margam. May we come in?'

'I was just on my way to work.'

'It's important.'

Hughes' face changed as though having two police officers appearing on his doorstep had set off alarm bells.

'Is your wife in?' Caren said.

'What's this about?' Hughes frowned.

Caren stepped in to enter the house as Hughes called his wife's name. 'Maria, the police are here.'

A woman, who looked to be the same age as her husband, emerged from the kitchen door. She had long dark hair, loosely tied behind her head.

'Do you have somewhere where we could sit in the kitchen?' Caren said.

Hughes nodded, and then he gave Huw a quizzical glance.

'What's this about, Gavin?' Maria said to her husband.

He shrugged but continued to frown.

Caren spotted a table at one end of the kitchen and motioned for Mr and Mrs Hughes to sit down.

'Is it about Emily? Jesus, is she all right?' Maria sat on one of the wooden dining chairs.

'I'm afraid I have some terrible news,' Caren managed her best serious voice. 'The body of your daughter was found this morning in the marina. We are treating her death as murder. I am most terribly sorry.'

A barely audible gasp caught in Maria's throat that she couldn't quite release. Her fingers trembled, the news hitting her like a physical blow, knocking the air from her lungs. For a moment, she shut her eyes tightly, as if by doing so she could halt the world from spinning out of control.

When she opened them again, tears brimmed at the edges. Her lips moved silently, forming words that never fully emerged, a prayer, a denial, or a desperate plea.

Maria's hands came up to cover her face, stifling the sobs that now wracked her body. Her shoulders shook, and when she finally found her voice, it emerged in a whisper, 'No, no, not my Emily, not my girl,' each repetition growing more broken, more heart-wrenching.

'There must be some mistake,' Gavin Hughes said, his voice trembling. He placed a hand on his wife's shoulder.

'I'm afraid not. We found her student services identification card. And there was a receipt from a tattoo shop in Swansea. We've spoken to them and they've confirmed that it was Emily's bankcard that paid for their work.'

Caren was pleased that Huw took the initiative and walked over to the kitchen cupboards, where he found glasses that he filled with water.

'I've arranged for a specialist officer to be present to support you in the next few days. They are highly trained to deal with families grieving.'

Gavin looked over at Caren, clearly unable to comprehend how he could reply.

'Was your daughter living at home?' Huw said.

He took his notebook out, ready to jot down the details. It was Gavin Hughes who replied, his voice almost breaking.

'No, she lived in a flat with students. We were so proud that she got a place at university.' He turned to continue comforting his wife.

'Do you have the address?'

Gavin nodded and, once he had extracted his mobile from his shirt pocket, dictated the details.

Caren recognised the name of the Swansea suburb.

'Do you know the names of the others sharing the flat with her?'

Gavin gave Huw an incredulous look, as if it was the stupidest question he had ever heard. Then he added, 'I can't remember.'

'Do you have any idea why she was at the marina?' Caren said.

'She had a part-time job there in one of the bistro pubs.'

'Do you remember the name?'

'The Hope and Anchor. We even went there once when she was working.' Gavin turned his head and tears filled his eyes as he stared out of the window into the back garden.

'How long has she been working there?'

He turned his head towards Caren. 'I can't remember. She learned about the place from her ex-boyfriend. I told her to be careful with him. I didn't think he suited her.'

'And what is his name?' Caren's thoughts immediately turned to the possibility she had a person of interest.

'Mark Tremain, and he works in one of the companies in the marina. He's involved in engineering or something related to engines. I never liked him and he has a hell of a temper.' His voice broke. Then he got up and paced around. 'When they broke up, he came to the house furious and shouting threats. Telling her she could expect all sorts if she didn't get back with him.'

'Do you have the name of the company that he works for?'

Gavin blinked heavily. 'No, but it won't be difficult for you to find him. There aren't that many companies in the marina.'

'Can you remember anything else about his work?' Huw said.

Gavin shook his head. 'There was something off about him. I'm sure he never liked me. I didn't feel I could ever trust him.'

The sound of the door opening grabbed their attention. Caren and Huw turned to see a man in his early twenties entering.

'What is going on?'

Gavin gestured towards the young man. 'This is our son, Tom. It's your sister. These are police officers...' But he couldn't finish the sentence, and he sat down and sobbed.

'I'm Detective Inspector Waits and this is my colleague Detective Sergeant Huw Margam. We've just broken the very sad news to your parents that Emily's body was found this morning. We believe she was murdered.'

'When did this happen? I mean, I spoke to her only a couple of days ago.'

Huw stood up and motioned for Tom to sit in his chair. But the young man ignored Huw.

'Can you tell me anything about your sister's movements last night?' Caren looked over at Tom, whose eyes were filling with tears, the colour draining from his cheeks. He shook his head vigorously.

'She was mixing with all sorts of people down in the marina and she was friends with that Rachel Scott. You should bloody well ask her about Emily.' Tom looked furious. 'She never should have got involved with her.'

Caren's attention was drawn to his last comments. 'What do you mean, involved?'

'I knew something like this would happen.' Then he stormed out.

Gavin replied. 'He never liked Rachel. He thought she was a bad influence on Emily. I never understood why that was the case.'

'Was Rachel Scott one of Emily's housemates?'

'No, and before you ask me I do not know her address but I think she lives in the Mayhill area.'

'And why did he think this Rachel was a bad influence on Emily?'

'You'll have to ask him yourself, but he reckoned she was involved with some organised criminals.'

Once the family liaison officer had arrived Caren nodded to Huw and they left.

Caren marched back to her car. 'Let's go and track down some of Emily's housemates.'

Chapter 6

Huw Margam sympathised with Caren's reluctance to inform Emily's family about the tragic news. The task was much better handled by the specially trained family liaison officers. Huw had admired the way Caren shared all the details with Emily's parents.

Huw couldn't imagine what it might have been like for Caren to have fellow officers standing at her doorstep to share the news of her husband's death. Had it given her an insight? She certainly had more empathy than he had seen with other police officers he had worked with.

He tapped the postcode for Emily's flat into the sat nav as Caren turned the car around and headed back into Swansea.

'Call the CSIs and get an update,' Caren said.

Huw did as he was told and put the call onto speakerphone so that Caren could listen. It was a one-sided conversation, as Susan Howard shared with Huw and Caren that the team was still hard at it. It was likely to take several hours, possibly even until tomorrow morning, to complete the search. 'If we have to extend the crime scene perimeter, then it could take a lot longer.'

'Do what you think best, Susan,' Caren said.

Once the call was finished, Huw added, 'It would have been so easy for the killer to dispose of the murder weapon in the water.'

Caren nodded. 'But not so easy to have discarded a set of bloodstained clothes.'

'Of course, boss.'

Huw knew his way around Swansea well enough, but he didn't know the location of the street the Hugheses had provided so he had to rely on sat nav. Eventually, they pulled up outside the terraced property where the sat nav announced they had reached their destination. It was typical student accommodation – wooden windows badly in need of a coat of paint and the small front yard awash with bins and detritus.

'Landlords of this sort of property never seem to worry about keeping up appearances.' Caren opened the car door. Huw joined her on the pavement and they walked up to the front door.

Caren knocked; a young woman appeared without much delay. Her eyes were bloodshot and there was evidence of tears all over her cheeks.

Caren didn't bother showing her warrant card, and once she introduced herself and Huw, she waved them inside.

'I'm Michelle. I suppose you've come about Emily. It's terrible, we can't believe it.'

Michelle had curly blonde hair and striking green eyes despite the tears. She had an open, inquisitive face, and she led them into a room at the rear of the property where two other students were sitting on sofas.

None of them seemed surprised to see Caren or Huw.

Both Charlotte Parry and Chloe Edwards introduced themselves without requests. They had the same evidence of tears that Caren had seen on Michelle's face.

Michelle moved a pile of magazines and an empty pizza box from a sofa and pointed an invitation for Caren and Huw to sit down. The room's furniture was old and battered, just like the threadbare carpet.

'How well did you know Emily?' Caren said. Huw had his notebook ready on his lap.

Charlotte took the lead. 'We were on the same course. We were both studying Psychology. We'd all been in halls of residence for the first year. Then we decided to share this house for the second year. I can't believe this has happened to her. We got on really well.' Charlotte sounded serious. She adjusted a lock of her dark brown hair over her right ear. 'Have you spoken to her parents?'

'We've just been there. They were distraught, as you might expect.'

Chloe Edwards sat with her legs curled up on the sofa. She had a petite frame and when she spoke she sounded intense. She wore multicoloured layers, which Huw thought probably qualified as bohemian. 'I knew her very well' – Chloe paused – 'she was very sensitive. And very artistic.' Chloe paused again, the emotion of talking about Emily too much for her.

'Are you on the same course as Emily?' Caren said.

Chloe shook her head, avoiding any eye contact, simply staring at her fingers, which she was threading together.

'I understand Emily worked at a pub – the Hope and Anchor in the marina. Can you tell me if she was working there last night?'

Michelle responded first. 'Yes, she loved it there. Charlotte and I called at the pub. I didn't particularly like the place, but Emily seemed to be in good spirits.'

'How long had she worked there?'

'A while – I can't remember,' Charlotte replied. 'I can't believe this has happened.' Her voice trembled.

'How had she been recently?'

Caren immediately sensed a tension between Charlotte and Michelle as they exchanged a look. Chloe looked away as though she didn't want to be part of the unspoken messages.

'We need to know everything about Emily, so whatever you can tell us about her is going to help.'

'It was nothing, I suppose,' Michelle said. 'But she had a lot more money than usual. And far more cash than I've seen her with in the past. Unlike the rest of us, Emily wasn't hard up recently. She'd been buying expensive clothes and enjoying eating out.' Michelle ran out of steam and gave another glance at Charlotte.

'And she had been seeing a lecturer on the course,' Charlotte announced in a tone that suggested she wasn't going to add any more detail.

'What is his name?' Surprised by this revelation, Caren could sense Charlotte's reluctance. 'If it was common knowledge and if it was connected to Emily then you need to tell me his name.'

'Johann Ackland.' Charlotte realised his identity wasn't a secret now. 'And he flaunted his money and status. He could be really charming and personable.'

Michelle pitched in again, now that Charlotte had shared the details about Ackland. 'Emily could be entirely different when she was with him. She had got us to promise not to tell anybody about her and Ackland. She had mentioned something about a long trip away and that he was taking some sort of sabbatical.'

'What did she mean by that?'

Michelle shrugged. 'Emily could be a daydreamer at times. I think she was completely seduced by Ackland.'

'Did she think she had a future with him?'

'I can't say. That might be true.'

'Do you know if Johann Ackland is married?'

'Emily got the impression he was unconcerned about his marriage and that he was more worried about his status in the department,' Charlotte said.

Huw glanced over at Chloe, who had said nothing and didn't seem to want to contribute anything. But he sensed she had something on her mind. 'Do you know anything about Ackland, Chloe?'

She shook her head a little too quickly. Huw knew from working with Caren she would have sensed Chloe had more to share with them.

'When we spoke to Emily's parents, they mentioned that her previous boyfriend, Mark Tremain, had been at their property in a hell of a rage. What do you know about Tremain?'

'She had a fling with him for a couple of weeks.' Michelle sounded authoritative. 'He thought she was taking things seriously, and when he realised that wasn't the case, he became angry and upset.'

'I understand he works in one of the companies in the marina?'

Charlotte and Michelle looked at each other, but this time

Huw sensed nothing other than sorrow that their friend had died. 'Emily had a circle of friends around the marina, and that's how she met him. Apart from that, I know nothing about him.'

'Are you familiar with Rachel Scott, who was friends with Emily?'

The reaction of Charlotte and Michelle was unequivocal. 'Neither of us liked her,' Michelle said, nodding at Charlotte. 'She mixed with the wrong sort of people and… Well, she was in a group of people Emily knew from the marina.'

'Is there any other important information about Emily?'

Charlotte and Michelle shook their heads but Chloe seemed to have retreated into herself as she curled up on the sofa. She was chewing on a nail, studying it carefully.

Huw made a mental note that they needed to speak to Chloe again without her two housemates being present.

'We need to look at Emily's room,' Caren said.

Charlotte got to her feet. 'It's next to mine on the first floor.'

Huw followed Caren and Charlotte as they made their way upstairs and along the landing. Charlotte stopped and pointed at a door. 'We all trust each other, and we never lock our doors usually.'

Pushing open the door, Caren stepped into the room. For Huw it brought back memories of his room when he had been an undergraduate. The single bed pushed against one wall had a neatly placed duvet. The furniture looked cheap and old, from the chipped surfaces, but Emily had clearly attempted to make it look comfortable and homely. An old mantel had a set of scented candles on it. Caren opened the wardrobe and Huw noticed the clothes hanging from a rail.

'I'll look through the drawers,' Huw said.

He worked his way down through the chest of drawers near the wardrobe. It gave him a feeling of borderline voyeurism having to trawl through clothes of a murder victim in circumstances like this. If there was anything of significance, a full search team would be needed. Once he reached the bottom drawer, he found a shoebox at the rear.

He stood and set the box on a bedside table. Once he opened it, Huw realised there was more to Emily Hughes than her student persona. There was a carefully folded stash of money. Immediately, he found a pair of latex gloves from his suit pocket. 'Something you should see here, boss.' Caren joined him as he reached for the first bundle. 'There must be a few thousand pounds here, maybe even five or six thousand.'

'This could be important. We'll need to find out how Emily came by that money.'

Chapter 7

Before leaving the home of Gavin and Maria Hughes, Caren had spoken with her mother briefly, asking her to collect Aled from school. The first day of any inquiry was always going to be demanding. She needed to quickly learn everything about the murder victim and her life.

Operational support had been tasked to track down the address for Rachel Scott, and once they had left the home Emily Hughes had shared with her three student friends a message reached Caren's mobile. She read the details of Rachel Scott's address. Huw had received the same information.

'I need to talk to my mum about Aled,' Caren said after she had opened the car with her remote for Huw.

She watched as he got in and tapped the postcode into the sat nav. She felt lucky that at least he knew his way around Swansea, although he found the sat nav helpful.

Caren didn't have to wait long for her mother to answer the phone. 'Aled's fine. I'll give him some tea and take him home later. Just give me an idea of when you might be back.'

'Thanks, Mum.'

'There's been something on the news about a body found in the Swansea Marina this morning.'

Her Mum, Ann, would know that Caren couldn't discuss the details with her. 'It's the body of a young woman. I'm in Swansea now, interviewing one more person. It's probably a few hours until I get home.'

Caren spoke to Aled, inquiring about his day at school and assuring him that his Mamgu would take care of him until she got home. It pleased her that her son seemed to take the disruption to his daily routine in his stride. He enjoyed spending time with his Mamgu and she knew that her mother relished her time with him.

'It should only be twenty minutes to Rachel Scott's place,' Huw said when Caren got back in the car.

Caren glanced at the sat nav screen, started the engine and drove off. She followed the directions carefully enough and listened to Huw's instructions.

A large noticeboard announced that the block of flats belonged to a housing association. The footpaths leading up to the main entrance needed to be cleaned and pressure washed to be free of weeds. None of the cars in the car park was less than five years old, Caren guessed. She parked and they walked over to the entrance.

As she did so, she picked up messages from Rhys Davies confirming that he and Alice Sharp had finished their preliminary work with the various pubs and other hospitality premises around the marina. A full house-to-house team had also started. Another message from Susan Howard updated Caren, mentioning that the CSI team would work late into the evening, likely completing the search by morning.

Caren replied to each of the texts with a simple thumbs up as she joined Huw. He had already spotted the name of Rachel Scott on one buzzer which he pressed. They waited. There was no reply. Huw pressed again and moments later a slurred voice emerged from the loudspeaker.

'Yes.'

'Police, we need to speak to Rachel Scott.'

A metallic sound followed by a click indicated the opening of the front door to the downstairs lobby. Huw was the first inside and Caren followed him up to the first floor, where they found Rachel Scott's front door slightly ajar.

'Rachel Scott?' Caren pushed open the door with her foot.

A voice called out: 'In here.'

Caren led the way into a narrow hallway. A collection of fleeces and thin softshell jackets hung from a row of hooks. The door to a lounge was open.

Rachel was sitting on a battered leather sofa, her feet propped up on an improvised coffee table made from bits of an old pallet. Several posters of various surfing locations adorned the walls and in one corner was a large surfboard. Her eyebrows were well-shaped, and her cheekbones were high, framing her face elegantly. Caren sensed a defiance in her slightly upturned eyes. Neatly cut, healthy-looking auburn hair would have completed the appearance of an attractive woman, were it not for her pale complexion and make-up ruined by tears.

'Have you come about Emily?'

Caren nodded, pleased that she didn't need to go through the formalities of flashing warrant cards – simply rank and name. They sat down and looked over at Rachel.

'We've spoken with Emily's parents and they told us about your relationship with her. Do you have any details about her life that could assist us in our inquiry?'

'I can't believe she's gone.' Rachel picked up a glass from the floor and sipped the clear liquid. It wasn't her first drink that day, Caren guessed from the slurring.

'How long had you been friends?'

'We met when she came to join a group of us to go surfing. When she began, she wasn't very good, but she enjoyed it.'

'Did you socialise with her?'

'Sometimes. She worked down in the Hope and Anchor in the marina and occasionally I called in to see her.'

'What do you do for a living, Rachel?'

'I work for a company that makes surfboards. They sell them all over the world.'

Huw made his first contribution. 'We'll need the name of your employer and your full personal details.'

'None of your business,' Rachel snapped.

'It's all part of the inquiry and perfectly routine.' Huw sounded utterly reasonable.

'Why? Do you think I killed her?'

'Why would you think that?' Caren said.

'Her family and her friends didn't like me.'

'Even if that were true, why would we think you are responsible for her death?'

She straightened and then sat up in her chair, her manner changing and her voice striking a challenging tone. 'You can't trap me that easily.'

'We're not here to catch you out, Rachel. We hope you can shed some light on Emily Hughes' background and possible motives for her murder.

Rachel's eye contact suddenly veered away and her glance darted around the room. 'Perhaps it was one of those stalkers targeting women in Swansea. Your lot have been useless at catching the man involved.'

'You haven't answered my question whether you know of anything or anybody who might want to see Emily dead.' Caren's tone was serious and determined. She wasn't going to allow herself to be sidetracked by Rachel Scott's attitude.

'No, of course not. Everybody liked her.' Rachel wasn't convincing.

'Did Emily have a boyfriend?' Caren decided she wasn't going to disclose any of the information they had learned so far. Something was off about Rachel's reaction.

Rachel shrugged. 'Nobody serious. There was Mark Tremain, he works in the marina.'

'Anyone else?'

Rachel shook her head but didn't look at Caren.

Caren fished out one of her cards from her jacket pocket and handed it to Rachel. 'If you think of anything else, please contact me.'

Rachel stared at the card but said nothing, and Caren nodded to Huw for them to leave.

'She knows a lot more than she's telling us,' Caren said as she pointed the remote at her vehicle. 'Let's get back to headquarters and one of the first things we do is a full PNC check and background search against Miss Rachel Scott.'

Chapter 8

First thing the next morning, Caren found an email in her personal inbox from the solicitors handling her late husband's estate, explaining the details of the meeting at the coroner's inquest the following week. But the inquest was far from her thoughts, as she faced the pressing new inquiry into Emily's murder.

She tapped out a simple reply, confirming she would meet them as suggested. Then she turned to the day-to-day practicalities of making certain her son ate a proper breakfast before she prepared his bag for school. He had just gone to sleep the previous evening when she arrived home. After her mother had left, she crept up to Aled's bedroom and had sat by the side of his bed watching him sleeping. Although she loved her work as a detective, a day like this – when she hadn't been able to collect her son from school, make them both an evening meal and read him a bedtime story – was something she regretted.

The solicitors had warned her that Alun's previous relationship with Miss Hale might well mean a claim against his estate. But once she had concluded everything, she could move on with her life. The warning that Miss Hale might well be attending the inquest had surprised Caren, causing her to feel anger and shock. Were her feelings directed at Miss Hale or at Alun?

'Come on, Aled. You need to go to the toilet before school or else we'll be late.'

'I've already been,' Aled protested. 'Will you be picking me up from school today?'

'I hope so. Yesterday was very busy.'

Aled nodded. 'Was it another murder?'

It always surprised her how easily he had become accustomed to the reality of her job.

'Come on, time for school.'

Caren lingered at the school gate to watch her son talking

animatedly with some of his friends as they walked to their classes. It pleased her enormously that he had settled into the school after losing his father and having to move home.

As she drove away, she immediately switched to the demands of the inquiry. She made mental notes of the priorities to make progress. After parking, she walked through the corridors of Western Division headquarters to the Incident Room.

She pushed open the door and the sound of conversation quickly stopped as she entered. The officers on her team greeted her with the customary 'good morning, boss' as she strode over towards the board. The image of Emily Hughes and a marina map were on it.

After she had arrived at headquarters the previous afternoon they had reviewed progress, but Caren had made no final decisions about priorities for the second day until she had some sleep.

'Rhys and Alice' – Caren nodded at both officers – 'I want you both talking to the marina management company. We need a list of all owners of yachts, boats, flats, and houses in the marina. And you can coordinate with the house-to-house team too.'

'Yes, boss,' Rhys Davies replied. 'I've requisitioned a PNC check against Rachel Scott and Mark Tremain.'

'And we've requested a more detailed background search into Rachel Scott,' Alice added.

'Good,' Caren said. 'There was something odd about Rachel Scott's replies to us yesterday. Before we talk to her again, I want to learn more about her. And also check out the company where she works.'

Caren's mobile rang and she saw the number for Susan Howard, the crime scene manager. Caren had left the box recovered from Emily Hughes' bedroom at the forensic department the night before for basic fingerprint checks to be undertaken.

'Morning, Caren. We were able to recover two sets of

fingerprints from some of the bank notes you left with us. We'll go through them all, of course, but it's going to take some time. One set belongs to Emily Hughes, but so far the other fingerprints don't appear on the national database.'

'Thanks, Susan. Send me more details when you can.'

It simply meant that the second person who handled the bank notes didn't have a criminal record. But that didn't mean that the person wasn't known to the police.

Caren shared the information with her team, who nodded their understanding.

'And I want a full search done against Emily Hughes' background. I want to know if there are any references to her in intelligence reports. There must be an explanation for why she had such a substantial amount of money in her room.'

'Maybe she did a lot of overtime,' Alice sounded her usual cynical tone.

Rhys grunted a surprise. 'Come off it, Alice. That's far too much money for that. And if it was overtime, there'd probably be a paper trail from the bar where she worked.'

'Don't be soft, not if she was paid in cash.'

Caren interjected. 'Contact the owner of the Hope and Anchor in the marina. Find out everything about the hours she worked and how much she earned. Establish if there is any possibility she could have earned this money legitimately. In the meantime, we're going to talk to Ackland.'

It was mid-morning by the time Caren and Huw arrived at the University's Psychology department. A woman on the reception who seemed to double up as a secretary and telephonist stared at Caren and Huw's warrant cards as though she couldn't believe the two officers were standing there.

'We need to speak to Johann Ackland. I understand he's a lecturer in the department.' Caren smiled.

'Yes, of course. I mean, Dr Ackland is one of our senior lecturers. But I think he may be taking a tutorial at the moment.' The woman clicked through into her computer screen and stared at a spreadsheet of a timetable, its cells filled with different colours.

'Can you please inform us of Dr Ackland's whereabouts?'

'Yes, I've found it. He has a tutorial starting in five minutes. So can you come back later? I can schedule a proper appointment for his diary.'

'That won't be necessary.' Caren added forcibly: 'We'll see Dr Ackland now. The tutorial can wait. Just tell us where we can find his office.'

The woman appeared lost, unsure how to respond to Caren and Huw.

'It's T34. On the first floor, halfway down the corridor.'

Without bothering to thank the woman, Caren swiftly turned and made her way towards the staircase they had spotted earlier in reception.

Ackland's name was displayed on the door to his room with his title as senior lecturer. Caren knocked and entered uninvited.

A man about six feet tall was standing by a small desk gathering papers together. He had dark brown hair thinning at the crown and wore a pair of well-pressed chinos and polished Chelsea boots. A well-tailored blazer hung on a coat stand behind him.

'Dr Ackland?' Caren said.

'Yes, and who are you?' Ackland looked over at Caren with striking intense blue eyes.

Caren produced a warrant card, and Huw did the same. Caren watched for any sign of realisation on Ackland's face about why they were present.

'I have a tutorial starting in a few minutes. Can this wait?'

'Are you aware that Emily Hughes, one of your students, has been murdered?' Caren stared into the man's face.

'Yes, of course I mean it was tragic, very sad.'

'We need to ask you some questions. The tutorial can wait for now.'

Ackland frowned and gave a brief sigh of irritation. He waved his hand towards two chairs for visitors and took his seat at the desk.

'I'm not certain I can help you.'

We'll see about that, Caren thought.

'How well did you know, Emily?'

'She was one of my students. And she was very conscientious.'

Caren was convinced Ackland had been expecting them. He had made no suggestion they speak to her personal tutor or any of the other lecturers in the department who would have been familiar with Emily.

'How would you describe your relationship?'

How was Ackland going to reply to a simple, open enough question?

'As I said, she was one of my students.'

'The information we have, Dr Ackland, is that you and Emily were close, intimate. Is that true?'

'It's none of your business.'

'It is when it's murder, Dr Ackland. Now, I'll ask you once again, were you intimate with Emily Hughes? Because if you're not prepared to answer our questions, we can always conduct this interview at the nearest police station under caution.'

Ackland remained silent for a moment. He pinched his lips tightly closed and Caren thought she saw his jaw twitch.

'Yes, if you must know, we were having a relationship. I would hardly call it anything serious.'

'You were sleeping with one of your students,' Caren exclaimed.

Ackland was taken aback by her bluntness and blinked vigorously. Then the smooth persona took back control. 'That's a very coarse way of putting it, Detective Inspector.'

'Did you see Emily the night before her body was discovered?'

'I had been on my boat the afternoon before Emily's

body was found. But I wasn't there in the evening. I have a yacht in the marina and I was preparing for the new season. It's a great place to relax and unwind.'

'Did you take Emily to your yacht?'

'Yes, we went there together a couple of times.'

Ackland was now getting into the swing with smooth, confident replies.

'Can anyone confirm the details of your whereabouts that evening?'

'I was at home.'

'Was your wife with you?'

Ackland stiffened perceptibly and adjusted his position on his chair. 'Yes, of course.'

'Is your wife aware of your relationship with Emily Hughes?'

'It's none of your damned business.' Ackland sounded angry.

'Luckily, Dr Ackland, I get to decide what is my business and it looks to me that you are heavily involved in my inquiry. So the sooner you understand that and cooperate, the better it will be.'

Ackland said nothing, but sat back in his chair, giving Caren an angry scowl.

Before they left, Huw interrogated Ackland about the timings of his visit to the marina, and noted down in his notebook the details the lecturer provided.

Caren led Huw out of the room and down to reception, where she asked for details of where she could find Emily Hughes' personal tutor. 'I think we do a full background check on Ackland.' Caren said to Huw. He nodded back. 'I didn't like him for one moment.'

Chapter 9

'I've been expecting to hear from you.' Dr James Barker, Emily's tutor, was a small, intense man in his sixties with a crumpled jacket, a weathered white shirt and a blue tie knotted at an odd angle. 'I've left a message at your headquarters.'

'Headquarters?' Caren said.

'Yes, in Cardiff. That's where you're from, surely, if this is a murder inquiry.'

'I'm the senior investigating officer and I'm based at Western Division headquarters in Carmarthen.'

'Oh, I see.'

Caren couldn't make out Barker's accent but it was rich and suggested a public-school education.

'What can you tell me about Emily Hughes?'

'I was her tutor. My role was to support her and be a sort of mentor.'

'Did you teach her in the Psychology department?'

Barker shook his head. 'Only the first year. Then she chose options in the second year that didn't come under my purview. You need to talk to the lecturers in the department who actually taught her.'

'We've already spoken to Johann Ackland?' Caren made the statement sound like a question.

'Have you indeed, and what did he have to say?' Barker realised as he finished the question that Caren couldn't respond. 'But of course, you can't tell me.'

'What do you know about Emily Hughes?'

'She was a delightful girl.' Barker relaxed as he began sharing his knowledge of Emily. 'She was well liked and had lots of friends. I'm sure she had a promising career ahead of her in whatever field she pursued. She was an excellent student, and I'm certain she would have graduated with good honours.'

'Do you know of anyone who might have had a reason to kill her?'

'No, of course not, of course not. The whole thing is quite preposterous. In her first year, she volunteered to assist with a group that helps a homeless charity in the city. I suggest you speak to the person in charge there, but from what I understand, they valued her input. Not many students would give up their leisure time to help in a local homeless centre.'

'And you have the details of the group that Emily was part of?' Huw said.

'I've got it here somewhere,' Barker said, scrambling through one drawer in his desk.

'Can you provide the name of the charity in the city that the University group supports?'

'Yes, of course, give me a moment.'

Caren and Huw watched in silence as Barker searched the various papers in the drawers of his desk before finally announcing with relish that he had the details. Huw jotted them down in his notebook and they thanked Emily's tutor and left.

St. Hubert's, a former chapel, was located near the main University buildings. A professional board replaced the sign that had once advertised the denomination and Sunday service schedule. On it was written 'St Hubert's Hostel'. There was reference to a website and a mobile telephone number as the contact details, together with a Facebook page.

High above the door, carved into concrete, was the word 'Bethany'. 'It was a common name for an English-language chapel years ago,' Huw said.

Caren had learned to defer to Huw's knowledge of history. The denomination that established the chapel would probably be pleased to see it now being used to support less fortunate members of society.

The chapel still had its original substantial wooden doors, but modern locks had been added.

Inside the old entrance lobby, there was a locked door and a window by its side. Caren pressed the bell and soon enough a face appeared staring at Caren and then at Huw, who displayed their warrant cards. 'Give me a minute.'

On the journey to St. Hubert's, Caren and Huw discussed the possibility that Emily's killer might have a connection to the hostel. And that meant speaking to all the staff.

Moments later, the door opened, and Caren and Huw were ushered in.

'Follow me through to my office.' The manager had introduced herself simply as Andrea.

At the end of a corridor on the ground floor of the old chapel she had a small office.

The functional space had filing cabinets, and on top of a small bookcase an electric kettle, mugs, sugar, and tea bags. Andrea took a seat behind a desk which was reasonably tidy. Far tidier than Dr Barker's that they had seen at the University.

'I'm not certain I can help you. I've heard about what happened to Emily, which is tragic.'

'Did she come to help at the hostel regularly?' Caren said.

'She was part of the voluntary group that helped from the University. I can't tell you how often she has been here. She was always friendly and supportive.'

'Did she ever have any difficulty with any of the hostel users?' Huw said. 'Did anyone get violent with her or threaten her in any way?'

'Nothing like that happened. I can't think of any users of the hostel who might get violent.'

'Do you have a list of the regular users?'

'We do, but some of them don't give us their proper names and some point-blank refuse to cooperate. We're not in the business of collecting personal data, Detective Sergeant.'

'We appreciate that,' Caren interjected. 'But we're in charge of the murder inquiry and we need to identify anybody that might have had a motive for killing Emily Hughes.'

'I'll need a formal written request from you, I'm afraid, before I can send a list of the users.'

'We'll need the names of staff members too.'

'Of course, I'll get the details for you. Emily came a couple of times with a woman called Rachel Scott as well. You might talk to her. They seemed to be good friends.'

Caren shared a surprised look with Huw.

'I don't think I can help you any further.' Andrea got to her feet.

Caren left her business card on the desk. 'Contact me if you think of anything else that could be of interest or help to us in the inquiry.'

Chapter 10

Rhys Davies was more than happy for Alice Sharp to drive. She always seemed to complain he drove too slowly. Once they'd completed the work Inspector Waits had assigned them, they had left headquarters and headed down for the A48 and then along the M4 towards Swansea before turning off to the marina.

Alice was convinced she knew a shortcut, but it had led them down a couple of dead ends and she had cursed loudly. Rhys decided against making some pithy comment. After all, Detective Constable Alice Sharp was his senior in years and experience, even if not in rank. And she often reminded him that that was the case. He had a lot to learn from her, although he often thought that her cynical and jaded take on life suggested she was looking forward to retirement.

They eventually located the mobile incident room parked near the marina entrance. They walked over after parking and discovered a harassed-looking uniformed sergeant talking to two elderly ladies. 'I want to reassure you both that the Wales Police Service is doing absolutely everything it can and all the information you have provided will be considered most carefully. He tipped his head towards Rhys and Alice. 'These detectives are part of our extensive murder investigation team.'

'Murder!' exclaimed one of the women, as if hearing the word for the first time.

'And now if you'll excuse me.' He ushered both women out.

Satisfied they were out of earshot, he turned to Rhys and Alice. 'They're convinced they saw somebody carrying an axe along the quayside on the afternoon Emily Hughes was killed.'

'Typical,' Alice said. 'Time wasters can be a real waste of time.'

'Hilarious.'

Despite Alice's comments, she would know full well that house-to-house enquiries and statements from residents could often lead to a breakthrough.

'After talking to the marina manager, we'll come back to catch up on the house-to-house.'

'I've just had a list of all the flat and homeowners in the marina, so it'll be easier to identify who has been spoken to.'

Rhys and Alice left the sergeant, agreeing on a time to speak to him for an update, and headed to the marina office. It was a modern detached building constructed in a position that gave an excellent view over most of the marina basin. Rhys had already counted three CCTV cameras located in prominent positions near the building. Two more were attached to the fascia boards.

He yanked open the door to the marina building and took the stairs to the first floor, Alice close behind. A preliminary search of the official website had given Rhys the name of the marina manager as a Captain Maynard.

Rhys identified the operations room from the sign on the door. It was a long, wide room with various computers and enormous monitors that displayed the coastline around the Swansea Bay area in precise detail. A man in his seventies, short and with a paunch, glanced their way.

'We're looking for Captain Maynard,' Rhys said, producing his warrant card. 'Police.'

Maynard nodded and gestured towards the door labelled 'Marina Manager', indicating that it was his office.

'I suppose you've come about the murder of that young girl.' Maynard sat at his desk. Rhys and Alice each sat in a visitor chair.

'Did you know her?' Rhys said.

Maynard shook his head.

'We'll need all your CCTV footage for Sunday afternoon and evening. And into the early hours of Monday morning.'

'No problem I'll get that sent over to you. But there are other CCTV cameras around the marina.'

'Do you have details of the people who keep their yachts here?'

'Only the ones that use the marina run by the city. The sailing club uses their own section of the marina area. They'll have the names of their members. We have a list of the visiting boats and yachts. Just their names and the details of the yachts.'

'How many are there?'

'Altogether between the city and the sailing club, several hundred.'

Rhys' heart sank at the prospect of contacting them all. It could take hours, days even.

'Do you have a contact for the sailing club?' Alice said.

'You'll find everything on their website,' Maynard said.

Maynard launched into an explanation of how the sailing club was different to the city council-run marina. Then he gave them a potted history of the marina and extolled the virtues of spending a day at the maritime museum a little further down the coast. The marina manager was clearly very proud of what had been achieved from the industrial legacy after years of neglect. Rhys cut short the history lesson.

'Thank you very much, Mr Maynard, for your time, but we have another appointment.'

They left Maynard and headed downstairs.

'I think we've had enough of his history lesson for one day,' Rhys said. 'Let's speak to the bar manager at the Hope and Anchor.'

It was a short walk to the pub, which was situated in the middle of the marina development. Rhys pushed open the door and noticed the large expanse of windows looking out over a seating area.

James Carver had a leathery complexion and a cheerful outlook to life as he smiled broadly at Rhys and Alice as they approached the bar. Clearly hoping that they were going to be big spenders, he looked disappointed when he stared at their warrant cards.

'We'd like to speak to you about Emily Hughes,' Rhys said.

'Of course.' Carver led them to a room behind the bar. Three members of staff were sitting inside and Carver shooed them away, telling them to get ready for the lunchtime service. Carver and his visitors sat around a table. 'It's terrible what's happened to Emily. I can't believe it, she was really nice. All my customers thought the world of her.'

'Had she been working here long?'

'Not long, but it feels like she's been a fixture here. We have lots of regulars who enjoyed chatting to her and she had a charming personality. There are two old ladies who started coming here regularly once they'd met Emily. They'll be devastated.'

'We understand she was working on the evening before her body was discovered?'

Carver nodded. 'Yes, she was doing a shift until eleven.'

'How did she seem? Did she seem frightened?'

'No, I wouldn't say so.'

'And is Emily paid in cash?'

'No, she's paid directly into her bank account. All the staff here are paid that way and, before you ask, that includes any tips.'

At least they knew that working in the pub hadn't given Emily the cash she had stashed in her room.

'What do you know about her boyfriend, Mark Tremain?'

'He was in that night. He had one too many drinks at the bar. Emily had a thing with him in the past, but I thought it was over. He was an odd character. He couldn't hold his booze and he'd get angry and argumentative.' He gave a frustrated shake of his head.

'Did you see him argue with Emily that evening?'

'No, but he'd had an argument with Johann Ackland the previous night.'

The reference to Ackland focused Rhys' attention.

'Why were they arguing?'

'Ackland and Emily were an item and Tremain was furious. Ackland has deep pockets, and he splashes money around, making an impression with everyone. He's the exact opposite of Tremain.'

'And was Emily working that Saturday night when Ackland and Tremain argued?'

'She kept out of the way. I had to throw Tremain out, eventually.'

'Do you know where Tremain works in the marina?'

Rhys and Alice listened carefully to the instructions Carver gave them for McCarthys the chandlery workshop where Tremain worked. Before leaving they asked Carver if he had any CCTV cameras inside the building. He confirmed they had one on the outside but that it was broken. What was the point? Rhys pondered.

'Let's talk to Tremain,' Alice said as they stood outside the Hope and Anchor.

With so many CCTV cameras Rhys reckoned it would only be a matter of time before they'd be able to plot exactly the route Emily had taken from the pub. He joined Alice as they walked through the marina towards the chandlery workshop, a sprawling collection of buildings that serviced the yacht and boat industry. It took them some time to find the manager in charge.

'He's on his day off.'

'Do you have Tremain's home address?' Alice said.

Once they had the details, Rhys and Alice returned to their vehicle and she tapped the postcode into the sat nav. Alice reached the property outside Swansea in half an hour, despite city traffic. Tremain lived in a poorly maintained cottage down a track thick with weeds and lined with hedges that hadn't been trimmed for years. No activity, no car, no bicycle in sight. After banging the door and walking around the rear, Rhys turned to Alice.

'Let's get back to headquarters. We've got hours of

CCTV footage to review.'

Chapter 11

Unexplained amounts of cash always prompted a suspicion of involvement in the drugs trade. And Emily Hughes' hoard meant identifying if she was known to the officers dealing with drug-related crime. Detective Inspector Simon Williams coordinated investigations into those sorts of offences. Caren called her colleague, who told her he could allocate a few minutes for her later that afternoon.

After their conversation, Caren checked her watch. Despite not usually eating before a post-mortem, she was hungry and they still had some time until their trip to the mortuary. She suggested to Huw grabbing a quick sandwich and coffee.

'I know a place nearby,' Huw said.

His directions were clear and a few minutes later, Caren found a slot to park outside Bella Cucina.

They found a table and sat down.

'Christopher and I come here often. The owner has an interest in a coffee roasting company. We buy our coffee beans here.'

Huw was warmly greeted by a waiter who appeared at their table.

'I tell the boss you are here.'

Caren ordered a ham and cheese panini with a flat white. Huw had his sandwich with a bottle of sparkling San Pellegrino.

Moments later, a stocky man in his fifties with a distinctly Mediterranean complexion came over to the table. He gave Huw a bag with a loaf inside. He smiled at Caren.

'This is for you, Mr Huw. Tell Mr Christopher it was baked this morning to a new recipe.'

Huw looked inside the bag, and Caren could see what looked like a sourdough loaf.

'Thanks, I'll tell him.'

'And remind him about our bakery course.'

'I will.'

As they waited for their lunch, Caren scanned her surroundings. The Italian café seemed to be flourishing. A beautiful rich smell of coffee filled the place. Leather sofas were arranged in one corner, and the tables and chairs looked expensive.

'The owner runs bakery courses and events promoting speciality Italian desserts. They are very popular.'

Caren glanced at her watch, conscious they had to get back to headquarters.

'My boss in Northern Division was a stickler for making the coffee the right way. I've seen him take a sip from a coffee mug and then throw away the rest.'

'He'd get on fine with Christopher then.'

Their sandwiches arrived and they finished their lunch in silence. The bread had been excellent and the filling fresh. Her flat white had been delicious. No wonder the place was a success.

On the journey from Swansea, Caren spoke briefly to Susan Howard asking for an update on the CSI's work. Susan confirmed they hoped to get finished later that afternoon. Then she got Huw to message Rhys Davies and Alice Sharp to make certain they got back to the Incident Room by the end of the afternoon for a catch-up session.

It meant that she would have to call her mother and arrange for her to collect Aled from school. She did that after parking in the slots reserved for visitors near the mortuary. They walked over to the entrance and the pathologist, Dr Nigel Langmore, was already waiting for them.

'Good afternoon, I'm glad you're prompt.'

Nigel led them through into the mortuary. Caren sensed the cool temperature on her skin and the smell of antiseptic tickled her nostrils. Attending post-mortems was an essential part of her job as the senior investigating officer but she doubted she would ever become truly accustomed to a post-mortem. She admired the dedication of medical professionals who spent their careers carving up dead bodies. She had learnt too that pathologists help the living too by examining tissue samples from suspected cancers.

A mortuary assistant pushed in a trolley with the body of Emily Hughes covered in a white body bag that Nigel unzipped with a flourish. He stared down at the corpse with a mixture of interest and fascination clear on his face.

'This is the post-mortem of Emily Hughes, twenty years of age,' Nigel dictated her date of birth from memory. Then he got to work examining the dark ugly laceration across Emily's neck. 'The deceased suffered a catastrophic injury to her neck and the wound looks so precise it almost suggests someone used a thin wire ligature of some sort as a garrotte.

The pathologist continued, saying nothing for a few moments. He moved Emily's head from one side to another. 'There would have been some blood loss from this injury.' He looked over at Caren. 'And that means the killer would likely have some blood on his hands and probably clothes.'

Caren nodded and asked, 'How was the injury caused?'

'It's difficult to be exact but a wire of some sort could have caused the injury.' He fell silent and re-examined the injury again. 'Whatever it was, had been wrapped around her neck causing mechanical asphyxiation. The ligature strangulation, which you might refer to as garrotting would cut off the blood flow.'

He turned his attention to Emily's eyes and spent a few moments examining each. 'An asphyxia telltale sign of strangulation is a phenomenon known as petechiae. It's basically small red or purple dots around the eyes caused by bleeding under the skin due to a huge increase in pressure in the veins due to strangulation, or in this case garrotting.'

'Would it have taken a strong person to have done this?'

The pathologist pondered before replying. 'It's difficult to speculate. It depends if they used some sort of spindle to wind the wire, which would need some planning.'

Once he had finished examining the wound he turned to

inspect the rest of Emily Hughes' body. He started with her feet and worked up the body. 'There were signs of dust and dirt on her trousers which suggest she had been kneeling.'

'So the killer could have attacked her from behind, pushed her to the ground and then pulled the wire tight until she had died,' Huw said.

'Top of the class, detective sergeant,' Langmore said. 'That would seem logical. Which in part would answer your question, Caren, of whether a strong person was needed. The element of surprise offers significant strength in itself. I'll check the wound in more detail but I cannot see any sign of a rope. So the wound was probably caused by a wire of some sort. Especially to cut so deeply.'

Once he had finished with the body, he began the Y incision of the chest and abdomen dictating as he removed each of the organs of the body. Caren had learned to compartmentalise her emotions. This was part of her job. Emily Hughes was dead and they had to find her killer. That was the only priority. She glanced over at Huw and noticed a hand over his mouth. Perhaps they shouldn't have had that sandwich at lunchtime after all. He stared at the pathologist, not even acknowledging Caren.

Before he started on the skull, he announced. 'Everything I've seen so far would suggest that she was a fit and healthy young woman.'

Caren nodded briefly. She wasn't being invited to comment.

Then Nigel reached for the saw that would slice open Emily Hughes's skull. The sound always reminded her of the DIY power tools Alun and her father used. Soon enough Nigel Langmore examined the brain carefully and then placed into a stainless-steel receptacle on the table by his side.

Caren had seen enough.

'So can you give us a formal cause of death?'

'Strangulation causing asphyxia.'

'And time of death?'

'It's difficult to be precise because she had been in the water. Do you know when she was last seen alive?'

'She was working in a pub in the marina until eleven.'

'I can give you an upper limit of sixteen hours from when she was found given her liver temperature at the scene. But given the water it may have been a lot less than that.'

Caren nodded. 'Thanks.' At least they had a reasonable timeline for when Emily may have last been seen. And they had a cause of death.

'I'll send you my full report in due course.'

'Thanks, Nigel.'

Caren jerked her head at Huw telling him to follow her out and as soon as they were outside the mortuary both stood for a moment taking in the afternoon sunshine.

'I don't know how they do it,' Huw said. 'Cutting up dead people all day, and the smell…'

'Makes you glad to be alive. Let's get back to headquarters.'

Detective Constables Rhys Davies and Alice Sharp got to their feet when Caren and Huw arrived at the Incident Room. Caren had told them before: she wasn't a stickler for that sort of formality and she had insisted they were not to call her 'ma'am'. When they both acknowledged her with a simple 'boss', it reinforced for her that she was in charge.

Caren walked up to the board as Hugh took his seat by his usual desk. She looked at the image of Emily Hughes.

'The post-mortem confirmed that someone used some sort of ligature to kill Emily,' Caren said, adding that the pathologist believed a wire must have been used.

'Looking for that sort of weapon could be as easy as searching for a needle in a very big haystack,' Alice said.

Typical of her to strike a negative tone at the beginning of an inquiry, Caren thought.

'Hopefully the crime scene investigators will turn up something from their search around the marina.' Caren would not countenance the possibility the wire or cable or whatever else had been used as the weapon wouldn't be found. She turned back to look at her team. 'Bring me up to date with what happened today.'

'We've ruled out that she would have earned all that cash from the Hope and Anchor. They pay all salaries through the electronic banking system,' Rhys said.

'I'm seeing Detective Inspector Simon Williams later. I've asked him for any intelligence that Emily Hughes could have been involved in the drug trade.'

Knowing that there was no realistic way for Emily Hughes to have legally earned the cash she had stashed in her cupboard, it had to mean she had somehow gained the money unlawfully. Caren turned back to look at her face on the board. 'I wonder where she got all that money?'

'Once we know the answer to that I reckon we'll crack the case wide open,' Huw said.

'I've been working my way through some of the CCTV footage the harbourmaster has sent us,' Rhys said. 'But I'm waiting for quite a lot of footage from other cameras in the area.'

'Good, we need to be able to establish a timeline and a route for her journey from the Hope and Anchor to the likely spot where she was killed. It's going to narrow things down.'

'We've had the preliminary results of the background checks on Mark Tremain, boss,' Alice said. 'He has a history of violence and burglaries. And he was a suspect in various burglaries from Southampton marina several years ago. He was charged with possession of stolen items including valuable electronic equipment from several yachts.'

Caren looked over at his face on the board. 'Before we talk to Mark Tremain, get more details about his background. And has anybody been able to follow up with the officers from Swansea city centre about the stalker women have been complaining about?'

'I spoke to a sergeant who promised to get back to me,'

Rhys said.

'Chase it. And Huw and I called at St Hubert's Hostel earlier. Apparently, Emily Hughes helped there regularly with her friend Rachel Scott in tow occasionally. Get the names of the staff members run through the system. And do background checks on Rachel Scott.'

Rhys and Alice nodded their confirmation. Caren read the time and realised Simon Williams was late, which meant she was going to be much later getting home to Aled. She walked over to her office, but she had been sitting for only a few minutes when she heard the voice of Simon Williams in the Incident Room.

'Sorry I'm late,' Simon said as he stood in the doorway to Caren's room. He had a strong jawline and an open, interested face. His hair was neatly cut and Caren noticed a few streaks of grey. His navy suit fitted his slim build perfectly.

She had just completed tapping out a message to her mother telling her she was almost finished for the day. She waved her fellow officer in and he sat on one of the chairs.

'I've done some digging around into this Emily Hughes but I can't find anything to suggest she is linked to the drug trade. Do you have anything else that would help me narrow down the search?'

'She was in a relationship with one of her lecturers at the University, a Johann Ackland, and a previous boyfriend, a Mark Tremain, has got a history of violence and handling stolen property.'

'I'll run the name through our system and circulate the other officers on my team. But you should be aware there is a history of low-level social drug taking amongst the yacht owners that has come to our attention. It's all personal use stuff and never justified an intervention from us. Are you aware of the burglaries that have taken place around the marina?'

Caren shook her head. 'No, I'm not.'

'It might be relevant.'

Caren nodded. 'We'll get onto that first thing in the morning.'

Chapter 12

Caren hadn't spotted her friend Susan Howard dropping her son at school that morning. It probably meant that Susan had started work early. Her husband, Dafydd, often did the school run early. Contacting the forensic team was one of Caren's priorities.

She arrived at the Incident Room at the same time as Huw Margam.

It always pleased her he was prompt, particularly at the beginning of an important inquiry. She was getting to know him much better now, having worked with him for several months. He could be reserved, but she always felt she could rely upon his good judgement.

'Morning,' Huw said. Caren returned the greeting. They stood by the Incident Room board for a moment looking at the image of Emily Hughes and now Mark Tremain's and Johann Ackland's, added yesterday.

'How did you get on with Detective Inspector Simon Williams?' Huw said.

'His team has got no intelligence linking Emily Hughes to the drug trade. But he told me about a series of burglaries in the marina area.'

'And you believe it could be connected to Emily's murder?'

'We need to look at every angle.'

Rhys Davies and Alice Sharp arrived together and the sound of their conversation filled the Incident Room. They exchanged greetings with Caren and Huw and moments later, before Caren could assemble priorities for the day, Susan Howard walked in.

'Morning, Caren,' Susan said. 'We should have finished in the marina by lunchtime. But I wanted to tell you we believe we've found the spot where Emily was murdered.'

'Excellent,' Caren said. 'We'll get down there later this morning and you can show us.'

Caren pointed over at the map of the marina on the board and then asked Susan to show her approximately where she believed Emily had been killed. The crime scene manager studied the map carefully and pointed to an area near a block of flats. 'I can be more exact when I see you later. Can someone send me a copy of this map so that I can be accurate?'

'I'll get that done,' Rhys said.

'We've also been able to recover a strand of hair from Emily's clothing. I've sent it for forensic analysis and marked the request as extremely urgent. We should have the result without delay.'

'Anything else? Scraps of clothing, skin particles?'

Susan shook her head. 'My guess is that Emily was frantically trying to remove the ligature clawing against her own skin. And the killer was probably wearing gloves, but nobody is clever enough not to leave a fragment or a trace. It's just that we haven't been able to find it, forensically at least.'

'Thanks, Susan.'

Once Susan Howard had left, Caren turned to the rest of the team.

'We've got to prioritise establishing precisely the route Emily Hughes took from the Hope and Anchor to where she was killed. Huw and I will go down to the marina this morning – I want to talk to the Commodore of the sailing club. So I want you, Rhys, focused on coordinating with the house-to-house team speaking to the homeowners near the possible route of her journey.'

Rhys Davies nodded his understanding. 'Do you want me to finish off viewing the video footage?'

Caren tipped her head at Alice. 'Both of you get onto that too. Someone must have been walking around the marina. Somebody must have seen something.'

'I'll do some digging into Mark Tremain's background as well, boss,' Alice said.

'And what do we know about Tom Hughes, Emily's

brother?'

Rhys piped up. 'I did a preliminary search against his name and there's nothing on the Police National Computer. And there is no mention of him in any intelligence reports.'

Something from their meeting with Mr and Mrs Hughes and Tom had concerned Caren. A comment he had made suggested he expected something bad to happen to his sister. 'We'll go and see Tom Hughes after we visit the Commodore.'

Caren retreated to her room and started searching for the officer in charge of the burglaries. She knew that different complaints coming into the Wales Police Service at different times might not always be joined up together quickly. So she might be looking for two or more officers who had originally been tasked with investigating. Until it had become apparent there was a pattern involved, it might never be allocated to a single team.

Frustration grew in Caren's mind as she was passed from one officer to another in the Swansea area divisional command before being bounced to two officers at headquarters in Cardiff who promptly denied any involvement.

Eventually she spoke to a chief inspector responsible for supervising the teams in Swansea.

'There have been burglaries of flats and houses. They were all empty at the time and the usual valuables were taken: TVs and computers,' the officer said.

'How many have there been?'

'How is that relevant? One is too many.'

'I don't know. I've got an open murder inquiry and my victim worked in the marina and had a large stash of money in her home.'

'Must have been drugs. You know what it's like amongst these middle-class sailors with too much money. A bit of cannabis and cocaine is like a glass of wine to you and me.'

'We don't believe there's any connection with drugs.'

The chief inspector grunted disbelievingly.

'I've just put together a small team who are looking into the burglaries. One of the officers discovered that a couple of the flat owners reported a domestic burglary at their empty homes in Cardiff too. He thought it was too much of a coincidence.'

Caren sat back and pondered for a moment. She never liked coincidences.

'I'd really appreciate if your team would keep me informed.'

The DCI seemed pleased when the conversation finished. Caren got to her feet and gave Huw a shout. 'Let's go.'

Chapter 13

Alice Sharp had enjoyed her time with Detective Inspector Sammy Evans, DI Waits' predecessor. He was tough and uncompromising, just the sort of police officer Alice wanted to be. She admired the new detective inspector for the hard work she put in and Alice knew she could rely on Caren to be supportive.

Even so, she still missed the Sammy Evans approach to policing – knocking heads together, pushing the rulebook and encouraging that sense of excitement in his team. Police officers like Evans were a thing of the past. Everything had to be dealt with correctly these days.

When DI Evans had retired, Alice had worried that she and Rhys Davies and Huw Margam would be moved to another team. Even though Rhys Davies was young and inexperienced, she quite enjoyed working with him. He was a typical country boy, a little wet behind the ears, but very dedicated. It hadn't surprised her that Huw Margam had taken to working with Detective Inspector Waits so easily. He had a natural self-confidence she envied.

Alice's husband worked in one of the supermarket distribution hubs on an industrial estate outside Swansea. After he had met Huw and Rhys and DI Sammy Evans socially on one occasion he had described Huw as a posh git. It had brought a smile to Alice's face.

'I'll get started on the footage the harbourmaster sent us,' Rhys looked over at Alice.

He was wearing a serious look that morning. He always did at the beginning of an inquiry. But when he smiled, one cheek would pucker more than the other. For the son of a farmer he had impeccably tidy hair. His hands were rough, which she put down to years of helping on the farm. Rhys often made comments about labouring as a teenager. He had dark eyes that when he smiled could look full of life. It made Alice realise how much of an age gap there was between them, and she ruminated about how old she felt compared to some of these young detectives.

'If we're not able to get anything from the CCTV footage then God knows how we're going to make a case,' Alice replied.

'Don't sound so cynical.'

Alice didn't respond. She had more than her fair share of criticism for what she thought was down-to-earth advice or comment. Her task that morning was to build a background picture of Mark Tremain. After all, at the moment he was their principal person of interest.

Emily Hughes had been stupid enough to sleep with one of her lecturers, which Alice thought was bad enough. So she was keeping an open mind about the prospect that Johann Ackland might be involved. After all, he was a man with a status in life and a reputation to protect. But Mark Tremain was her priority.

She opened the results of the Police National Computer check. Mark Tremain had a conviction for assault on a woman, six years previously when he had been working in a chandlery in Southampton. The second entry was for a conviction at the Southampton Crown Court when he was given a suspended sentence for handling stolen property.

It took Alice an hour to track down the detective constable in the Hampshire police who had been responsible for managing the inquiry.

'We always thought that Tremain was part of a larger conspiracy to steal items from the chandlery and yachts on the south coast. Sailing is big business here.'

'Were there many others involved?'

'He faced prosecution alongside another man who received a prison sentence. At the time we reckoned that Mark Tremain was lucky not to have had an immediate custodial sentence.'

Alice knew exactly what the officer meant. Justice could be a lottery when sentencing depended upon the judge on the day.

'What is Mark Tremain doing now?' the officer asked.

'He's working in a chandlery business in Swansea Marina, and he's linked to a recent murder.'

The officer sounded surprised. 'Jesus, murder. I would have said that's way out of Mark Tremain's league.'

'But he's got a conviction for assault.'

'Not the sort of violence that would give him a propensity for murder.'

Before she finished the call the officer promised to send her the file of papers relating to the case. Then she got down to completing details of Tremain's home circumstances. She knew he was single and had lived in Southampton before moving to the Swansea area. It had taken her several searches to pin down the exact details of all the addresses where Tremain had lived. He had lived nowhere for more than a few months. Certainly not putting down roots and definitely not on the property ladder, as he was now a tenant of an old cottage on the outskirts of the city.

Alice put together a list of the homes and printed out a copy of the photograph taken of his cottage. Then she pinned an image of the old property underneath his photograph. She turned to look over at Rhys who was gazing at his monitor. She offered to make coffee, and Rhys gratefully accepted. She traipsed through into the kitchen near to the Incident Room and returned a few moments later plonking a mug onto a coaster on his desk. Rhys mumbled his thanks.

Mark Tremain had moved employers as frequently as he did homes. Before joining the company in the marina, Tremain had worked in a sheet metal-working company in the Swansea Valley before moving to a company making double glazing.

Tremain's date of birth and his employment record were the first part of his history and once the email had arrived from the Hampshire Constabulary with Tremain's case file, she was able to get some more details about his family, including a brother who lived in the Swansea area.

When she had the bare bones of Mark Tremain's life in place, she turned to his social media accounts. It always amazed her how much modern policing relied on discovering links on Facebook or Instagram. She didn't understand TikTok, but knew it was important in any inquiry.

She scrolled through the images on Tremain's Facebook page. She was looking for a connection to Emily Hughes. It was easy enough to unfriend someone on Facebook, but in Alice's experience few people did that. Eventually, Alice found he was friends with Emily Hughes. It didn't surprise her that Emily's Facebook account was still in existence. She knew of people whose Facebook page was still alive many years after they'd died. Was it laziness or a desire to pay homage to the deceased? Alice thought it was a bit weird.

Alice was pleased to find an email with Mark Tremain's financial details when she checked her inbox. The Wales Police Service had a standard protocol for working through bank accounts. She would start at the most recent and work her way back until she had built a detailed picture.

There were regular payments into the account from Mark Tremain's employer, but recently there had been small irregular cash deposits. Alice fumbled for the calculator on her desk and tapped in the numbers, and she was surprised to find that over £3000 had been deposited. It made the difference between keeping Mark Tremain solvent and struggling to pay his debts. And he had quite a lot to repay.

Alice sat back and pondered. A large amount of cash had been recovered from Emily Hughes at home and now cash was deposited into Mark Tremain's bank account. Was there a connection?

Alice got up to stretch her legs and walked over to the board. 'I've just been working on Tremain's finances and it would seem he has a sugar daddy as well.'

Rhys looked up. Alice continued: '£3000 has been paid into his account in cash in the past eighteen months.'

'You need to tell the boss.' Rhys got to his feet and joined Alice, putting both hands to the small of his back and stretching. 'I've still got hours of this footage to look at.'

Alice pointed to the map pinned to the board. 'Mark Tremain has convictions for handling stolen goods from the Southampton marina when he was working in that area in the sailing industry. Maybe he and Emily Hughes had a nice little number. She gets to know a lot of the yacht owners from working in the Hope and Anchor. She tips off her boyfriend who steals the items and then flogs them. They split the money but for some reason she decides she wants a bigger slice of the action.'

'She gets greedy and decides that she can do without Tremain. But he finds out and…'

'Very good, Constable Davies, we'll make a detective out of you yet.'

'So all I have to do is find footage of Mark Tremain in the marina holding a piece of wire that he later uses to kill Emily Hughes.'

Alice walked back to her desk. 'I'm sure that would be most helpful.'

Before calling Inspector Waits, Alice decided she would complete some background checks on Rachel Scott. She would not dismiss the possibility there was some connection with the drug trade – unaccounted-for hoards of money and unlikely deposits into bank accounts always suggested the murky world of illegal drugs was involved.

The Police National Computer search against Rachel's name came back clear. But her name popped up as being involved with low-level drug selling. It hadn't been anything the officers involved could take to the Crown Prosecution Service. But it suggested to Alice that there was more to Rachel Scott. She emailed the officer her request, asking for any information he had.

It was a little before lunch when Rhys shouted out for Alice to join him. 'You won't believe this.' He waved his hand inviting her to join him.

'What have you got?' Alice said, looking over his shoulder at the monitor.

'I've found a camera which has got somebody running through the marina at eleven thirteen pm.'

'Can you identify who it is?'

Rhys shook his head. 'We'll need to do a public appeal.'

'I'll call the boss.'

Chapter 14

Caren looked down at the stone surface at which Susan Howard had pointed, speculating that the mark there looked like an unsuccessful attempt to wash away a bloodstain. Caren knew that removing blood was exceptionally difficult.

'It's difficult to think what the killer was trying to achieve,' Susan said.

'Luckily, we don't have to discover that.' Caren looked up at the building by her side. No CCTV camera visible and no street lighting in the adjacent area made the spot where they were standing the perfect setting for an unobserved killing.

A cool, sharp gust of wind reminded Caren that this was a waterside location. It carried the smell of seaweed, salt and oil.

Susan continued: 'The location is quite isolated from the rest of the marina. She was probably heading to an exit that's a shortcut to the town itself.'

Caren nodded. Emily Hughes was literally a few feet from safety when the killer had struck. This wasn't a random, opportunistic attack. The killer knew exactly what he or she was doing, and where to strike.

'I'll need photographs of this area,' Caren said.

'I've already asked one of my team to do that,' Susan said. 'We've completed a detailed search of this area and I believe she was dragged into this alleyway where she was probably forced to her knees and then killed.'

'And the killer seems to have known exactly where there were no CCTV cameras,' Huw added.

Susan then took two steps behind her and indicated for Caren and Huw to join her. They stood on a piece of waste ground from which it was a short walk towards the marina basin. 'Once Emily Hughes had been dispatched we think she was probably dragged towards the marina itself where she was pushed in. It's a blind spot for the CCTV cameras.'

'Which suggests the killer knew the locations.' Caren wasn't looking for confirmation, but Susan and Huw murmured their agreement.

'We will have completed the full forensic search later this morning. We'll tell the uniformed officers they can then complete their house-to-house enquiries with the homeowners and business owners.'

'Thanks, Susan,' Caren said. 'Send me a full report when you can.'

Caren and Huw left the crime scene investigators to complete their work and walked over to the sailing club, where they had a meeting with the Commodore. A short distance from the city marina, the building the club occupied reminded Caren that yacht owners had two options for mooring: either pay at the club or through the city marina itself.

The main entrance door squeaked a complaint as Huw forced it open. The sound of a vacuum cleaner filtered through from the area to their right where two cleaners were busy at work. Through a glass partition Caren glimpsed two men at a table, studying a map.

She had to force another door to open and Caren walked over to both men. 'We're looking for the Commodore of the sailing club.'

'That's me, Charles Holloway.' A tall thin man walked over to join them.

Caren and Huw had their warrant cards ready, but he didn't bother examining either. 'Follow me.' He led them up a flight of stairs to a suite of rooms on the first floor.

Furniture filled the small room and the walls were covered with photographs of sailors and certificates for sailing honours. A wooden chair creaked when Caren sat down. Commodore Holloway's desk chair was equally old and battered. Huw scanned the surroundings, clocking all the photographs before sitting next to Caren.

'I'm the senior investigating officer in charge of the

inquiry into the murder of Emily Hughes.'

'Of course, of course. Terrible, absolutely terrible.' The accent definitely wasn't Swansea, more south coast of England.

'We need the names of all the yacht owners that moor their yachts in the marina you administer.'

'I'll get straight onto it.' Holloway clicked into his computer and without looking at Caren asked for an email address. She passed over one of her cards. Once he had typed in the details, he turned to Caren. 'I'll send you the details as soon as we finish. I thought I had them reasonably easy to hand, but they update the data at the beginning of every season and I wouldn't want you to have outdated information.' He sat back in his chair and Caren could see him taking a moment to compose his thoughts. 'But you can't possibly suspect anybody associated with the sailing club being responsible for this heinous crime, can you?'

'We need the information as part of our routine enquiries.' Caren knew she was sounding like somebody from a TV crime drama. But it was true. 'Did you know Emily Hughes?'

'I can't say I knew her personally, but some of the staff here and the club members have told me she was on the staff of the Hope and Anchor. They provide all our catering and so Emily must have been a regular at our parties and balls.'

Imagining guests in long dresses and dinner jackets attending a ball in the ramshackle premises they were sitting in struck Caren as a little unlikely.

'It might help if we could have the names of your other flag officers and the directors or administrative staff here at the club,' Huw said.

Huw's comfortable use of the right terminology impressed Caren.

Commodore Holloway shared the details of the vice and rear commodores, confirming also that he would email the details. It was the name of the resources director, Johann

Ackland, that immediately caught Caren's attention.

'Dr Ackland, the university lecturer?' Huw said.

'Johann and his wife are both very active sailors, and they take part fully in the social life of the club. Harriet Ackland is the membership secretary and extremely efficient at it, I might say.'

'How many club members do you have?'

'There are well over four hundred. Not everyone has yachts, some are just social members.'

'Do you have any information about which of your yacht owners have properties in the marina area?'

Holloway frowned. 'No, we don't have that sort of information. But I have heard complaints about a spate of burglaries recently both from the yachts and their homes. Some of them are furious. Quite a few have lost some very valuable kit from their yachts. A lot of marine equipment has been stolen. Stuff like that can cost thousands to replace.'

'Have all the homeowners and yacht owners reported these thefts?' Caren said.

'I don't know. I suspect not, as some will feel they have nothing to gain by doing it. I'm sorry to have to say this, Detective Inspector, but some of the members don't have a great deal of faith in the Wales Police Service to investigate thefts from yachts.'

'I can reassure you, Mr Holloway, that the Wales Police Service will treat every complaint with the utmost seriousness.'

Holloway rolled his eyes.

'I suggest you circulate your members, inviting them to report it to us if they have been the subject of a theft or burglary.'

Holloway nodded. Caren got to her feet and she and Huw left the sailing club.

The mobile rang in Caren's jacket pocket as she headed back to the car. She recognised Rhys' number.

'We've been able to establish that Mark Tremain has

been depositing cash into his bank account to help him pay various credit card debts over the past eighteen months.'

Caren paused and stood for a moment as she listened to Rhys' explanation about Tremain's background.

'And from footage on the night of the murder, I've spotted a man running in the marina area. But we can't identify him.'

'We might need to do a public appeal. He might have important evidence. And in the meantime, do a full background search on Johann Ackland and his wife.'

'Yes, boss.'

Caren turned to Huw. 'Before we speak to Tremain, there's someone else we need to speak to.'

Chapter 15

Before leaving Swansea Marina, Caren made a call to the local divisional police station in Swansea. She found the inspector in charge and explained why she needed two uniformed officers to invite Mark Tremain into headquarters for an interview. She didn't want to waste any time by acting as a taxi herself. Before speaking to Tremain, she wanted to iron out a concern in her mind.

'Let's go,' Caren said, once she had finished the call.

It didn't take long for them to drive the short distance to the home of Gavin and Maria Hughes. The family liaison officer's vehicle was parked in the drive outside, and two vehicles were occupying the paved area in front of the house.

'We need to find out if Emily's parents or her brother have any explanation for the cash we found in her flat. And we need an explanation from Tom what exactly he meant by those comments when we saw them initially.'

Huw nodded.

They left the vehicle and walked over to the property.

'Ma'am,' the FLO said formally once she'd opened the door.

'We need to speak to Tom Hughes.'

'He's watching TV.' She tipped her head at the door to the sitting room.

'We'll speak to him first but tell Mr and Mrs Hughes we need a word with them as well.'

Tom Hughes was sitting watching a science fiction series on a streaming service.

'We need a word, Tom.' Caren sounded forceful but not hostile.

It took a few seconds for Tom Hughes to work the remote to silence the television. Caren and Huw sat down.

'When we were here on Monday you made some comments about Emily's friends, and particularly Mark Tremain.'

'Have you arrested him yet?'

'All I can tell you is that we are doing everything possible to find your sister's killer. But we need your help. What do you know about Mark Tremain?'

Tom gave Caren and then Huw an angry look.

'You should fucking arrest him.'

'Do you know something specific about Mark Tremain that is going to help us?'

'He was involved with some bad shit. A friend of mine told me all about his connections. Tremain had more cash than he could ever have legally earned. All he did was fix engines for fucks' sake.'

'What did this friend tell you?'

'That Tremain was involved with a man called Gerard Rankin. You people know all about him. He's Swansea mafia. If you want to scare somebody or if somebody owes you money then Rankin is your man. He's got his finger in lots of different pies.'

Caren looked over at Huw, who gave her a knowing nod as though the name Gerard Rankin was familiar.

'If he was involved with Gerard Rankin, what was the connection?'

'This mate of mine had seen Mark with Rankin a couple of times. When he heard Mark was involved with Emily, he told me she should be super-careful.'

'Who is this friend of yours?'

'Don't be mad. I'm not going to tell you.'

Caren decided not to push the issue. She was already making some progress with Tom Hughes. She was pleased when Huw butted in and sounded reasonable with his question.

'You've been very helpful so far, Tom. The team is dedicated to finding Emily's killer and bringing that person to justice.'

Tom gave a nod of acknowledgement.

'Is there anything else you can tell us about Emily's

personal life that might help us identify somebody with a motive?'

'What do you mean?'

'Did she argue with anybody? Did she ever tell you she was frightened?'

Tom glanced at the door into the hallway. 'Emily and that other bloke...'

'You'll need to spell it out?'

'That lecturer she was going out with. I saw them in a nightclub in town. He was all over her. I spoke to him when he was at the bar. I told him straight to leave her alone. He just sneered at me as though I was a piece of dirt.'

'Were you always this protective of your sister?'

'I looked out for her. We were best mates until she started seeing Tremain and Ackland and....' Caren sensed he couldn't articulate his feelings. 'Things changed after that, and she was never the same.'

'And who exactly do you mean by "that lecturer"?'

'Ackland, of course. He has a swanky yacht in the marina. And I discovered he has a wife, so I felt quite tempted to go and see her. Tell her exactly what was happening so that she could put a stop to it.'

'And did you?'

'No, of course not.'

'Do you think that Ackland could have been responsible for killing her?'

'How would I know?' Aggression returned to Tom's voice.

'And your parents don't know about her relationship with Ackland?'

'No, and I don't want them to. I want them to remember Emily without him in the picture.'

'That's not going to be possible.'

A look of angry frustration crossed his face. His eyes narrowed slightly.

'And you should talk to Rachel Scott – after all she was

the one who introduced Emily to Mark Tremain.'

'Why do you think she might help?' Caren hoped her questioning would encourage Tom to share something more specific, something they could use directly with Rachel Scott.

'It's nothing. I don't know anything that would help you about Rachel Scott. I just didn't like her.'

Caren wondered whether there was anybody Tom Hughes liked.

'How often did you see Emily?'

'All the time… Why do you ask?'

'I want to know about your relationship with her. What did you know about her life?'

Tom Hughes shrugged.

'Did she ever mention to you having more money than usual?'

Now his eyes opened wide.

'No, she never did. Why?'

'We found a large amount of cash in the room of the home she occupied with the other students. Do you have any idea how she came by that money?'

'It was probably that Mark Tremain or even Rachel Scott. They can tell you.'

Despite Caren's continued questioning, it became apparent Tom Hughes had no further helpful information for the inquiry. As Tom pointed the remote at the TV, they left him, and the room filled with the sound of an action sequence from a far-off planet.

They found Mr and Mrs Hughes sitting at the kitchen table, the FLO tidying up the sink.

Caren pulled up a chair and sat looking over at Mr and Mrs Hughes. It had only been two days since they had learned of their daughter's death, and Caren couldn't imagine how it must feel. Losing a child was against the normal chronology of life. She remembered how empty and desperate she had felt after Alun had died. It had felt like an eternity, but now she had accepted his death and was determined to move on with her life despite knowing her marriage had been a lie. After all, she had her son to look after.

'Have you made any progress?' Gavin Hughes said. His skin was pale and his eyes sunken. He looked as though he hadn't eaten anything for the last two days.

'It's still very early in the inquiry, Mr Hughes,' Caren replied softly, 'but we have a number of lines of enquiry. There is one thing we wanted to ask you.'

Hearing the question, Maria Hughes raised her eyes and she and her husband looked over at Caren.

'We found a stash of money – a little over five thousand pounds – in a drawer in Emily's room. Do you have any explanation of how she came by that cash?'

Caren stared intently over at Mr and Mrs Hughes, looking for any glimmer of recognition but they both looked dumbfounded.

'I've no idea.' Mr Hughes sounded surprised. 'She certainly didn't get it from us. I don't have that sort of cash lying around. We are not rich people. We've done everything we can to support Emily while she was at university. But… Five thousand pounds.' He shook his head. 'I've no idea where she got that money from.'

'Had you seen any change in Emily recently?'

'No, nothing,' Mr Hughes said.

Maria Hughes nodded, agreeing with her husband. Soon afterwards Caren and Huw left Mr and Mrs Hughes, and the FLO saw them to the door. She walked out to the car with them.

'They're both taking it very badly,' the FLO said. 'Family members have called, but they still need to sort out the funeral.'

Caren nodded. 'Do what you can to help and keep me posted.'

Back in her car, a message reached Huw's mobile. He turned to Caren and announced, 'Mark Tremain is in a cell in headquarters.'

'Good, let's get going.'

Chapter 16

Caren sat at her desk finishing a hurried sandwich and a banana she had bought at the canteen en route back to her office. She and Huw had been finalising the plan for the interview with Mark Tremain.

An email from Susan Howard, which Caren had read when she had returned from Swansea, confirmed the strand of hair removed from Emily Hughes' clothing belonged to Mark Tremain gave her a welcome boost. Thank goodness for forensic laboratories working quickly, Caren thought. She had emailed Susan an acknowledgement with her thanks.

It gave them the ability to build a better and more complete picture of Mark Tremain.

Huw stood by the door to her room, and she waved him in. He plonked a mug with his unfinished coffee onto a coaster on her desk. 'I've been reading some of the background of Mark Tremain from the police in Southampton. He gave them the runaround for a long time.'

Caren nodded. 'And he has a temper. He's probably been getting away with assaults for years. Often people are too afraid to make a complaint, particularly women, and that encourages violent behaviour.'

She got to her feet and gathered together the papers on her desk. 'Let's see what he has to say for himself.'

The custody suite at headquarters was like many others Caren had been to while serving with the police. Often the smell of urine or vomit would linger, despite the efforts of the cleaning staff. Cleaning fluid would be sloshed around the place, contributing to the lush cocktail the officers would have to breathe in most days. She had worked as a custody sergeant for a brief period when it had been made clear to her that preferment depended on doing a stint in the custody suite. She had made certain it was as short as possible, pleased – ecstatic even – when the opportunity arose to work as a detective in one of the teams at Northern Division.

Sergeant Daniel Thorpe, on duty that afternoon, was a familiar face and he smiled broadly. 'Detective Inspector Waits. Welcome to the wonderful world of the Wales Police Service's hospitality.'

Having a decent sense of humour would make working in the custody suite bearable.

'It's lovely to see you again,' Daniel said. 'You'll be delighted to hear that Mr Tremain has availed himself of the very best legal advice.'

Caren paused and narrowed her eyes, uncertain, exactly, what Daniel was saying.

'It's not that bloody Ifan Llywelyn, is it?' Huw said.

'Excellent, your deduction skills are unrivalled. We'll make a detective out of you yet, Detective Sergeant.'

Caren groaned. She had come across Ifan Llywelyn on her first murder case. He was a former detective who had been a valued member of Western Division until he had retired. Then he had gone over to the dark side, as one of his former colleagues said, retraining as a police station representative. It meant he could advise suspects in the custody suite and during interviews. His background gave him a unique advantage.

'I've allocated you one of the interview rooms which has digital recording equipment,' Daniel said, a serious tone taking over his voice.

Once Caren knew where the interview would take place, she walked through with Huw who made certain all the equipment was ready just as Mark Tremain entered with Ifan Llywelyn.

'Good afternoon, Detective Inspector,' Ifan said.

Caren nodded, giving Ifan a brief smile. 'We're going to be conducting this interview under caution, but your client isn't under arrest.'

'Noted.' Ifan was tall and thin with a head that Caren guessed he had shaved that morning as it glistened in the artificial light of the interview room.

Tremain sat next to Ifan. His long, unkempt hair spread

across his shoulders and he wore a greying T-shirt under a zip top with the name of the company he worked for sewn into the material. His work trousers had a dozen different pockets. He had dark eyes, a little too close together, and he hadn't shaved that morning, which gave him an intense look.

Formalities completed, Caren looked over at Tremain.

'I'm investigating the death of Emily Hughes. Are you aware of who I am talking about?'

'Yeah, of course.'

'We believe she was killed sometime after eleven pm last Sunday evening. A yachtsman found her body on Monday morning in the marina.'

Caren looked at Tremain, knowing it wasn't a question but hoping he might volunteer some response. But he looked at her blankly.

'Were you in a relationship with Emily Hughes?'

'Yeah, of sorts. We went out for a while.'

'When did the relationship finish?'

Tremain shrugged. 'I can't tell you. I'm not much good with dates.'

Huw butted in. 'Was it recently or in the past two months?'

'Weeks, I suppose.'

'Why did you break up?'

He shrugged again.

'Is it true that Emily finished with you?'

Tremain looked at Ifan, who gave him a brief nod.

'Were you angry that things hadn't worked out?'

'Yeah, I was pretty upset.'

Caren continued: 'Let's come back to your relationship with Emily Hughes a little later.'

Caren sorted the papers on the table in front of her so that she had Tremain's bank statements readily at hand.

'We completed a standard search of your financial records and several cash payments were made into your bank account over the last eighteen months. We'd like you to explain how you got that money?'

'I'm not certain I see the relevance of this,' Ifan said.

'It'll become clearer once we are further ahead in the interview.'

'It's none of your business.' Tremain's voice sounded hard-edged.

'Everything is my business if it relates to a murder inquiry. Where did you get that money? Is it money you've got from selling drugs?'

Tremain grunted. 'Oh, for fucks' sake.'

'If it's from work you've done legitimately, please tell us so we can check it out with the people involved.'

'Go to hell.'

'A substantial sum of money was recovered from Emily's room in the shared house. Her possession of money and your unexplained cash deposits indicate a potential connection. So what is it?'

Tremain sat expressionless, just shaking his head.

'Let's come back to your relationship with Emily Hughes. Did you fight with Johann Ackland at the pub in the marina after you found out about him and her being in a relationship?'

'I was drunk.'

'So do you admit having an altercation with Johann Ackland about his relationship with Emily Hughes?'

'She'd been leading me on. She was telling me how much she loved being with me but she'd been seeing Johann Ackland all the time.'

'And Mr and Mrs Hughes, Emily's parents, have confirmed that you showed up at their property in a foul temper threatening Emily after she broke up with you. Is that true?'

'They never liked me.'

'The fact that she broke up with you must have made you pretty angry.'

'Yeah, suppose it did.'

'And you were angry enough to fight with her, weren't you'?

Tremain straightened in his chair. 'I don't know what you mean.'

'You've got a history of violence, Mark. You were sentenced in the Southampton Crown Court to a period of imprisonment for assaulting a woman several years ago. From what I've read about the case you blamed her for everything. Exactly as you're doing now.'

'This isn't fucking right. You can't hold against me something that happened years ago.'

'We've recovered a strand of hair from Emily's clothes and DNA analysis has proved it belongs to you. On the night she was killed did you argue with her?'

'No, of course not. Don't be mad. But.... we did argue a few days ago... and I may have.'

'May have what?'

'Things got heated and I may have shoved her.'

'What does that mean?'

'Exactly what I've said. That must be how my DNA is on her jacket.'

'Were you trying to reason with her so that she'd come back and re-establish her relationship with you? Did things spiral out of control and you lost your temper entirely?'

'Don't be mad.'

'Did you fight with Emily Hughes because of her relationship with Johann Ackland? And we shall be undertaking a search of your property. It would be good for you to give us an explanation now for any substantial sums of cash that we might find.'

'I must say, Detective Inspector, this strikes me as a bit of a fishing expedition,' Ifan said.

'We have evidence Mark argued with Ackland and there are fragments of his DNA all over Emily Hughes' clothes.' Caren looked over at Mark Tremain. 'We find that extremely suspicious.' Caren paused. 'Did you kill Emily Hughes?'

'Of course not. And you've got no evidence against me. I don't know how she got the money. How the hell would I know? You need to talk to Rachel Scott. Maybe she knows. She thinks she knows everything about everybody.'

'What do you mean by that?'

'Nothing, nothing.'

Once the interview was completed Mark Tremain was escorted back to his cell. Caren and Huw retreated to her office in the Incident Room. It always amazed Caren how thirsty and hungry she could become after an interview, and she demolished a chocolate bar Huw had brought along with the coffees from the kitchen.

'We won't get the results of the search of his house until the morning,' Huw said.

Caren checked the time, pleased that she'd be able to leave work at a reasonable hour. Her mother had already collected Aled from school, but she was determined to have an evening meal with him, play some games, enjoy his bath time, and read him a story in bed. She got to her feet. 'Until then, he's not going anywhere.'

Chapter 17

When Aled heard his mother coming into the house through the back door he ran towards her. He did his best to wrap his arms around her legs. He led her by the hand, wanting to show her something in the lounge. Ann smiled at Caren.

'He's been building a set of dinosaurs with his Tadcu.'

Caren was pleased that Aled's Tadcu, her father, had made the time to be with them that afternoon. His work as a lecturer left him little time to see Aled.

Several plastic dinosaurs in various stages of construction covered the coffee table.

Aled took great pride in showing his mother everything they had done since he had arrived back from school. 'Aled has been building all these himself.' Trevor beamed at his daughter.

Caren sat cross-legged on the floor as Aled showed her some of the toys he had created. It amazed her he knew the names of the different dinosaurs. He had images of dinosaur species on his pyjamas, T-shirts and on one of the duvet covers, though his favourite was a Spider-Man one.

Soon enough, Ann and Trevor made their excuses and left. Caren thanked her parents profusely for collecting Aled from school. She could never do her job without their support.

'Let us know about tomorrow,' Ann said as she was leaving.

'Of course, I'll message you.'

Caren prepared a meal for herself and Aled and she listened to him as he told her about his day. He sounded grown-up, discussing his friends, their actions, and the teachers' responses. It filled her with pride and immense contentment that Aled had settled well into his school. Uprooting him from his home in North Wales for a new life in Carmarthen had always made her feel apprehensive.

He never inquired about his father; she pondered if he ever reflected on him. He'd probably have no recollection of him. She had photographs and videos ready and waiting for the right moment to share them with him. And ever-present in the background were Alun's parents. They'd probably want to have contact with Aled in due course, but so far she hadn't heard from them. She hoped they would leave any such contact until after the inquest into his death had taken place.

And she wondered if they knew about Miss Hale. What did they think of their son when they'd discovered he had a child with another woman?

She fried sausages, dropped some French fries into the air fryer and put a glass bowl full of baked beans into the microwave. Aled tucked into the food with relish. Once they had finished, she gave Aled a pot of fruit yogurt while she had some stewed fruit, with plain yogurt that she found at the bottom of the fridge. He gazed at her dessert and, as he was halfway through his own, announced, 'Swaps?'

Caren smiled and then burst into laughter. 'Of course.'

Knowing he'd find the fruit in her bowl too tart she put a small dollop on the spoon he was using. He grimaced his dislike. It was moments like this she wouldn't have missed for the world.

After she had cleared away the dishes and they sat and watched some television together – his favourite was the Welsh version of Paw Patrol and the brilliant Bluey. Then it was bath time and pyjamas before she read to him in bed. He had a settled routine of having to read three books, some of which he flicked through quickly, others he was content to have read to him carefully.

Once he was ready for sleep she kissed him lightly and settled him under the duvet.

Back downstairs, she found a bottle of Pinot Grigio in the fridge and poured herself a generous glass. Her mobile had pinged with messages, all of which she had ignored until Aled was in bed.

A message from David Hemsby brought a smile to her face.

I was so looking forward to seeing you this week. The Welsh class has been postponed. But there's a social event at Susan Howard's home on Saturday night. Will you be going?

Caren had seen the messages from the person running the Welsh class informing her that they had postponed the class. She double-checked again and saw a message from Susan in the WhatsApp group that included David Hemsby and the others that were learning the language inviting them to her home that Saturday evening.

She and David Hemsby had both been attending the Welsh class as their respective employers expected them to develop basic proficiency in the language. Starting a relationship with another man so soon after Alun's death wasn't something she had expected. But David was handsome and kind and understood the demands of her work. How would she describe their relationship? They had been on a few dates. Their intimacy had extended to a few kisses but nothing more. Did she want there to be more? She wasn't certain at that moment, but she knew she didn't want to be living alone for the rest of her life. And she wanted Aled to have a father figure.

She tapped back a message. *I'm in the middle of a new case but I should be there.*

His reply was instantaneous. *Lovely, looking forward to seeing you again. Is it the murder of that poor girl in Swansea Marina?*

If I told you, I'd have to kill you. Then she added a winking face emoji.

Look after yourself. Don't work too hard. How is Aled?

Thanks, Aled's good. Building dinosaurs earlier. Now fast asleep in bed.

She took another sip of wine and turned to replying to Susan Howard's message, confirming she hoped to see her on Saturday night. In return, she received two thumbs up. Caren valued her friendship with Susan Howard. It had been lucky that they had struck up a good relationship immediately. She valued Susan's professional approach to managing a crime scene and knew she could rely on her if her parents weren't able to assist with childcare. They had even had some outings as a family with Susan, her husband Dafydd and their son Ieuan.

There were messages from the search team supervisor confirming they had completed a search of Mark Tremain's home and that a full report will be emailed in the morning. But there was nothing to help the inquiry, which frustrated Caren. It meant they couldn't justify holding Mark Tremain in custody.

A text from a number she didn't recognise reached her mobile.

I need to speak to you.

Caren tapped back a message. *Who is this?*

It's Chloe. I shared a house with Emily.

I can see you tomorrow morning

A pause preceded the final reply. It gave the details of a café in Swansea and time – 9 AM.

I'll see you then.

Caren tapped out a message to Huw about the meeting with Chloe and then she spoke to her mother, doublechecking she could take Aled to school.

Then she wondered what on earth Chloe had to tell her.

Chapter 18

Caren allowed herself enough time to park in one of the multi-storey car parks in the middle of Swansea. Aled had been left at her parents' home first thing that morning and she knew her mum would make certain her son had something to eat before school. She hadn't bothered with coffee or breakfast and felt distinctly caffeine deprived when she parked. She walked over to the café where they were meeting Chloe and slipped into a bench seat at a table near the rear a little after eight-forty. She ordered coffee and toast when a waitress came over to take her order.

She didn't have to wait long for Huw, and he sat down opposite her as her belated breakfast arrived. Huw shook his head when the waitress asked if he wanted to order.

'I've just eaten and had a strong coffee. Christopher has been experimenting with a new bean variety from Guatemala.' Caren nodded and ate her toast. Listening to Huw regaling her about Christopher's coffee-making routine reminded her of her previous boss Inspector Drake in Northern Division. It was almost tiring watching him fuss over the precision he employed to make coffee. Caren was happy enough having a cup of instant.

'Did Chloe say anything about what she wanted to discuss?'

'No, she just asked if we could meet. This place was her suggestion.'

Huw scanned the premises. Faded prints of various European cities in pine frames hung on the walls. The Formica-topped tables were clean, each with a collection of condiments at the end. From the friendly conversations and familiarity, it seemed that most of the customers knew the owners and the staff. The place had a buoyant trade in takeaway coffees and sugar-coated doughnuts. She tasted the coffee – it wasn't bad at all and even Detective Inspector Drake would find it palatable.

Caren crumpled the paper napkin she had used to remove

crumbs from her mouth and dropped it onto the plate by her coffee. 'There was something off about Chloe when we spoke to her and the other two girls at the house Emily shared with them.'

Huw nodded. 'Let's hope she's got something important to tell us.'

Caren finished her drink as Chloe pushed open the door and walked into the café, spotting them instantly. She sat down alongside Huw and smiled over to the waitress who had served Caren earlier. Chloe was clearly a regular, as a double espresso was delivered moments later.

'What did you want to talk to us about?' Caren said.

'I don't think Michelle or Charlotte gave you a complete picture of what Emily was like.'

Chloe added a teaspoon of sugar to her drink and pulled a spoon through it carefully.

'What do you mean by that?' Caren said.

'I was good friends with Emily. I met Rachel Scott at about the same time as she did. Rachel is a complex character. She could be vivacious and clever and funny but she was bad at saying no and she got herself into all sorts of scrapes. But she'd go out of her way to help people. Did you know that Emily helped out in that homeless centre?'

'Yes, we've spoken to Emily's tutor at the University who told us about her volunteering there. We've also visited St Hubert's.'

'Rachel helped out there too. They were really supportive of that centre. They asked if I'd go but I didn't want to get involved. I admired them for doing that.'

'Is there anything else that you want to tell us?' Caren said.

Chloe took a sip of her drink. 'I've been to parties with Emily and Rachel in a flat in the marina.'

'Were Michelle or Charlotte there too?'

Chloe shook her head. 'No, they didn't go. Emily and Rachel were friendly with a Kate Evans. I think she has a flat in the marina and she has a serious drug habit.'

'You have an address?'

'No, and don't ask me about the location. You know how it is after a few drinks… And all the apartment blocks look the same.'

'Tell us more about these parties.'

'You need to speak to Kate Evans. And I saw Johann Ackland there and he was obviously with Emily.'

'Did you know anyone else at those parties?'

She shook her head. 'No, I assumed they were friends of Kate Evans. Emily knew some of those present, so I guessed she knew them from the Hope and Anchor.'

'Was Emily dealing in drugs?' Caren immediately thought such activity would explain the cash recovered from her room.

'No, but she was a regular user – recreational only, it was nothing serious.'

'So was Rachel Scott dealing in drugs?'

'I can't say. I don't even know if Kate was dealing, but somebody supplied drugs for the parties, mostly cannabis but sometimes I saw some coke as well. Emily warned me to keep party secrets to myself.'

'Did you see Emily with Mark Tremain?'

Chloe nodded briskly. 'I saw her with him quite often until she broke up with him. He took it badly, very badly. I don't know what the hell she saw in him.'

'Did Mark Tremain know Kate Evans?'

Chloe gave Caren a puzzled look. 'I don't know. I didn't see Kate more than a couple of times.'

'There have been several burglaries of properties in the marina recently as well as thefts from yachts and boats moored there. Did Emily talk about those?'

Chloe shook her head.

'Did anybody mention the thefts and burglaries?'

'No, they were just parties.' Chloe's voice turned a little agitated. 'Jesus, you don't think Emily was involved in anything like that, do you?'

'Did she tell you about the large amount of money she had in cash in her room?'

Now Chloe looked startled.

'Did she share with you how she came by that money?'

Another head shake, this time with a frown.

'Can you describe Kate Evans for us?'

Huw had his notebook ready as Chloe dictated the description of the woman. Early thirties, short, non-descript brown hair to her shoulders and an unhealthy complexion.

'When we spoke before, your housemates said that Emily seemed to have more money recently. Do you have any idea where the money came from?'

Chloe shook her head. 'No idea. But she had been buying all these fancy clothes and boasted sometimes about going for expensive meals.'

Once they knew how Emily had accumulated the money Caren sensed they'd be one step closer to finding her killer.

'I've got a tutorial first thing.' Chloe got to her feet.

'If there's anything else you can recall about Emily contact me.'

Caren paid the bill and as she left with Huw a message reached her mobile. She turned to him. 'Super wants me back at HQ.'

Chapter 19

Rhys Davies drafted a press release relating to the man seen running through the marina on the night Emily Hughes was killed, which would need approval from the public relations department. He felt a sense of achievement that DI Waits had entrusted him with this job. He couldn't recall her predecessor, Detective Inspector Sammy Evans, doing anything similar.

He emailed a draft of the copy he had prepared to Alice for her feedback as well as sending it to the boss. She and Huw were interviewing one of Emily's housemates first thing that morning, so it would be ready for her when she got back. He hoped his draft wouldn't require significant alterations.

'Good job, Rhys.' Alice looked up from her monitor. 'It's early in the inquiry, so hopefully the press and public will respond. It's a long shot, though.'

Rhys felt rather deflated at Alice Sharp's lack of enthusiasm. But it would be up to the detective inspector and the public relations department to decide how to proceed.

He had already pinned a picture of Johann Ackland and his wife Harriet to the board as persons of interest. An email had arrived first thing that morning with the financial details needed to build a picture of Johann Ackland. He had a substantial mortgage on the property he jointly owned with his wife. The team knew little about her at present, apart from the fact that she worked at the University, and that she had her own finances, which were far healthier than her husband's. She had savings in her own name, whereas Ackland had credit card debts and a bank overdraft. The boat in the marina was in his name and subject to a loan secured on it. Once the detective inspector was back Rhys would provide her and the team with a summary.

He got back to the work of building a detailed background picture of Johann Ackland. It was easy enough to find details of his CV from the staff page on the University's website. It confirmed Ackland had been employed at the

University in Swansea for four years. Before that he had been at another university in the Bristol area, but the CV Rhys downloaded gave little information about his career before that. Ackland's entry on LinkedIn was more helpful and gave greater detail.

Rhys began assembling a detailed analysis of Ackland's employment history. Searches of the various university websites gave him contact names and telephone numbers. It created the impression of a seamless transition up the ladder of academia.

Researching Ackland's background might well alert him to the work they were doing building a picture of him, but Ackland knew by now that he was a person of interest in their inquiry. Ackland's Facebook account had several hundred friends and, without examining the information on each, it was difficult to establish who would be helpful. Once Rhys was satisfied he had built a complete picture of Johann Ackland's academic background, he made the first phone call to South Dean University. It took a few minutes to track down an administrative assistant at the right department.

After he had introduced himself and explained the confidential nature of his inquiry, he asked: 'I'm hoping you might help me with some background details about Johann Ackland, who worked at the University.'

'I'm sorry I can't discuss anything about him. You'll need to speak to the academic registrar.'

The call was ended abruptly. It made Rhys feel as though he were at fault. But he had been businesslike and polite, so it made him suspicious. It took another few minutes to track down the office of Mr Van Noort, the academic registrar.

'I don't know how I can help.' Van Noort's voice was defensive and brittle.

'Can you confirm the details of his employment at the university?' Rhys recited the dates he knew from the outline he had prepared.

There was a pause before Van Noort replied. 'Why do

you want this information?'

'It's part of a routine background inquiry.'

'Routine inquiry, I see.'

'Are the details I've just given you correct?'

'I'm not prepared to answer any further questions. If you want us to reply, then formally write in and our lawyers can deal with you.'

The second call that morning finished hastily.

After a moment of reflection, Rhys made a third call to the institution mentioned on Ackland's CV before South Dean University.

This time Rhys avoided the Psychology department altogether at the Mid-Somerset University and asked for the HR department, hoping for more success than he had achieved with South Dean University. The voice at the end of the call introduced herself as an executive assistant.

Rhys repeated the introduction and the reason for his inquiry.

'Before you say any more, I think you should talk to Professor Moon.'

Rhys couldn't object or respond as there was a pronounced clicking sound and then elevator music until the voice of a middle-aged, well-educated man spoke in an aggressive tone. 'And what the hell do you want to know about Johann Ackland?'

'It's all part of a routine inquiry. I just wanted you to confirm if he had been employed with your department for the three-year period he mentions in his curriculum vitae. It's nothing complicated.'

'Complicated, huh.'

'I'm sorry?'

'Let me tell you, Detective Sergeant—'

'Constable'

Moon ignored him. 'Whatever you've been told by Johann Ackland, be extremely careful. He was not here for three years. We quickly discovered after he was appointed that much of his previous curriculum vitae was questionable, particularly some of the research papers he alleged he was responsible for. Anyway, what is this inquiry about?'

'It's a routine matter and I'm not at liberty to discuss the details.'

'Then be very careful indeed of Ackland. You need to write to us if you need all this confirmed.'

And with that, Rhys' third conversation that morning came to a sudden end.

Rhys sat back in his chair, wondering if what he had just been told impacted the inquiry. He looked over at Alice who was gazing intently at the monitor on her desk.

'The universities where Ackland claims to have been employed previously really gave me the runaround. We may need to do more research to uncover the truth about his career.'

Alice grunted an acknowledgement before adding. 'I'd kill for a cup of coffee, Rhys. And once you're back, I think I've got some interesting footage for you to see.'

Rhys did as asked, traipsing through to the kitchen near the Incident Room. He found the biscuits Alice liked and added them to a tray with the two mugs of hot drinks. She was still poring over the screen when he returned.

'You won't believe this,' Alice said.

'Thanks for the coffee, Rhys,' Rhys said in best attempt at sarcasm.

'Don't throw the toys out of the pram. Pull up a chair and look at what I've found.'

Alice crunched her way through her first chocolate digestive as Rhys pulled over an office chair.

'I found this footage a little after 11.00 pm. It's from a camera on the main marina building.' Alice clicked 'play' and the footage began. On the right-hand side yellow lights twinkled around one side of the marina. The opposite side was shrouded in darkness.

'Nothing's happening,' Rhys said.

'Wait.'

Moments later a figure emerged from the darkness on the left-hand side, skirting around the marina area clearly trying to keep out of the well-lit area. Alice froze the frame and enlarged the image. 'There, can you see him?'

Rhys peered at the screen.

'It's Johann Ackland,' Alice said.

'But he told the boss he wasn't at the marina the night Emily was killed.'

'The boss hates it when people lie to her.' Alice had a determined edge to her voice. 'And you won't believe this either, but I have found footage of Mrs Ackland with that Rachel Scott earlier that evening. They were standing under a light so there's no question about their identities.'

'Show me.'

Rhys and Alice watched in silence as the footage played on the screen.

'This could be really important,' Alice said.

They watched the footage a second time.

Alice announced sternly: 'We'll need to tell the boss as soon as she's back.'

They didn't have long to wait before Caren and Huw walked into the Incident Room.

Chapter 20

Superintendent Brooks was troubled by Caren's failure to request a face-to-face review following the discovery of Emily Hughes' body at the start of the week. Now that it was Thursday, Superintendent Brooks realised his discomfort was probably misplaced. Caren Waits was an excellent detective. He had learned that from the two inquiries she had conducted since joining Western Division. Her appointment was more than justified, silencing the voices of criticism from other senior officers. Were they all simply too misogynistic for roles in a modern police force?

He had messaged her that morning, requesting her presence for a formal review. As she was driving back from Swansea, he scanned through the standard pro formas she had sent him with an outline of progress. Speaking to the officer in charge of the inquiry was no substitute for paperwork, however. Over the years, working with Detective Inspector Sammy Evans could be frustrating as he kept so much to himself and at least Caren Waits had none of his bad habits. And for that, Brooks felt pleased.

Caren arrived soon after he had finished reviewing all the updates she had emailed. His secretary showed her in and Brooks waved her to one of the visitors' chairs.

'I'm sorry if I'm late. I needed to get up to date with Detective Constables Davies and Sharp,' Caren said.

'I wanted to hear from you first-hand about the inquiry.'

Caren nodded.

'I understand you've released Mark Tremain.'

'He's got previous convictions for violence and several years ago he was involved with handling stolen goods from a marina in Southampton.'

'And is it your belief the recent thefts and burglaries from the Swansea Marina are linked to Emily's murder?'

'I'm keeping an open mind at the moment. The money we recovered from the room in the house which she shared would suggest a link to the sale of illegal drugs.'

'Have you considered the possibility of a connection to the sex industry?'

'We've spoken with her housemates, and none mentioned anything like that going on. And I spoke to one of them separately this morning who told us about parties she had attended with Emily Hughes and a woman called Kate Evans in Swansea Marina.'

'Kate Evans?'

'It's a new name that hasn't appeared in the inquiry so far. And do you know a Gerard Rankin?'

'Of course I bloody do. Rankin has been involved with organised crime for longer than I care to remember. Swansea mafia and all that.' Brooks realised Caren needed more of an explanation. 'In his twenties Rankin did a four-year stint for robbery. Ever since then he's kept his nose clean. By that I mean squeaky clean. He doesn't use a mobile, nor emails. But that doesn't stop him overseeing a criminal gang that no team in the Wales Police Service has prosecuted successfully.'

'So why would Gerard Rankin be involved with Mark Tremain? It was Tom Hughes, Emily's brother who told us that he'd seen Rankin with Tremain.'

Brooks leaned back, exhaling deeply. He hadn't heard the name Rankin associated with a current investigation for a long time. 'Last I knew about Rankin he was living in a villa in Spain.'

'Could Rankin be behind the burglaries and thefts from yachts in the marina?'

Brooks nodded. 'Small scale for him, but it could be someone further down the food chain. How could they be connected to your murder inquiry?'

'Emily Hughes had a substantial quantity of cash we cannot account for. Somebody might have been paying her for her silence.'

'Or cooperation?'

Caren nodded. 'But she might have got greedy.'

'Money always makes for the best motive.'

'We've also been investigating the background of Johann Ackland, a lecturer at the University. He lied about his whereabouts the night Emily died. We have footage proving he was in the marina, despite his denials. And we've uncovered footage of Mrs Ackland in the marina the night Emily was killed. We're going to be talking to them both later.'

'Good, excellent.' Brooks managed a soft tone to his voice and nodded his appreciation. 'And I've also seen the press release circulated about the mysterious individual running in the marina. I understand it was drafted by one of your team – good work, by the way.'

'It was Detective Constable Rhys Davies.'

'What do you make of him?' Brooks answered his own question before Caren said anything. 'I didn't initially think he was cut out for a career in policing. But he has surprised me. My first impression was that he might be better as a farmer.'

'Rhys is very conscientious, sir. He and Alice Sharp work well as a team.'

'I recall your predecessor complimenting Alice Sharp. I think he felt she shared his approach to policing.'

Brooks looked over at Caren, wondering whether she would take the implied invitation to comment from his last remarks. She kept silent.

'So the persons of interest you have for Emily Hughes' murder are Johann Ackland, with whom she was involved romantically. And Mark Tremain, her former boyfriend. I guess Mrs Ackland is in the mix too.'

Caren didn't reply immediately. 'Mark Tremain has a strong motive. He was devastated by the end of his relationship with Emily and he knew she was seeing Johann Ackland.'

'And you still have the mysterious individual seen running in the marina.'

Caren nodded her head and, before she could say

anything further, her mobile bleeped with a message. After reading it she abruptly stood up. 'I need to go, sir. Tom Hughes, Emily Hughes' brother, has been arrested for assaulting Rachel Scott, who is also a person of interest.'

Brooks waved a hand, sending her on her way.

Chapter 21

Caren and Huw raced down the outside lane of the M4 in a pool car, its lights flashing, sirens blaring on their way back to Swansea. Huw had expedited getting a copy of the Police National Computer search against Rachel Scott. There were no results, nothing of interest. It surprised Caren, as she had felt that there was something about Rachel Scott they had missed. They pulled into the main car park at Morriston Hospital and, after putting the *On Police Business/Heddlu Swyddogol* notice onto the top of the dashboard, Caren hurried over towards the entrance of the emergency department.

After passing through two automatic doors, Caren came to a window where the member of staff opened her mouth to enquire about Caren's ailments, but thought the better of it once she saw Caren's warrant card pressed against the glass.

'I need to speak to a patient called Rachel Scott.'

The woman tapped into her computer. Caren glanced into the waiting area and at least two dozen ill-looking faces looking over at her.

'I'll get the department manager to speak to you.' The receptionist picked up the telephone and Caren listened to the one-sided conversation. It was brief and, once concluded, she got to her feet and pointed to Caren's right. 'She'll meet you through those doors.'

Caren paced over and a woman wearing scrubs and a lanyard with her identity card hanging from her neck greeted her. 'We were told to expect you. Please follow me, Detective Inspector.'

The woman led Caren and Huw down the corridor, past trolleys and patients in wheelchairs to a side ward. She pushed open the door, its kick plate scuffed and dented with age. Inside, sitting upright on a bed, was Rachel Scott – her face pale and tired. Standing near the bed was a woman in her forties, wearing a worn sweatshirt and baggy jeans, and Andrea, the manager of St Hubert's Centre. Caren recalled her from her visit to the homeless shelter.

'This is my mum, Jean,' Rachel said.

'This is terrible,' Jean said. 'Are you going to charge him?'

'We shall need to speak to Rachel,' Caren said.

'I came as soon as I heard,' Andrea said. 'Rachel was due to help out this weekend and she's such a valuable contribution to the team. And I wanted to show my support, especially after…'

Caren nodded.

Andrea looked towards Rachel. 'If there is anything we can do.'

'Thanks.' Rachel said. Her mother gave Andrea a warm smile.

A nurse was finishing bandaging Rachel's arm. The bruising on her face around both her eyes was a stark red.

'What do you want?' The nurse had a high forehead and dark, intense eyes. Caren guessed that his accent was somewhere from London.

'Police. We need to talk to Rachel.'

'It'll have to wait until I've finished.'

Caren glanced at Rachel, who appeared well enough for a brief chat. 'No, it can't wait. We won't be long.'

For a moment, the nurse gave a double take, as though he wanted to throw his weight around.

'It won't take long.' Caren added with a smile.

Reluctantly, the nurse retreated, as did Jean and Andrea, but before closing the door on Caren and Huw, the nurse added: 'Five minutes, then I'll come and check on her again.'

Caren didn't respond. With the door closed, she looked at Rachel. 'Who did this?'

'It was Tom Hughes. He saw me in town.' Rachel's nostrils flared and she raised her voice, the anger evident. 'He came racing after me, cursing and shouting. Telling me I was to blame for Emily's death.'

'Why would he do that?'

For a moment, Rachel averted her gaze, as though she

wasn't ready to confront the truth. 'I don't know. I don't know – he's mad.'

'Did anyone else see this attack on you?'

Rachel nodded briskly. 'I was with a couple of my friends. They pulled him off me. And someone called the police because officers arrived really quickly.'

Caren nodded. On the journey to Morriston Hospital, Huw had related a message confirming that Tom Hughes had been arrested at the scene and had been taken to one of the stations in the city.

'You need to be honest with us, Rachel. Why on earth would he attack you?'

'Like I said, he was drunk and off his head.'

'I don't think you're telling us the truth, Rachel. There must be more to this. Why does he believe you were responsible for Emily's death?'

Rachel gave a brief shrug and then looked over at Caren and then at Huw.

'What were you and Emily involved with?'

'Nothing, nothing. He's mad.'

'I need you to be honest with me so that I can find Emily's killer and help you.'

Rachel didn't reply, but settled into a non-committal pout.

Caren decided there was nothing further she could achieve with Rachel and that her priority now was to interview Tom Hughes. She jerked her head at Huw, signalling they had finished. He turned and opened the door.

'About time!' The nurse angrily barged into the room.

Caren headed back to the car.

'What did you make of that?' Huw said, as Caren started the engine.

'I can't help but think that she knows more than she's telling us. Once she's been patched up and discharged, I want to interview her again.'

'I agree, boss. Maybe there was something going on

between her and Emily and Mark Tremain. He is our prime suspect in my book. He's got form for violence and would know his way around selling stolen goods from the burglaries and thefts from the yachts.'

Caren didn't reply. She negotiated her way out of a roundabout. 'Get the postcode for the police station in the city so that we can interview Tom Hughes.'

Huw did as he was told and moments later tapped the details into the satnav.

It wasn't a long distance, but the stop-start journey took them far longer than Caren had expected. Unaccustomed to driving in the middle of a city, she found all the delays and traffic lights and complex junctions frustrating.

Once they parked in the car park for the Swansea Central police station, they made their way to reception and the civilian at the desk showed them through after they presented their warrant cards. The custody sergeant was dealing with a drunk driver when Caren and Huw arrived. They waited for the usual formalities to be concluded – he emptied his pockets, confirmed his full name and date of birth. When asked if anyone should be informed, he shook his head. He wore an old, ill-fitting suit over a white shirt, gossamer-thin with age. Officers led him through so he could blow into the machine that would test his breath, although there was little doubt about the result.

'I've spoken with the injured party at the hospital,' Caren said.

'Tom Hughes is in one of the cells,' the custody sergeant said. 'You'll have to record the interview the old-fashioned way – on tapes.'

Caren nodded. A full digital recording suite was only used for the most serious offences. And there was nothing to suggest that Tom Hughes was responsible for the death of his sister.

'Is it really a valuable use of the time of a detective inspector?' The sergeant raised an eyebrow. 'One of the uniformed officers would have done this interview, surely? It is only an assault.'

'He may have relevant information in relation to an ongoing murder inquiry. His sister was killed earlier this week.'

The custody sergeant now raised both eyebrows.

'Tell us where the interview room is.'

Once the custody sergeant had provided them with the tapes and directed them to the right room, Caren sat and gathered her thoughts. Rachel Scott wasn't telling them the truth. Tom Hughes was doing the same. Now he'd have an opportunity to explain himself.

One of the custody suite officers showed Tom Hughes in and he sat opposite Caren and Huw. His hair was dishevelled and his pale skin made him look tired. There was a strong smell of stale alcohol on his breath.

Tom had refused the opportunity of having a solicitor present, so Caren got started after she had dealt with the formalities of introducing everyone in the room.

'You have been arrested for assaulting Rachel Scott. Did you attack her?'

'She was responsible for Emily's death. I've told you before and you've done nothing about it.'

'I'll ask you again: did you assault Rachel?'

'She was walking, bold as brass. She grinned at me and raised the middle finger as though she couldn't give a shit about Emily.'

'Did you assault her?'

'I kept thinking about Emily. And yeah, I lost it.'

'You need to tell me why you think she was involved in Emily's death.'

'I told you before, Rachel introduced her to some bad people.'

'Can you be more specific? Did you ever see Rachel with Emily?'

'I know they were all mixed up with Mark Tremain.'

'You've told us all this before. Unless you're going to cooperate with us then there's no chance at all I can put in a good word with the custody sergeant.'

Tom sat back in his chair and folded his arms, pulling them tight against his chest. 'It was drugs. That's how she got all that money, I'm sure of it. I followed her one night and saw her and Rachel going into one of the flats in the marina. I got asking around some of my mates. They all told me Emily and Rachel had been to a flat where a girl called Kate Evans lives.'

'Do you know this Kate Evans?'

'No, and I don't want to. She is bad news. She's a serious user but she is Teflon-coated. And you know why? Her old man is a policeman.'

'What the hell do you mean "old man"?'

'Her father is a retired officer. Kate bragged about how he could protect her if there was any shit going on.'

Caren glanced over at Huw, who shook his head slowly, confirming he did not know what Tom meant.

'Do you know the name of Kate Evans' father?'

Tom laughed. 'Of course I fucking don't.'

Huw took over the questioning, as Caren completed her notebook with the details Tom had just shared with them. 'Do you have the address where this Kate Evans lives?'

'Of course I don't. But I can take you there.'

'That's not how this works.'

'Works for me.'

'We'll decide what works for you.'

Caren took back the initiative and turned to Tom. 'As you've admitted the assault on Rachel we'll make the appropriate representations to the custody sergeant, but for now you're not going anywhere.'

They took Tom to the custody sergeant's desk where the officer didn't take long to decide that Tom Hughes was going to enjoy the hospitality of the Wales Police Service at least until the following morning when he'd sobered up.

Caren and Huw left after the formalities were concluded.

She noticed the time, surprised that it was so late. She made a quick call to her mother, telling her she was on her way back home. She didn't speak to Aled, she'd hug him tightly and pull him close once she was in the warmth of her own house.

'Is there any chance Kate Evans is Detective Inspector Sammy Evans' daughter?' Caren said to Huw as they sat in the car leaving the police station.

'I don't know. He never mentioned his family. It was as though they were strangers to him.'

'We need to find out where she lives.'

Chapter 22

The following morning, Caren rushed to get everything ready so that she could take Aled to school. Her mother had taken care of washing and tumble-drying his uniform so that he had a fresh set of clothes. She didn't know what she would do without her mother supporting her with all the domestic arrangements. Tomorrow was a Saturday but with a current inquiry she'd be at work, which meant Aled being with his Mamgu and Tadcu again.

Once he was ready and his bag prepared, Caren bundled Aled into the car and drove to his school, where she parked. He held her hand and once he saw Ieuan, Susan Howard's son, he called out and ran over to his friend.

'Morning, Caren,' Susan said. 'How are things going?'
'Busy.'

Susan wouldn't expect her to discuss the case in public.

'I expect you will be working tomorrow. Aled can come and spend the day with Ieuan, if that helps.'

Caren didn't hesitate. 'My mum was going to look after him, but I'm sure she'll be fine with him playing with Ieuan. Let me talk to her. I'll message you later.'

Susan nodded. Both women strolled over to the school gate and watched as their sons walked to the main entrance. Caren trotted back to her car, switching to the priorities for the morning. After parking at headquarters, she called her mum, who was delighted Aled had the opportunity of spending time with his friend. Her mum saw Aled often enough and probably secretly enjoyed having a Saturday free.

Caren made her way to the board after pushing open the door to the Incident Room. Huw was already at his desk and they exchanged morning greetings. Rhys Davies and Alice Sharp arrived as Caren was shrugging off her jacket. Her first task that morning was to make a call and arrange to interview Johann Ackland later. It was brief, and he sounded businesslike. After she confirmed the arrangements, she walked back into the Incident Room.

'Boss.' Caren nodded an acknowledgement at both detective constables.

'We'll authorise the release of Tom Hughes later this morning,' Caren said. 'But he told us yesterday that Kate Evans who was connected to Emily and Rachel Scott is the daughter of a police officer. Do either of you know whether Sammy Evans has a daughter?'

'He never talked about his family,' Alice said.

'I can't believe he wouldn't have mentioned his family at some point.'

'He kept his family life completely private,' Rhys added.

'Somebody must know about his family – if he has kids. I'll make some calls, but for now I want both of you' – she nodded at Rhys and Alice – 'to collect Tom Hughes from Swansea Central police station and take him to the marina so that he can identify the flat where he thinks Kate Evans lives.'

'Is he doing that voluntarily?' Alice said.

Caren nodded. 'And after that, talk to Mrs Ackland. I want her to explain herself about her visit to the marina on the night Emily was murdered. Find out if she's got anything to say about her husband and Emily Hughes.'

Caren glanced at Johann Ackland's image on the board. 'We're going to speak to Ackland. I've spoken to him, and he's working from home today. So you can see Mrs Ackland at the office where she works.'

'I've had an update from the team in Swansea dealing with the stalker in the middle of the city,' Rhys said. 'There's still nothing to report. They have uniformed officers working through hours of footage to see if they can identify anyone of interest. I got the impression they were short-staffed and that it's not being prioritised.'

'Typical,' Alice said. 'Attacks on women are never given the priority they need.'

Caren looked over at the officers at their desks. 'We are going to give the murder of Emily Hughes the utmost priority.'

'None of the staff at the St Hubert's Centre have any sort of record,' Alice said. 'And before you ask, boss, I have searched against the names of some of the users of the centre, but without full names it's difficult.'

Huw piped up: 'It's difficult to think that any of the people using the homeless shelter would have a motive to kill Emily Hughes.' Then he moved over to the board and stared at the image of Johann Ackland and his wife.

'Unless the murder was a random attack, being in the wrong place at the wrong time' – Alice sounded cynical – 'we might never find her killer.'

'She was garrotted, for Christ's sake,' Huw said. 'That's hardly the action of a drive-by killer. And I've seen Mrs Ackland before, somewhere. I think it might have been at the Bella Cucina.' When he saw Alice and Rhys' puzzled looks, he added, 'It's an Italian café in Swansea.'

'As always,' Caren said. 'We keep an open mind about everything. And at the moment Johann Ackland and Mark Tremain are the principal persons of interest. But before we leave I need to hear what you discovered about Ackland.'

Caren sat, Huw opened his notebook and Rhys outlined the flawed curriculum vitae of Johann Ackland.

Before leaving headquarters, Caren called Superintendent Brooks and enquired about Sammy Evans' family. Her senior officer confirmed what she knew already. Sammy Evans kept his private life to himself. He promised to call other colleagues who might know more details.

Huw drove that morning and as he joined the M4 he asked Caren, 'Do you think this Kate Evans might be a person of interest?'

'If she has a connection with this Gerard Rankin that everyone refers to as Swansea mafia, there is every chance she could be involved.'

Although Huw had tapped the postcode into the satnav

he only glanced at the directions occasionally. He pulled up at the address, a large detached house, and Caren guessed it was built in the Edwardian era for a wealthy merchant or business owner in the city.

'Nice place,' Huw said. 'A lot of these properties are popular with the staff from the University.'

Caren and Huw left the vehicle and walked over to the entrance. A Tesla was parked in the gravelled drive, its borders neatly cultivated. The property was clearly well maintained, and the escallonia hedges abutting the front wall were trimmed to a modest height.

Caren spotted the door videocam. What self-respecting university lecturer wouldn't have one? Caren's rented property certainly didn't, but once she could buy her own place it would be on her list of acquisitions.

Ackland appeared at the door as soon as Caren had pressed the bell. He was wearing the blazer she had seen on the coat stand in his office when they had first met. Underneath was a powder-blue button-down shirt that complemented his intense blue eyes.

'Come in,' Ackland waved a hand for them to enter.

He led them through into an office on the ground floor. The bookcases on one wall were filled with hardback academic tomes. Caren didn't spot any fiction – no Rebus novel or Stieg Larsson book in sight.

An expensive-looking leather sofa had been pushed against one wall. Ackland sat on a wooden-framed armchair. There was no offer of coffee or tea and definitely no chocolate biscuits.

'How can I help?' Ackland sounded as though he were in charge.

'When we spoke to you about Emily Hughes you indicated you hadn't seen her on the evening she was killed.'

'Yes, that's correct.'

'Dr Ackland we have video footage recovered from CCTV cameras in the marina that show quite clearly you were there. So why did you lie to us?'

Ackland didn't respond immediately. Then he crossed his legs and threaded the fingers of both hands together. Caren didn't like people who lied to her and now she sensed Ackland was teeing up to spin another lie.

'What time was that?'

Delaying tactic, always a sign of guilt, Caren thought.

'The footage records you in the marina at eleven pm although you seem to be making every effort to keep out of sight of the cameras. Why was that?'

Caren stared over at Ackland, waiting for a reaction. He struggled to keep direct eye contact with her. She could tell he was desperate to find a plausible answer.

'I must have been mistaken when I spoke to you before.'

'Mistaken. This is a murder inquiry, Dr Ackland.'

'I must have become confused about the time I left the yacht. Time goes so quickly when I'm working there.'

Caren looked over at Huw, and encouraged for him to pick up the questioning.

'We've spoken to your former colleagues at the Mid-Somerset University.'

Caren peered at Ackland, searching for a response, hoping for a sign he was feeling uncomfortable. But so far the smooth, polished exterior hadn't been penetrated.

'There are several inconsistencies and inaccuracies in your curriculum vitae. You have included details of a research paper to which you didn't contribute and there's also a question mark about your PhD thesis and the number of doctoral students you claim to have supervised.'

Huw paused and looked up at Ackland. The lecturer's face had darkened.

'Why did you lie in your CV when you applied for the post at the University here? Why should we trust anything you say?'

'You shouldn't listen to tittle-tattle from other academics.'

'My colleague has spoken in detail to the department of the Mid-Somerset University. I would hardly call it tittle-tattle.'

Ackland adjusted his position. Caren noticed the expensive-looking frame to the impressive seascape hanging on the wall behind Ackland.

'Does the head of your present department know of these untruths?'

'What has any of this got to do with your murder inquiry?'

'Why did you lie to us?'

'I hardly think petty jealousies and academic intrigue between colleagues is something that justifies your time and energy.'

'We'll be the judge of that,' Huw said. 'Because if it was the case that Emily Hughes became aware of your chequered past and threatened to expose you to the University authorities that would certainly give you a motive for her murder.'

'Don't be absurd.' Ackland raised his voice in the first show of emotion.

Caren decided to interject. 'Are you a regular drug user, Dr Ackland?'

His reaction was exactly what she had hoped for. 'How dare you. Of course not!'

'Was Emily involved with using or supplying drugs?'

Ackland's initial reaction was to look away immediately. She took it as a sure sign he would not tell the truth.

'No, of course not.'

'Have you ever been to parties with Emily where she or other guests used drugs?'

'Of course not.' Ackland sounded appalled at the suggestion.

'Have you ever visited a flat in the marina where a Kate Evans lives?'

Ackland's reply was too quick. 'No, never and I don't know who you're talking about.'

'I understand you have a substantial mortgage on this property.'

'And my wife and myself are regularly paying the instalments.' Ackland's eyes narrowed.

'You also have a large amount owed on your credit cards. And you've missed quite a few payments recently.'

Ackland clenched his jaw. Caren was convinced she had noticed Ackland's cheek twitching.

'I think this conversation has gone as far as it can. Please leave.' Ackland stood up, pushed his chair to one side. Caren nodded at Huw and they left.

As they walked back to their car a message reached Caren's mobile. The content made her stop. She turned to Huw. 'That was a message from HQ. Kate Evans is indeed Sammy Evans' daughter.'

Chapter 23

Acting as taxi driver or minder or whatever was the right word for taking Tom Hughes to the marina wasn't to Alice's liking. He was a toerag who needed to be prosecuted for assaulting Rachel Scott and hauled before the courts as soon as possible. She doubted he had any interest in cooperating with them.

And he smelled. Really badly. Her car would need to be fumigated if he sat in it too long. When they parked by the marina, she seriously considered leaving the doors and windows open, but she used common sense instead.

'If you do a runner before you've helped us, the boss will come down on you like a ton of bricks.' Alice got as much menace into her voice as she could. Tom Hughes wasn't impressed.

'Yeah, whatever.'

'The inspector wants to know if you can pinpoint exactly the flat where Kate Evans lives.'

Tom gave her another disinterested look.

'So can you remember what floor it was on?'

Tom shrugged noncommittally.

After half an hour trudging around the marina, they retraced their steps back to the vehicle. Tom had been singularly unhelpful. They had stopped at various locations so that he could familiarise himself with the surroundings. He had peered at the buildings, unable to identify the block of flats visited by Emily and Rachel.

'A fat lot of good you've been,' Alice said.

Alice unlocked the car with the remote. Rhys got into the passenger side.

'At least you can give me a lift back into town,' Tom said.

'What do you think I am, a taxi service? You can bloody well walk,' Alice said.

She drove away, leaving Tom Hughes with a sulk on his face.

'So, what do we know about Mrs Ackland?' Alice said.

Rhys had his notebook open on his lap, but he didn't need to consult it to reply.

'She comes from a wealthy family. Her father is a fancy wine merchant in Bristol and her mother is a solicitor who specialises in advising rich families. She is the beneficiary of several trusts and she's a researcher in one of the University departments. She and Ackland don't have any kids.'

'So it'll be interesting to hear what she has to say about her husband and his extramarital activities.'

Before leaving the marina, Rhys had tapped into the satnav the postcode for the address of the department where Harriet Ackland worked. Alice had to rely on the directions to reach the building and the absence of parking slots nearby meant she had to tour around until she found a space.

As they left the vehicle, Alice sent the inspector a message.

Finished with Tom Hughes – not helpful at all. Going to see Harriet Ackland.

The reply came almost instantly.

Good timing. We're about to interview Johann Ackland.

The department where Harriet Ackland worked occupied three terraced properties that were merged into one. Alice pushed open the substantial door to the end property, newly painted a glistening black. Beyond it was the hallway and a sign indicated that reception was a room to their left.

A man in his twenties, long ponytail and a flannel shirt, looked over at Alice. 'How can I help?'

'We'd like to speak to Mrs Harriet Ackland.'

'Is she expecting you?'

Alice flashed her warrant card at him. 'Police. Tell her it's urgent.'

He stood up and walked past them into the hallway before taking the stairs to the first floor. Moments later, Harriet Ackland accompanied him down to meet Alice and Rhys. The photograph they had on the Incident Room wall didn't do Harriet Ackland justice. She looked more refined, more attractive than the frumpy looking woman in the image on the board alongside that of her husband.

'Harriet Ackland,' she held out her hand. She had an open, welcoming face and a well-to-do accent. 'How can I help?'

'Is there somewhere we can discuss matters in private?'

She must know why we're here, Alice thought.

Harriet turned on her heel and led Alice and Rhys through into a small conference room she accessed with a security card. The smell of furniture polish lingered in the air. Harriet waved a hand at the chairs surrounding the glistening conference table.

Once they had all sat down, Alice looked directly over at Harriet Ackland. There was a wariness in her eyes now.

'We're part of the team investigating the murder of Emily Hughes. Are you aware of the case?'

'Yes, of course. She was a student at the University. Why on earth would you want to be speaking to me?'

'Did you know that Emily Hughes was one of your husband's students?'

'He briefly mentioned that she had been killed. Have you found who was responsible yet? I'm sure all the female students are worried. After all, there have been a lot of attacks in the city recently. Are they connected with this murder?'

'Are you aware that your husband was having an affair with Emily Hughes before she died?'

Alice searched for any sign of shock on Harriet's face. And she was rewarded with her blinking quickly and swallowing. It seemed clear enough that she was taken aback by the allegation.

'I don't know what you mean.' Her lips parted in amazement, and she gave Alice a stunned look.

Was that really the best reply she could manage?

'Did you know he had been sleeping with Emily?' Alice said.

'Of course not, this is preposterous. How dare you make

this sort of accusation against Johann. Surely you don't suspect him of being involved?'

'We are pursuing several lines of inquiry. And your husband's relationship with Emily Hughes is part of that.'

'This is intolerable. I think you had better leave now.'

Alice stayed exactly where she was.

'Were you aware of the allegations about Johann's association with students at the Mid-Somerset University?' Rhys said.

'That was preposterous nonsense too. A student just out of school became infatuated with him.'

'Do you do a lot of sailing with your husband?'

'We met at the University sailing club, if you must know. It's an interest we share – it makes a marriage so much stronger to share interests. So, all the tittle-tattle you've had the gall to regurgitate isn't going to affect that at all.'

Rhys produced a photograph of Emily Hughes and pushed it across the table at Harriet. 'Emily Hughes worked at the Hope and Anchor, a public house in the marina. She was a regular when the pub provided bar services to the sailing club. Do you remember her?'

Harriet peered at the image, giving it a good long, intense look. 'No, I don't recall her. After all, there'd be lots of bar staff at sailing club functions. I'd hardly pay them any attention.'

The second photograph Rhys produced was of Rachel Scott. Alice wondered if Harriet would walk straight into their trap of denying she knew Rachel as well.

'Do you know this woman?' Rhys said.

'Yes, I believe I do. I can't place her, though.'

Harriet stared over at Rhys, a defiant edge to her eyes.

Rhys persisted. 'When did you see her last?'

Was Harriet Ackland clever enough to calculate that her encounter with Rachel would have been recorded on CCTV?

Harriet looked away, answering with a dismissive voice. 'I can't remember.'

'We've recovered a lot of footage from the CCTV cameras around the marina and we have a record of you meeting Rachel Scott on the evening Emily was killed. We'd like you to explain your movements that evening. What were you discussing with Rachel?' Alice's tone was uncompromising and firm.

Harriet didn't miss a beat, replying with self-confidence that surprised Alice. 'Yes, of course. I remember now. I was on the yacht earlier, if I recollect correctly, although I can't be exact about the times. When I left, I bumped into Rachel Scott. We had met at some do at the sailing club and I can't recall how we got talking – probably a couple of glasses of wine too many. You know how it is, Detective Constable.'

Alice knew better than to try and engage with this woman. 'What did you discuss with Rachel?'

'Nothing in particular. Nothing important.'

Rhys butted in. 'Do you enjoy your position as membership secretary of the sailing club?'

'Very much so. My father was a member of the Cowes Yacht Club on the Isle of Wight for many years. It's wonderful to carry on the family tradition.'

Alice glanced over at Rhys, who gave a shake of his head indicating he didn't think there was anything further to ask Harriet Ackland.

'Thank you, Mrs Ackland,' Alice said as she pushed a card across the table. 'If you can help us in anyway in relation to the inquiry, please contact me.'

As they retrace their steps to the car, Alice turned to Rhys. 'What did you make of her?'

'She's a smooth operator, that's for certain. I think she knew about Emily Hughes.'

'You didn't tell me that the staff at the university in Mid-Somerset had told you Ackland had relationships with students there.'

'They didn't. I was making that up. Just to see what her reaction would be.'

'And she took the bait. Which means she probably knew he was having a fling with Emily Hughes.'

'Which might make her a suspect. After all, she comes across as a woman with very high regard for her standing in society.'

'I'll google the Cowes Yacht Club later, but I bet you it's one of the poshest in the country.'

'We better get back and tell the boss.'

Chapter 24

Saturday morning, Caren drove Aled to Susan Howard's home for his playdate. On the journey there, all he talked about was what he and Ieuan would do. He frequently mentioned ice cream. It pleased Caren that her son was so comfortable with the Howard family, but she felt a little guilty that she couldn't spend time with him herself. Once the inquiry was done, she would take a break and enjoy time with Aled.

Aled had disappeared into the house quickly after Caren had kissed him. Susan had reassured her he would be fine with them. Caren's mum was going to be babysitting later that evening so that Caren could return to Susan's home for a social with her fellow students from the Welsh class.

'I won't be working all day,' Caren said.

'I should hope not too. You're coming back tonight, aren't you? I'm sure David is looking forward to seeing you.' Susan smiled.

'I'll see you later.' Caren didn't want to get into a discussion on Susan's doorstep about her relationship with David Hemsby. She wasn't quite certain whether she wanted to call it a relationship. It felt disloyal, somehow, to her late husband for her to be seeing another man. Then she scolded herself for being absurd. Alun was secretly seeing Miss Hale before he was killed. She was being utterly old-fashioned about hanging on to a distorted memory of her marriage.

As she thought about David, the coroner's inquest into her late husband's death to be held on Monday in Cardiff loomed large in her mind. It was one small step towards finalising Alun's affairs.

She had been trying to avoid contemplating the possibility that Miss Hale would be there. But she wasn't going to think about her. She had to spend the morning with her team so that she could justify Monday morning at the coroner's court.

When she arrived at the Incident Room, an officer she

didn't recognise was deep in discussion with Huw Margam, both men standing by the board.

Huw was wearing a light navy jacket over immaculately pressed chinos and well-polished brown brogues. The officer alongside him was equally smartly dressed, and it made Caren feel slightly untidy in comparison. He had a well-cut grey suit and a white shirt with immaculate double cuffs, complete with fabric links. A flat stomach suggested a conscious effort to manage his diet and keep fit.

'Caren' – the man smiled warmly, his teeth perfect – 'DI Peter Jenkins.'

Caren recognised the name but couldn't place the face. Her puzzlement must have been obvious.

'We spoke about the series of burglaries at the marina.'

'Yes, of course,' Caren said.

Behind her, the sound of Rhys Davies and Alice Sharp arriving filled the Incident Room. Both officers exchanged morning greetings with Caren and Huw and Peter. Rhys and Alice were dressed casually, not the usual smart outfits required during the working week, although there could be little difference between a weekday and the weekends during a murder inquiry.

'I wanted to bring you and your team up to date with the latest information we have about the various burglaries around the marina area,' Peter said.

Caren sat in a chair by an empty desk. Peter remained standing by the board.

'The burglaries have all taken place in a fairly well contained area. They were all empty properties owned by people with yachts.' Peter turned to the map of the marina on the board. He then explained, from memory, which impressed Caren, where the various burglaries had taken place, pointing to the relevant apartment blocks.

'The number and frequency of the burglaries suggest a careful plan.'

Caren noticed Rhys was taking careful notes while Alice

looked uninterested, but Caren knew she was paying attention.

'We recently had intelligence from a reliable source that has implicated Mark Tremain as being involved.'

'Is this covert human intelligence source trustworthy?' Caren was the first to sound sceptical about evidence a CHIS provided. Despite all the careful procedures to ensure that any information was reliable, often material gathered this way was suspect.

'We have no reason to believe it is anything other than dependable.'

'How would this fit into our murder inquiry?' Huw said.

'Tremain works in the marina and would be privy to information about when the property owners were likely to be absent.'

'That wouldn't be difficult, boss. After all, the majority of the properties are second homes and they'll be empty for most of the time.'

Caren nodded. 'We know Tremain has form for handling stolen property. Somehow, he involves Emily Hughes and gives her money for her participation.'

'Maybe she kept watch, making certain Mark Tremain wasn't interrupted.' Rhys sounded animated.

Caren continued: 'And when she ended their relationship, Tremain decides she is a loose end that needs to be disposed of.' There was a silence while everyone pondered exactly the implication of what she had said. 'And she was two-timing Mark Tremain with Johann Ackland. So it certainly contributed to the red mist descending.'

Peter folded his arms and frowned. 'It might be the case. He certainly has a motive. Perhaps my team might assist and coordinate matters in relation to building a case.'

'We've had evidence that refers to Gerard Rankin, who is connected with organised crime in Swansea. Has his name appeared in your inquiry?' Caren said.

Peter looked puzzled. 'No, Rankin's name hasn't

appeared so far. Last I heard, he was spending a lot of time in Spain. Sun and sangria and all that.' Then he glanced back at the board. 'I'll circulate my team and get the officer in charge of our CHIS to establish whether there is any connection with Rankin.'

'Thanks.'

'I've emailed details of all the burglaries and the various items stolen. There's a cross-reference to various burglaries in the Cardiff area from properties owned by yacht owners in Swansea. There are so many for it not to be a coincidence. There may be burglaries at properties outside Wales owned by people with homes in the marina. Unless we have specific information from other forces in England, we will never know.'

Huw picked up another thread that was on Caren's mind. 'Have you come across a woman called Kate Evans? Her name has cropped up in the inquiry. We believe she is Sammy Evans' daughter.'

Peter whistled under his breath, and before replying he glanced over at Caren. 'Your predecessor.' He said nothing further, but Caren knew he had more to add. 'I knew nothing about Sammy Evans' family and we don't have a Kate Evans on our radar.'

Peter continued for another hour, outlining the progress his team was making. Once he had finished, Alice volunteered to make coffee and returned with the drinks for everyone and a plate with a collection of chocolate biscuits. 'It's Saturday, after all,' Alice said.

'Let's see what you've done to Sammy Evans' office.' Peter had a coffee mug in one hand and a half-eaten biscuit in the other.

The formal part of Peter's visit to the Incident Room was at an end. Caren guessed he wanted to gossip as one inspector to another. She led him through into her office where he sat down in one of the visitor chairs, scanning and nodding approvingly at the same time. 'Sammy Evans was a dinosaur.

He was a good cop, but he could twist and break the rules.' Peter nodded at the collection of cacti Caren had added to the room. 'I love the plants, and the landscapes are a lovely touch.' He gazed over at the set of three oil paintings Caren had on one wall. They were all of mountain scenes in North Wales and they gave her pleasure every time she came into the room, reminding her that there was more to life than simply work.

'How are you fitting in?'

'It's been a bit of a steep learning curve.'

'It must differ from Northern Division.'

Caren nodded. Peter continued: 'Have you found your way around the area?'

'My parents live in Carmarthen and my son has started in one of the local primary schools.'

Peter didn't respond, which suggested he knew all about Caren's family. There'd be gossip about her, she was certain of that.

'It's lovely to see an office with a feminine touch. Maybe you could come and give me some advice about my room when you get a chance.'

Caren smiled noncommittally. Peter finished his coffee and leaned forward in his chair. 'I'm sure you've got a lot to do. If there's anything I can do to help, then please contact me.' She noticed for the first time his blemish-free complexion and his healthy-looking brown eyes. He really was quite handsome. He didn't remind her of Alun for one minute. 'Perhaps you'd like to meet up for a drink one night. I can share with you all the gossip about Western Division.'

Caren was taken aback. She wasn't expecting an invitation but she smiled. 'That'll be nice, thank you.'

Peter left soon afterwards and Caren got back to the analysis of the case. She pulled a sheet of paper from a drawer in her desk. She wanted to make sense of the various threads in the inquiry. It would enable her to pull at some more aggressively and discard others.

In the middle of the page, she wrote the name 'Emily Hughes'.

To the top right, she added the name Johann Ackland and drew an arrow from Emily to his name. What would have been Ackland's motive for murdering Emily? Had she decided to expose the fraud that he was? Tell his wife about their relationship? He had certainly lied to the inquiry. But was that enough?

To the bottom right of Emily Hughes' name, she added Mark Tremain's. She felt a growing sense that Tremain was implicated in Emily's murder. If Peter's information was correct and he was involved with the burglaries, that sort of criminality would give him a motive for protecting himself.

Opposite her husband, Caren added the name Mrs Ackland. She had learned from the summary when Rhys and Alice had returned to the Incident Room the evening before, that Harriet Ackland had acknowledged she was in the marina the evening Emily Hughes was killed. Was she trying to protect her own reputation? Or was she simply disposing of her husband's lover?

At the bottom of the sheet, Caren added the names of Rachel Scott with a series of question marks and underneath her name she scribbled 'Tom Hughes protective brother'. And finally she added Kate Evans. She was about to review all the evidence and statements when Rhys Davies appeared at the door to her room.

'Something you should hear, boss.'

Caren got to her feet and followed the detective constable out into the Incident Room. Rhys was back at his desk, clicking into his computer.

'I've double-checked all the dates DI Peter Jenkins gave us. I've been able to cross match the dates of the deposits into Tremain's bank account and all took place within a week or so of the burglaries.'

'Which suggests that if he was the person responsible for the burglaries, he was being paid in cash by disposing of the stolen goods,' Alice said. 'You know what they say – follow the money.'

Caren nodded. 'Get all that put together as a detailed analysis.'

She read the time then decided that she would have a hurried sandwich at her desk for lunch. Then she'd collect Aled by the middle of the afternoon so that she could have at least a couple of hours with him before her mother arrived to look after him that evening.

Chapter 25

Caren had dispelled the guilt she had sensed earlier that day by spending time with Aled, playing with his favourite toys, watching some cartoons he loved, and then reading to him before her mother arrived to look after him for the rest of the evening.

During Aled's early years, she had had no social life. She didn't want him to feel left out, but she also knew the demands on her time as a detective often made it impossible to have a nine-to-five job and a normal family life. Her career and her now developing circle of friends would be impossible without the support she had from her parents.

She had bought some new clothes recently from an online store. The soft new jumper and smart jeans made a welcome change from the standard black trousers and navy jacket she seemed to wear incessantly at work. Tonight, she invested extra attention on her make-up. Looking in the mirror, she double-checked her appearance, making certain she looked presentable.

As she stared at her reflection she pondered briefly on her time with Western Division. Two challenging inquiries had been completed. Both cases were difficult in their own ways, with the culprit serving long prison sentences in each. She had made a mark, demonstrated to her superintendent she was a capable detective. And with her late husband's estate concluding, Caren felt she could look to the future with confidence. She drew a hand over her eyebrows, moved her head to one side, checking her make-up. Then she walked downstairs where her mum was reading to Aled.

Ann looked up and smiled. Aled complained that she had stopped and encouraged his Mamgu to continue. Caren leaned down and kissed her son.

'I won't be late.'

Ann nodded, made a movement with her eyes that suggested Caren should leave and that she had everything under control.

It was a short journey through the streets of Carmarthen to Susan Howard's home and once she had parked, she walked up the drive to the property. She didn't have to wait long for Susan to open the door.

'You look lovely,' Susan said. Then she whispered. 'David Hemsby's here and he's asking about you.'

'I hope I'm not late.'

'No, of course not.'

Caren smiled and followed her friend through into the open plan kitchen cum dining and seating space. David spotted her immediately and walked over, wine glass in hand. He gave her a welcome peck on the cheek and moments later Susan appeared with the soft drink Caren had asked for.

'Good to see you again,' David said. 'I hope you've done more revision than I have.'

Caren thought that was highly unlikely. He seemed to be a dedicated student, and from their previous conversations, he was committed to learning Welsh. He had even mentioned aiming to apply for the Welsh Learner of the Year competition at the National Eisteddfod. It was a prestigious award made to those who had learned Welsh and used it in their everyday work and home life.

Caren knew that if she was to become proficient, she'd need to persuade Superintendent Brooks to free up more of her time outside of urgent inquiries to learn the language.

All the students from the class were standing around an island in Susan's kitchen area although Caren spotted one or two faces she didn't know. Dafydd, Susan's husband, was playing the gracious host, making certain that everyone's glasses were filled and offering canapés. A buffet had been laid out on the table nearby. Caren hadn't realised how hungry she felt until she saw the selection of cold meats, potato salad dressed with chopped chives, and various salads.

The course tutor, Llinos Parry, made a point of announcing that everyone should try to make certain they spoke to each other using as much Welsh as they could. She encouraged them all to make mistakes, making clear in measured tones that practising Welsh was the only way they would get better.

Llinos explained that the unfamiliar faces were Welsh first-language speakers there to encourage students to polish their skills. Each student had to introduce themself and share something of their lives. Caren suddenly became quite nervous about showing to the guests present how poor she was at the language and how little time she really had to practise.

A person she spoke to complemented her on how proficient she had become. Another encouraged her to be developing her skills by talking to Aled, and he was especially pleased that he was going to a Welsh medium school. 'That's the only way we're going to save the language for the future,' he added in a serious tone.

By the end of the get-to-know-you session, Caren felt quite exhausted by the effort it had taken her to be thinking in Welsh about her conversations. But she also felt that she had switched off completely – which meant she had enjoyed every moment.

The food was just as delicious as she first thought it would be, and David Hemsby made certain he sat with her as she ate the meal. His grey stubble was darker than she recalled, but he still had the lively eyes and full lips she found attractive. He was engaging company, and she enjoyed spending time with him.

'Are you very busy with that case of the young girl in the Swansea Marina?' David said.

'I've been rushing up and down the M4 more than I care to remember.'

'And how is Aled?'

'He's good.'

'We must do something together again.'

This reminded Caren that they had spent a day at the National Botanical Garden as a sort of get-to-know-you session for Aled to meet David. It had gone well and David had pressed her about arranging more outings for the three of them. He had suggested the Techniquest in Cardiff and the National Gallery in the city. Caren wasn't certain she wanted her relationship with David to develop at quite the pace he wanted. So she'd suggest they go out, just the two of them, until she was more certain if their relationship was going to be serious.

Perhaps she might feel differently once everything was finished with Alun's estate. When Caren realised the time, she made her excuses and left. David walked with her to her car and they kissed and embraced. 'I'll call you,' Caren said.

On the journey home she felt pleased she had relaxed that evening, despite knowing that no matter how far she banished the inquiry to a corner of her mind it would still be there in the morning.

Chapter 26

After Rachel had been discharged from the hospital, her mother had spoiled her rotten. The morning after her assault she had felt bruised and exhausted, but a decent night's sleep had done her the power of good. By Sunday morning she had been able to go out with her parents for lunch at their favourite pub.

When she returned home from her family meal, a couple of texts reached her mobile from her friends Donna and Liz, who must have been colluding to invite her out for a drink that evening. It would be great to see her friends again, so she replied confirming she'd meet them at the time and place they'd suggested.

Her mum wasn't happy about her going – the grimace on her face made that clear – but knew she shouldn't stand in her way. 'Don't be late back. You need all the sleep you can get.'

'Of course, Mum. Don't worry. I'll get a taxi home.'

Both her friends were waiting for her in the first pub. Donna jumped to her feet when she saw Rachel and, after confirming her choice of drink, Rachel sat down with Liz.

'Tell us everything,' Liz said.

'I'll wait until Donna gets back.'

'Of course.'

A band was playing cover versions of eighties songs on a stage at the back of the premises. But they weren't loud enough to interrupt the girls. Once Donna returned, they got down to the serious business of hearing all about Tom Hughes' assault on Rachel.

Rachel had known both her friends since their days at the same primary school. They knew each other well and were the closest of friends. The faces of Donna and Liz changed from incredulity to surprise and then astonishment at the events that had seen Rachel end up in hospital.

'He was always a wild one.' Liz sounded important.

She gave them the detail of every stage of her visit to the emergency department. When she told them about the smart, fit-looking nurse who had looked after her, both girls giggled.

'I'm sure he goes to the gym. You should have seen the muscles on his arms.'

'I thought you were going to say "his abs" for a minute.' Donna winked at Rachel.

'And the policewoman who came to interview me gave the doctor a rollicking.'

'Have they arrested Tom Hughes?' Liz said.

'He was held overnight in the cells and when he was released, a condition of his bail is that he doesn't go anywhere near me or within a hundred metres of the house.'

'Are you afraid he might attack you again?' Liz said.

Rachel shook her head. 'He's not that stupid.'

'I hope he goes to jail,' Donna said. 'It's the least he deserves for having beaten you up.'

Rachel nodded, but she knew that Tom must have been devastated by his sister's death. She had been shocked at Emily's death, but she couldn't really imagine how he must feel. But it didn't excuse the assault which still made her angry at him.

After the second bottle of Kopparberg cider, Rachel relaxed. They went over to listen to the band, but gradually became bored and all three decided they'd set off to another pub. The Foresters Arms was full of students and Liz had to wrestle her way to the bar, using her elbows. She returned with their drinks. The place was too noisy for them so they moved on after they'd finished them.

Deciding to visit the Hope and Anchor didn't take much thought. Rachel and her friends knew it would be quiet on a Sunday evening. They laughed and joked as they sauntered through the city centre, down past the National Waterfront Museum. The smell of seawater and seaweed mixed with a hint of oil from the boats and yachts in the Tawe basin and the marina drifted in the air.

Donna led the way and pushed open the door of the main entrance. A waitress they knew well stopped to make a fuss of Rachel. She enquired how she was feeling and looked pleased when Rachel reassured her she was on the road to complete recovery, explaining she was only at the hospital for a bandage after a knock. Her injuries weren't that bad.

The three friends found a comfortable table to sit at in one corner and Rachel left to buy the drinks, returning with a tray. Another bottle of her favourite cider, and a vodka and tonic each for Donna and Liz.

'I don't know how you can drink that stuff all night,' Donna said, glancing at the bottle in Rachel's hand.

'You don't know what you're missing.' Rachel took a glug of her drink.

'Have they found who killed Emily yet?' Donna said.

'Did the woman detective tell you anything?' Liz added.

'No, nothing. I don't suppose she could have told me anyway.'

'I think it's that stalker who's been terrorising girls in the middle of the city. They have done nothing about that, have they?' The anger clear in Donna's voice.

'You were friends with Emily,' Donna said. 'Have the police asked you who you think might have killed her?'

'I told them I've got no idea who killed her.'

Rachel missed Emily so badly it was like a physical pain. Her outward certainty didn't match the trepidation she felt. Donna and Liz's fascination with the snippets of information Rachel shared showed on their faces as they interrogated her for every detail.

'It must be terrible being involved with the police,' Donna said.

Liz nodded, taking a decent mouthful of her drink.

A text from her mother asking how she was reminded Rachel of the time. 'I'd better be getting back.'

'Want us to come with you?'

Rachel shook her head. 'No, I'll be fine. I'm going to get a taxi.' She knew there was a taxi rank at the entrance to the marina, a short walk from the Hope and Anchor.

She got up and thanked her friends, telling them how much she had enjoyed the evening. She retraced her steps but decided to get some evening air, so she walked around the marina, passing several blocks of flats. It was an area she knew well. She didn't feel any unease. After all, there were CCTV cameras everywhere.

She walked past shops and commercial buildings and workshops, all locked up for the evening.

When she reached an area without any lighting, she picked up her pace. She glanced around troubled by an unease the darkness created. Her body's own protection mechanism warned her there was somebody behind her and her pulse spiked.

She didn't sense any danger until it was too late.

She couldn't tell who it was.

She was about to turn and look over her shoulder when she felt the blinding pain as metal collided with her skull. There was an intense, searing pain. Then her body and face collided with the rough stone surface of the marina.

Chapter 27

After negotiating the scanner inside the entrance for the coroner's court in Cardiff, Caren spotted her solicitor looking out for her. Matthew Reynolds waved over at her and shook her hand warmly when she approached. 'Caren, good morning. How are you?'

She had recently instructed a new firm of solicitors in Carmarthen to deal with the final part of Alun's estate. She couldn't afford the time to travel for meetings with lawyers up in North Wales, when everything seemed to be straightforward. It was much easier seeing Matthew – a ten-minute car journey from her home and headquarters.

Caren wanted to tell him she was in the middle of a murder inquiry and ask how long this inquest hearing was likely to take.

'We can use one of the small rooms they allocate to families and their legal representatives.' Reynolds ushered her towards a substantial oak door. Before she left the main entrance hallway, she scanned the others present. She didn't know what Miss Hale looked like but thought that she'd probably recognise her. Apart from an usher, the place was quiet and in complete contrast to the Crown Court hearings Caren attended at the end of an inquiry. On those occasions, the court would throng with journalists, family members and onlookers.

An inquest into a death would hardly attract the same sort of attention.

Inside the small conference room, beside a large oak table stood a woman in her forties. Caren knew this would be the barrister Matthew had chosen to represent her at the hearing. She was plump and her black jacket had stopped fitting her several years ago. She had a kindly face and reached out a hand.

'Rose Hewitt. Pleased to meet you. May I call you Caren?'

'Of course.'

'I just wanted to take some time to explain to you exactly how matters will proceed today. You may not be entirely familiar with how a coroner's inquest is conducted.'

'I've never been to one before.'

'I'm sure you've got far more experience of being in the Crown Court.'

Caren nodded.

'It's a procedure for establishing the cause of death. It's not a confrontational forum in any sense of the word. The coroner determines how the inquest will proceed. He'll invite me to ask questions and I imagine he'll do the same for Miss Hale's representative.'

'I don't think there can be any doubt the determination will be accidental death as a result of the car accident.'

'Do we know if Miss Hale is here?' Caren said.

It was the solicitor who responded. 'I believe she is, and she is represented by lawyers too.'

Caren wanted to say some pithy remark about finally meeting the mysterious Miss Hale but decided against it. She was never likely to see this woman again.

'After the inquest, will we be able to complete the administration of the estate?'

'Yes, of course, Caren,' Rose Hewitt said. 'Now, let's go through some background detail.'

The barrister spent a few minutes asking about Alun and Caren's relationship and his employment history. As she concluded, the usher appeared at the door and announced that the coroner was ready.

Caren followed her lawyers out into the hallway and then into the court room itself. Oak panelling lined the musty room giving it an austere atmosphere. On the right-hand side Caren saw two lawyers and a woman who she guessed was Miss Hale. Her pulse quickened when Miss Hale turned her head to speak to one of the men at her side. She had long thin hair, immaculately brushed to fall naturally over her shoulders. She had a narrow chin, a high forehead and pretty eyes. Caren felt herself staring so she looked down at her fingers threaded together tightly. What had Alun seen in her? What had she seen in Alun?

One of the men sitting in the row at the front Caren assumed was the barrister representing Miss Hale. They didn't wear gowns as they did in the Crown Court. Everything was less formal, or appeared that way to Caren.

She had for weeks been mulling over how she would react when seeing Miss Hale. Would she go over and speak to her? Would she want to ask about Alun and the time they had spent together? The hurt she had experienced when she had first learned about Alun's infidelity still felt raw. The nights of disturbed sleep when she had woken, her mind full of anger directed at Alun and his memory, were still common.

Caren couldn't see Miss Hale's face properly now but she wondered how they had met. What did they talk about? Did Alun ever mention her and Aled? What did they talk about when they were in bed together? The very thoughts made her feel angry and betrayed.

Caren's rumination didn't last long, as the coroner entered.

'I'd like to extend my sincere condolences to Mrs Waits and Miss Hale on their sad loss.' It was the sort of announcement the coroner must have made a thousand times before. Caren nodded out of courtesy.

Caren had noticed the two road traffic officers she knew from her time in Northern Division sitting at the side of the courtroom, and one of them was the first witness called.

The testimony they gave was factual and uncontroversial. The coroner asked them to confirm their statements and Rose Hewitt asked some banal questions. Miss Hale's lawyer did the same, and Caren wondered why on earth everybody had turned up for the hearing. The coroner turned to the reports from the investigators of the traffic department.

Once the coroner had finished glancing through them, he asked Caren's barrister, 'Miss Hewitt, do you intend to call

Mrs Waits to give any evidence? I already have her statement and unless you think her formally giving evidence will add anything I don't need to hear from her.'

Rose Hewitt got to her feet. 'I don't think it will be necessary to call Mrs Waits.'

The coroner turned to the lawyer for Miss Hale. Caren blanked out his name but his reply was like Rose Hewitt's although he added: 'Miss Hale wishes it formally recorded she was in a relationship with Mr Alun Waits. And that she is the mother of his child.'

The coroner sounded annoyed when he replied. 'I'm not certain that is something within my remit. I can only determine the circumstances leading to Mr Waits' death. And the person responsible has been investigated by the Wales Police Service and successfully prosecuted through the courts. The only determination open to me is one of accidental death.' The coroner looked over at Caren and then at Miss Hale. 'It is so often the case in road traffic accidents that the loved ones of the deceased have to live with a death in tragic circumstances. And I must extend my apologies that there has been a delay in this inquest taking place.'

And with that, the coroner stood up, as did everyone present out of deference. The proceedings at an end, the coroner left. Caren glanced over at Miss Hale, hoping she'd look over at her so that at least they would have looked each other in the eye. Caren wasn't certain what could be achieved by doing that. She had no intention of approaching the 'other woman' to shake hands and offer condolences. She had seduced the man Caren loved, or had it been the other way around? Part of Caren wanted to know, another part felt repulsed by even wanting to have the information

Exploring her own emotions, Caren recognised the sourness she felt about Miss Hale. It had been hard enough listening to the circumstances of the car accident that caused Alun's death. With the inquest over, Caren simply wanted to leave, get in her car, and drive away from Cardiff.

She left the courtroom with her lawyers and stood in the hallway for a few moments watching as Miss Hale stood talking with her legal team. Miss Hale then glanced over at Caren. For a few brief seconds Caren looked directly at her, the other woman. She had pondered this moment – should she go over and say something? But what on earth did they have to say to each other?

Miss Hale seemed to move towards Caren, only to pause and change her mind. A look crossed Miss Hale's face sharing exactly the emotion Caren had been thinking moments before. Then she broke eye contact with Caren and made to leave the building.

'Caren,' Rose Hewitt said, 'everything is concluded now.'

Caren turned to face her barrister. 'Sorry. I wasn't paying attention.'

'I'm sure you're glad the inquest is over.'

'Does that mean we can finalise the estate?'

'Your solicitors have told me that Miss Hale has made a claim against the estate in relation to her child. At least now you can move ahead and deal with that.'

'How long will that take?'

'It depends,' Reynolds said. 'I shall need to see you again to consider discussing settlement terms.'

Caren nodded. Now it was about money. With the coroner's inquest out of the way, the insurance company would release the monies to Reynolds. The mortgage on the smallholding in North Wales could be paid off, and proposals made to Miss Hale to settle. Caren could move ahead with purchasing a new home.

Caren left the court building after thanking Matthew and Rose.

The air felt fresh on her face after the court's musty atmosphere.

She thought about getting a coffee and perhaps a sandwich before heading, back but a message reaching her mobile soon put paid to that idea. *Get back here now, boss - Rachel Scott's body has been found.*

Chapter 28

Caren accelerated hard out of Cardiff, negotiated the junction for the M4 and, after switching on the hazard warning lights, she powered the car into the outside lane. She had done a basic course years ago in advanced driving techniques and now hoped it would help make certain she got to the crime scene quickly. She received word that the CSIs were en route which meant she needn't take foolish risks, but even so, the speedometer nudged ninety miles an hour.

She was making good time, and luckily the traffic was light. After leaving the motorway at the junction for Swansea, she allowed the satnav to direct her to the marina. She spotted uniformed officers standing by a fluttering crime scene tape. One of the police officers volunteered to accompany her down to the crime scene once he and his colleague had examined Caren's warrant card.

'It's this way, ma'am,'

The officer kept up a brisk pace as Caren followed. She was pleased there were no members of the public milling around the marina area. In the distance, she spotted crowds of onlookers near to another section cordoned off by uniformed officers. Caren hoped they wouldn't be joined by television crews searching for a news exclusive.

On the journey from Cardiff, she had spoken with Huw Margam, who had confirmed the basic details – a little used outbuilding was visited that morning and Rachel Scott's body had been discovered. Caren had given him an indication of when she expected to arrive, adding that she didn't want the body moved until she got there.

The police officer escorting her slowed his brisk pace and pointed towards the gaggle of people surrounding what looked like a disused industrial unit. Huw Margam came over to Caren when he saw her.

'You got here in good time,' Huw said.

'Not much traffic. So, give me the details.'

'Someone working for one of the companies in the

industrial units nearby found the body this morning. They were looking for some equipment they thought had been stored here.' Huw jerked a hand towards the building.

Caren looked over and saw Susan Howard directing activity. Taking a moment, Caren scanned her surroundings. The blocks of apartments and the marina were some distance away. What immediately came to her mind was why on earth was Rachel in this area?

When Caren noticed that Susan Howard was looking over at her, she and Huw ventured over to join her.

'Morning, Caren,' Susan said. 'We haven't moved her, just as you requested.'

'Thanks.'

Having photographs of the victim taken from a hundred different angles and pinned to the board in the Incident Room was never the same as seeing the body. It made a personal connection she would take with her to the end of the inquiry. Caren steeled herself. Would she ever become accustomed to seeing a dead body? She reminded herself that it was her work. This is what she was paid to do, but if she took it home with her, she would probably never be the detective she aspired to be. So she shook off any reservations and walked over to Susan.

'It looks like she was struck at the back of her head, twice,' Susan noted.

Caren took a moment to look inside the deserted workshop. A dilapidated bench with a rusty vice stood empty and alone to one side. No sign of any hammer or spanners or chisels or wrenches. The body of Rachel Scott was lying a few feet into the workshop, just enough for the killer to have dragged her inside, enabling the door to be pulled closed afterwards.

Caren immediately thought about the clothes that Rachel was wearing when she had spoken to her the previous Thursday after she'd been assaulted by Tom Hughes. They didn't look the same. The jeans and top she was wearing looked expensive, and Caren wondered if she'd been out the previous evening. Had she been to any public houses or restaurants in the marina?

Caren's attention was drawn to the bloodied wounds at the back of her head and the puddle of blood that had formed under her body, stretching out into the main part of the workshop.

'Any sign of a murder weapon?' Caren said loud enough for Susan to hear her.

'Nothing yet.'

Caren moved back out of the doorway and joined Huw and Susan. The crime scene investigators began their work in the workshop.

'When's the pathologist due?' Caren said.

'Should be any time.'

'It looks to me as if someone struck her over the head and then dragged her body into the outbuilding and dumped it. Her killer possibly knew the workshop door was easily forced open.'

Susan nodded. 'Assuming that's true, the killer's clothes would be soaked in blood.'

'And if you look around, boss,' Huw said. 'There are very few CCTV cameras in this area.'

Caren tilted her head up and scanned the buildings. Huw was right. 'Again, it suggests the killer had some sort of knowledge about where a good place would be to attack Rachel Scott.'

'If you had any inkling about thinking the first murder was an opportunistic random attack, then everything about this case looks premeditated,' Susan said.

'Who's identified the body?' Caren said.

'The person who found her knew who she was.'

'Have the family been informed?' Caren recalled the kindly, warm face of Rachel's mother when she had met her at the hospital. Now she'd be seeing her again under entirely different circumstances.

'A family liaison officer is with the family,' Huw said.

A voice from inside the workshop called out for Susan's attention. She stepped over and spoke to one of her investigators, then she turned to Caren.

'You need to look at this,' Susan said.

Caren watched closely as the crime scene manager, wearing a hazmat suit and protective overshoes, stepped into the workshop. The investigator held up for Susan's attention what looked like a piece of metal. When Susan brought it out of the workshop and showed it to Caren, after she had slipped it into a protective evidence bag, she said. 'It looks as though we've found the murder weapon.'

'What is it?' Caren peered at the elongated piece of metal. One end had a protruding dimple shape while the other seemed to have a handle topped with a piece of yellow plastic.

'It looks like a winch handle,' Huw said.

'What does that do?'

'It's used on a yacht to efficiently crank lines and adjust sails with increased leverage,' Huw said. 'It's quite common with yachts, and there are probably dozens of them in this marina.'

'So all we have to do is find a yacht with a missing winch handle and we'll be that much closer to finding the killer,' Caren said. 'But I guess it won't be as easy as that.'

Caren noticed the same uniformed officer that had escorted her now doing the same for Nigel Langmore the pathologist.

Caren stood to one side as he got to work and it only took him a brief time before he rejoined Caren outside the workshop. 'It looks as though the cause of death is blunt force trauma from a large metal object,' Langmore said.

'We believe it was from the winch handle the crime scene investigators have recovered.'

Langmore glanced at the plastic evidence pouch and nodded. 'I'll give you a better idea whether it is the murder weapon at the post-mortem. First thing tomorrow, Caren.

Don't be late.' And with that Langmore left the crime scene.

Caren turned to Huw. 'We need to get the house-to-house team back here.'

'They've only just finished.'

'And we'll go and see the family. I wonder what she was doing here last night.'

Chapter 29

Huw had his mobile pinned to his ear as he and Caren walked back to her car. She could hear the instructions he was giving to the house-to-house team supervisor. The officer must have queried the instruction because Huw added, 'It's a new inquiry. Just get it done.'

Caren opened the car with her remote and, once inside, Huw tapped into the sat nav the postcode for Rachel's parent's home. It was a journey of eighteen minutes and Caren glanced at the screen for the first directions.

'Her death must be connected to Emily Hughes',' Huw said.

Caren nodded. 'Both girls knew each other.'

Caren blasted the car horn at two vehicles dawdling in front of her. They drove north to the Townhill suburb of Swansea. Eventually, the satnav announced they had reached their destination. She pulled up at the wide pavement and peered over at the semi-detached property. The front door was down a small side alley. Two heavily curtained windows on the ground floor looked out over a piece of weed-infested grass.

'And I bet you anything the electric Mini Cooper over there belongs to the family liaison officer.'

The Wales Police Service was making a big push to use electric vehicles as part of the Welsh Government targets for net zero. She had listened often enough to David Hemsby talking animatedly about the impact on the world if nothing was done to counter global warming. They left the vehicle and, standing on the pavement, Caren could see over the northern part of the city between the house they were going to visit and the adjacent semi.

They walked down the alley but didn't need to knock, as the FLO opened the door.

'Good morning, ma'am,' the FLO said. 'Mr and Mrs Scott are in the living room.'

She waved them through into one room in the front of the

house.

A large television hung over a mantelpiece and underneath was a dormant faux log burning gas fire. Mrs Scott sat at one end of a grey sofa, husband by her side. She was wearing the same jeans Caren had noticed at the hospital, but a different coloured sweatshirt. It was clear from the pale and fragile colour of her cheeks that the profound shock of learning her daughter had been killed had drained away any healthy features. Her eyes were wide and still full of tears. She gazed up at Caren, a flicker of confusion creasing her brow. Her husband simply looked blank, staring intently at something on the carpet at his feet.

She nodded in acknowledgement when the family liaison officer introduced Caren and Huw.

At least Caren didn't have to break the bad news. She always hated doing that.

'My condolences, Mr and Mrs Scott. I'm the officer in charge of the investigation.' Caren wanted to add 'Into your daughter's murder', but thought the better of it. 'I know this is a terribly difficult time, but I have to ask some questions.'

Mrs Scott had a lost expression, as though she couldn't fathom out what had happened. It was entirely different from the relief she had seen on her face at the hospital the previous week.

'Do you have any idea where Rachel was going last night?'

'She said she was meeting some friends,' Mr Scott replied, his voice breaking.

'Do you know the names of her friends?'

'I think… It was probably Donna and maybe Liz.' Mrs Scott creased her brow.

'They were her best friends,' Mr Scott added.

'Where can we contact them?'

Mrs Scott shook her head from helplessness rather than ignorance. Now her husband scrambled to his feet. 'I may have a number for Liz. I know her parents.'

The family liaison officer accompanied Rachel's father out of the room.

'This must be a difficult question, but do you know of anyone who would wish to cause Rachel harm?'

Mr Scott returned mobile in hand. He sat and thumbed through its contact list before shaking his head.

Caren repeated the question.

'It must be something to do with Emily Hughes.' Mr Scott sounded bitter.

'Do you know how she met Emily Hughes?' Huw said.

'They were in a group that went surfboarding off the beach or paddleboarding or something like that,' Mr Scott said. 'Rachel was friendly with Emily Hughes. And now our baby is dead. Are they both connected? Are you looking for the same person?'

'It's far too early to say.'

Caren picked up the questioning. 'What can you tell me about Rachel? What does she do for a living?'

'She worked in a clothing shop in town and she had been a part-time model,' Mrs Scott said. 'I can't believe it. I just can't believe it. Nobody would want to kill her, nobody she's.... I mean, was... Everybody loved her.'

'Did she live at home?'

'She had her own place, a flat in town. It wasn't much, but she loved the independence and moved out of here a year ago.'

The sound of a young woman's voice in the hallway drifted inside. Caren could make out snippets, but then the family liaison officer interrupted them.

'This is Rachel's sister, Jane,' the FLO said.

Caren and Huw excused themselves and allowed Jane the opportunity to grieve with her parents. They sat in the kitchen at the rear of the property while the FLO clicked the kettle on. The door to the sitting room had been left slightly ajar, and Caren could hear the sobs and tears and the obvious grieving emanating as Rachel's sister and her parents shared their sorrow.

'Rachel's parents gave me the details of where to contact Jane. Another FLO went to speak to her.'

Caren nodded. The family liaison officer made mugs of tea for Caren and Huw. Caren checked the time, conscious that every hour after the discovery of a body was precious in their investigation. They needed to find who Rachel had been with the previous evening and speak to them urgently. But a family had to grieve properly. After a few minutes, she decided she'd interrupt Mr and Mrs Scott and their daughter, but as she got to her feet she heard movement in the hallway and Jane walked into the kitchen.

Anger was clear on Jane's face. She stared at Caren and then at Huw, searching for answers.

Huw pulled out a chair by the table, silently suggesting she sit.

'I'll go and see how Mr and Mrs Scott are doing.' The FLO left the kitchen.

'I know this must be very difficult. But can you tell us anything that might help us with the investigation.'

Jane wiped away tears. Then she looked directly at Caren. 'I don't know. Do you think it's the same person who killed Emily?'

'Do you know where Rachel was going last night?'

'She was probably out with Donna or Liz. They were her besties.'

'Do you have contact details for either woman?'

Jane nodded and fumbled, scrolling through her mobile. She texted Caren and Huw the contact details for both.

'They were good friends. Rachel changed after hanging out with Emily.'

'What do you mean?'

'She became secretive, and she didn't confide in me as she once did. And I was with Rachel once when she met Emily, who gave her some money. They pretended it was natural, but she gave Rachel an envelope with a lot of cash.

'Did you ask Rachel what was going on?'

'She laughed it off. She said I was being silly, and it was none of my business anyway.'

'What did you think was going on?'

Jane shrugged. 'I'd seen Rachel with Mark Tremain in one of the cafés in town. I got the impression he was into drugs and stuff and, well… I didn't want to think about it. If Rachel was involved with selling drugs, she was mad.'

'Did she do a lot with Emily Hughes?'

Jane shrugged. 'They were always going on about parties in the marina. She invited me along one evening and there was this lecturer from the University there. He was a right smarmy character who touched me up and he was far too personal, making lewd suggestions.'

'Do you know his name?'

'It was an odd name – European.'

'Can you describe him?'

Caren stopped Jane as she was halfway through. 'Does the name Johann mean anything to you?'

Jane nodded. 'Yeah, that sounds right.'

Huw had been scrolling through his mobile as Caren had been talking to Jane. He passed over his mobile with an image of Johann Ackland on the screen. 'Is this the man?'

Jane briefly glanced before nodding confirmation. 'That was him.'

'Did she ever tell you she was frightened?'

Jane reached for a tissue from the box on the table and blew her nose loudly.

'She was just ordinary. She enjoyed going out, and she liked to help out at that homeless centre in town. I don't know anybody who would want to kill her. It's completely senseless.'

'If you think of anything else,' Caren said, pushing a business card across the table towards Jane. 'Contact me immediately. Don't worry about the time.'

Caren got to her feet with Huw, and the family liaison

officer saw them to the door. Caren walked back to her car trying to imagine the intensity of the raw emotion of losing a child in such circumstances. The grief that had overwhelmed her when Alun had died had made her feel as though she didn't know what to do with the rest of her life. But it couldn't be anything as bad as a parent whose child had died before them.

Huw was on the phone when they reach the car. 'That was Donna. I've arranged to meet her and Liz.'

Chapter 30

Driving back to the marina Huw explained to Caren that Donna and Liz were on the beach nearby. 'Beach' wasn't a word that he normally associated with this part of Swansea Bay. He naturally thought of a beach as a pretty, often convex feature, lined with warm sand and perfect for swimming. He knew that Swansea Bay had sand but there was nothing attractive about the post-industrial end of the bay despite the attempts to gentrify the area with modern apartment blocks, the marina and shrubs and greenery. It was much nicer towards Mumbles, where he lived with Christopher.

'They told me it was this end of the beach,' Huw said as they stood on the concrete promenade looking south.

Over to their left, Huw spotted the West and East piers pointing like fingers into the Bristol Channel. Beyond them were Swansea docks, the last part of the industrial history of Swansea to survive.

In the distance to his right Huw could just about make out two figures sitting on upright director-type chairs. He raised a hand and pointed, turning to Caren at the same time. 'I think they're over there.'

His brogues sank into the soft sand above the high-water mark and he complained he wasn't properly dressed. 'I'm more accustomed to the beach at the other end near where we live. Although we haven't walked on the beach recently because of all the building work on the sea defences at the moment.'

'There was a programme on S4C the other night about global warming. It's quite depressing what could happen with rising sea levels.'

'That would have been in Welsh,' Huw sounded puzzled.

'I'm trying to watch television programmes to improve my Welsh.'

'I should learn, and I'm quite ashamed I don't speak it, actually. My father does, but he never passed on the language to me.'

They were making slow progress across the beach. Their footsteps were heavy and Huw cursed inwardly that his shoes and socks would be full of sand soon.

'Aled goes to a Welsh language medium school.'

'It's easier if you learn the language as a youngster.'

Huw admired Caren for her determination to attend the Welsh classes. More and more of the officers promoted to senior roles were bilingual, and he wondered if he should ask to be sent on a course. He hadn't given up the prospect of preferment. But things were comfortable as they were. He wasn't certain he wanted to embrace the challenges of being a detective inspector.

'Did everything go smoothly at the inquest?'

'It was exactly as expected. The coroner made a determination of accidental death.'

'So you'll be able to wrap up your late husband's estate now? It's been a long time. I'm sure you must be very frustrated.'

Caren had never discussed the details of her personal life with Huw, but he could imagine bringing up a child on her own and combining it with a demanding career as a detective would be particularly challenging. She had mentioned before that the property she owned in North Wales needed to be sold so that she could buy her own place in Carmarthenshire.

'I just want to get everything finished after so many delays.'

They reached a section of the beach next to the Civic Centre car park where marram grass clung to a triangular-shaped corner of the sand abutting the Oystermouth Road. The two figures Huw had spotted earlier stood up and turned to face them as they approached.

'Are you Donna and Liz?' Huw said.

'I'm Donna,' the older replied. Once Huw had introduced himself and Caren by their full names and ranks, he asked. 'Were you with Rachel last night?'

As he cooled down, he felt the perspiration trickling

down his forehead. It was warmer than he had realised. A woollen suit and a white shirt and reasonably expensive silk tie weren't the ideal apparel for traipsing on a beach. So he loosened his tie and opened his collar.

'We feel like shit,' Liz said. 'We persuaded Rachel to come out with us for a bit of a pub crawl, as we thought it would do her good.'

'We'll need full details of exactly where you went,' Caren said.

It didn't take long for Donna to provide the names and addresses of the pubs they had visited before they eventually visited the Hope and Anchor in the marina.

'Why did you go there?' Huw said.

'It was one of those places that Rachel liked. She knew a lot of the girls working in the bar.'

'And it was where Emily Hughes worked. Did either of you know Emily?'

Donna was the first to respond. 'We met her a couple of times.' Liz nodded in agreement.

'Did Rachel tell you anything that made you suspect she was frightened of anyone?'

'You should talk to Tom Hughes about what happened to Rachel.' Donna added a serious tone to her voice. 'He beat her up the other day. What more evidence do you need?'

'Did either of you see Tom Hughes at the Hope and Anchor last night or at any of the other pubs you visited?'

Donna and Liz shook their heads.

'Did Rachel mention anything troubling her?' Caren said.

More shaking of heads.

'We're also trying to track down a Kate Evans who has been mentioned as part of the investigation. Do you know anything about her?'

Donna and Liz frowned. 'We've seen her around but I don't think she was friends with Rachel. She was a bit of a hanger-on.'

'We know that Emily knew a man called Johann Ackland and that she'd had a previous relationship with a man called Mark Tremain.'

'Yeah, we know Johann Ackland and his wife,' Donna said.

'His wife must know what he's like,' Liz added,

'I'm sure I saw her in the Hope and Anchor on Sunday night,' Donna said.

'And that Mark Tremain has one hell of a temper. I heard someone talking in the Hope and Anchor a while ago, suggesting he was tied up with some dodgy people who might have been responsible for the burglaries and thefts from the yachts in the marina. He was always flashing his money around, telling people how well he was doing.'

Huw looked over at Caren. Liz's information about Mark Tremain hardly coincided with the information the team had uncovered about his financial circumstances. The look on her face told Huw she shared his concern.

'When did Rachel leave the Hope and Anchor last night?' Huw said.

'She left about ten-thirty,' Donna said. 'She was going to get a taxi home. That's what she told us.'

A text reached Caren's mobile and she reached into her jacket. She turned to Huw and he could see on her face that they had to finish their meeting.

'We'll need your full contact details.'

He scribbled down the information they provided, and he walked over to the promenade as Caren said, 'Rachel Scott's place has been ransacked.'

Chapter 31

A marked police car was parked by the pavement outside the terraced property where Rachel Scott had a bedsit. A group of neighbours nearby were looking over animatedly at the front door waiting for something dramatic to happen. Caren looked at the time on the dashboard clock. Her focus that morning had been on the priorities for a new inquiry, but now she was away from the crime scene she needed to speak to her mum about Aled. She pulled up a little distance from the property and found her mobile. Her mum would want to know what had happened in Cardiff, but Caren didn't go into the details.

'Everything is fine, Mum,' Caren said. 'There was a verdict of accidental death, just as we expected.' Caren could sense her mother expecting more detail, especially about Miss Hale. 'But I can't talk. There has been another murder at the marina. I've no idea when I'll be home tonight.'

Before she could explain anything further, her mother added, 'Aled will be fine with me. I'll get your father to come over later to help.'

'Thanks, Mum,' Caren said.

She finished the call and then noticed a police officer emerging from the property. Meanwhile, Huw arrived in his car. Caren felt a mild sense of achievement as she had made the journey more quickly than Huw, despite the fact he lived in the Mumbles area. Although she reminded herself that he had a walk from where she had left him to collect his vehicle.

The police officer stood by the pavement and looked relieved when Caren arrived.

'I'm pleased you got here so fast, ma'am.' The officer introduced himself as Tony Williams. 'The bedsit is on the first floor.'

'Show me,' Caren said.

A burglary of Rachel's home was clearly part of their investigation. Caren hated coincidences. Rachel's murder the night before and now a break-in at her property were linked.

Williams led them up the staircase, its carpet thin and

grey with age. The smell of dust and second-hand cigarette smoke hung in the air.

'Who reported the burglary?' Caren said.

'The occupier of one of the bedsits arrived home and found the door to Rachel's bedsit open. She put her head in and when she saw the chaos, called us straight away.'

'Where is that person?'

'I've told her to stay in her bedsit for now.'

'Good, we'll talk to her once we've finished.'

The sound of conversation from the ground floor took their attention.

'That'll be the CSI team,' Williams said. 'I was told they wouldn't be far behind you.'

Caren and Huw snapped on a pair of latex gloves each and when Williams approached the door to Rachel's bedsit, he pushed it open gingerly. For a moment, Caren and Huw stood looking in at the carnage.

Moments later, an investigator appeared at the door. He whistled under his breath.

'I'm DI Waits and this is DS Margam. This bedsit belongs to a Rachel Scott. Her body was found this morning in the marina.'

'I'd heard Susan Howard's team is down there.'

'We need to find out exactly why someone would want to trash Rachel Scott's property.'

'Detective Sergeant Margam and I will talk to the person who discovered the place had been trashed. Have you got enough investigators in your team to get this job done quickly?'

The CSI looked around the room. 'Shouldn't take long.'

Caren stepped out into the hallway and noticed two other investigators already wearing hazmat suits and plastic covers for their shoes.

Williams took Caren and Huw to the second floor of the building and, after knocking on a door that had a number six hanging loosely by a single screw, didn't wait to be invited in.

Maureen, a woman in her thirties with flaming red hair, numerous bracelets and multicoloured jewellery, was sitting on the sofa sipping from a can of lager.

After introductions, Huw pulled over two old dining chairs.

'Is it true that Rachel is dead?' Maureen said.

'Yes, did you know her well?'

'Not really. Sometimes we'd have a coffee together or maybe go down to the local pub, but we weren't close.'

'Did she mention anything about feeling frightened?'

Maureen shook her head. Then she took another sip of her lager.

'Did you notice something out of the ordinary when you returned this afternoon?'

'What do you mean? This is like something out of one of those cop dramas. Could I be next?'

Caren didn't want to dismiss this woman immediately, but she needed to move on. 'Did you see anybody in the building that you haven't seen before?'

Maureen exchanged a worried look with Caren and Huw, appearing unable to understand and uncertain about seeking clarification.

'Did you notice any strangers here?' Huw said. 'Was there anyone who appeared suspicious or out of place when you arrived?'

Maureen continued to look utterly lost. After finishing her lager, she glanced at Caren. 'I don't remember. I wasn't looking out for anybody suspicious. I wanted to get home.'

Constable Williams cut their conversation with Maureen short by appearing at the door. 'The CSIs want to speak to you, ma'am.'

Caren gave Maureen her card and told her in stern terms that if she had anything that might be helpful, she should contact them immediately. Maureen nodded enthusiastically.

Retracing their steps to the first-floor bedsit, Caren stepped inside. The CSI in charge picked up a small plastic bag he had found. 'We found this in the kitchen units. I've done a field test and there's enough cocaine here to justify a charge of possession with intent to supply.'

'Anything else?' Caren inquired, thinking about the investigators' discovery.

'Nothing at the moment. A lot of old clothes. We've recovered three different fingerprint sets.'

'Good, let me know as soon as you have anything else. I want a report on that cocaine without delay.'

Caren didn't wait for a reply and ushered Huw out of the building. She delegated finding the names and full details of all the tenants in the other bedsits to Constable Williams and then stood for a moment by her car.

'If somebody broke into her property looking for something, it certainly wasn't that cocaine,' Huw said.

'I know, and that's what worries me. Maybe Rachel had a secret hoard of cash, just as Emily had. We need to discover what the culprit was looking for.'

Caren decided to speak to Tom Hughes on the journey back to headquarters. After his assault on Rachel the previous week, he was the prime suspect they needed to speak to. Had his temper and rage with Rachel got the better of him? As he blamed her for the death of his sister, had he been consumed by revenge?

The family liaison officer's car was still parked outside the property as Caren and Huw pulled up by the pavement. Caren had rung ahead to warn the FLO they would call, and she opened the door as they approached it.

'I've warned Tom Hughes to expect you,' the FLO said.

'How are Mr and Mrs Hughes?' Caren said.

'They are bearing up, I guess. Much as you'd expect, but Rachel Scott's death has unnerved them.'

The family sat in the living room and Mr Hughes muted the channel showing some banal daytime television. Until a family really came to terms with the death of a loved one, watching inane quiz programmes, and others on buying a property overseas, was a simple way of dealing with the long hours of the day. Mrs Hughes looked up at Caren and the look on Tom Hughes' face told Caren he was expecting her.

'We need to speak to Tom on his own. In the kitchen please,' Caren said.

She had been tempted to take him to the local police station and interrogate him under caution. But they had nothing at that stage of the inquiry to suggest he was responsible, other than his past behaviour towards Rachel.

Tom followed Caren and Huw and he sat by the table. Huw closed the door carefully.

Caren didn't bother sitting. They weren't here for a social call.

'You know why we're here. The body of Rachel Scott was found this morning, her head was caved in. We want to know exactly your movements yesterday and today.'

'I had nothing to do with her death. I did not kill her. Okay, I was angry with her, but that didn't mean I would do anything to harm her – I wouldn't do it.' There were noticeable shadows under his sunken eyes.

'Tell us where you've been.'

'I was working yesterday. I was doing an extra shift until five o'clock. Then I came home. I went out to the takeaway last night. And I was here this morning when that other woman arrived. Since then I've been playing games in my room.'

Caren tipped her head at Huw, who left the kitchen, acting on her implied instruction to check the details with Mr and Mrs Hughes and the family liaison officer. He returned moments later and nodded at Caren.

'I was not supposed to go anywhere near Rachel after I was released on bail.'

Caren looked down at the man sitting by the table. Even if he had been responsible for the murder of Rachel Scott, they still had the inquiry into Emily's death. Caren felt both deaths were connected, which meant Tom Hughes would not be a realistic suspect. She doubted whether he was really a sick enough person to kill his own sister.

'I told you before, Rachel and Emily have been playing a dangerous game with that Mark Tremain. Whatever he was up to, she should not have got involved with him.'

Caren turned and left. She spoke briefly to the family liaison officer, telling her to keep them fully informed about Tom Hughes' movements and how Mr and Mrs Hughes were getting on.

Caren returned late to the Incident Room with Huw. Alice and Rhys raised their heads from their work on their computers and greeted Caren. 'Boss'

Caren sat in a chair by a spare desk as Huw shrugged off his jacket.

'Can someone make me a coffee?' Caren said.

Alice stood up and went through to the kitchen. Caren told Rhys to wait until she was back before beginning a review of the activity that day. She paused to survey the images on the board. Somebody had already added a photograph of Rachel Scott, a prominent red dot added to the map showing exactly where her body had been found.

'Thanks, Alice,' Caren said when the constable returned with mugs of steaming drinks for the team. She had also been able to find two packs of different biscuits, judging by the variety on the plate.

'Chocolate digestives,' Huw said. 'My favourite.' He took two with his coffee.

Caren didn't count the number Rhys had taken and suspected that he hadn't either. He was young enough to not worry about calories. It made her realise she hadn't actually eaten anything at lunchtime. She couldn't even remember where she was at lunchtime. Then she remembered eating a KitKat she kept for emergencies in her car.

Caren took a mouthful of her coffee.

'Somebody murdered Rachel Scott last night using what looks like a winch handle. And her flat was trashed earlier today.'

Alice looked puzzled.

'It's to turn a winch on a yacht that manages the sails,' Huw said. 'They're very common on yachts.'

'We know she was at the Hope and Anchor last night with two of her friends, Donna and Liz, who we've spoken to earlier. I want all the CCTV from around the marina recovered and examined. There must be a record of her being there and hopefully the killer will be there too.'

'And an amount of cocaine was recovered from her bedsit that would be enough to justify a possession with intent to supply charge,' Huw said.

'So that gives us a link to the drug use in the marina,' Alice said.

Caren stood up and walked over towards the board. 'We keep an open mind. After all the person who broke into her bedsit might not have been looking for anything. The cocaine might have been planted.'

'I'll start checking her social media accounts,' Rhys said.

Caren nodded. 'And a full search of her background. Financials, job et cetera.'

'I think we can eliminate Tom Hughes as a suspect,' Huw said. 'We've seen him on the way back from Rachel's flat.'

Caren sensed waves of tiredness hitting her. She stared at the map of the marina on the board and then at the various images and names pinned to it that seemed to blend into one. 'It's been a long day. Early start tomorrow.'

Chapter 32

Caren woke in the morning convinced that she hadn't moved all night. She spent a few moments enjoying the peace before she had to get up and prepare Aled for school. The light leaked around the sides and bottom of the curtain. The radiator under the window rattled slightly, which she knew was a sign the boiler in the utility room had fired up. Soon she could go house hunting. She wanted nothing fancy, just enough for herself and Aled. It would be nice to have a garage and an extra bedroom and space so she could live comfortably with her son, especially as he was getting older. And more than anything, she'd have no mortgage. Although the claim Miss Hale's child had against Alun's estate still needed to be resolved.

She made a mental note that she needed to contact the solicitor in Carmarthen and pressurise him into making progress finalising Alun's affairs. The estate agents in North Wales had reduced the asking price of the smallholding she and Alun had owned to get a quick sale. It was empty of furniture and she could easily justify not visiting again.

But, perhaps for her own closure, she needed to go there on one more occasion to close the door on her memories of her married life with Alun. Her new life filled her mind with enthusiasm for future hopes and plans. A message reached her mobile after she finished dressing.

How are you? How did the inquest go? How are you feeling?

She must have mentioned to David her visit yesterday to the coroners' court at Susan's house. She felt pleased he had remembered and tapped out a reply.

Much as expected. I'm pleased it's over.
Are you involved in that Swansea Marina case?
Yes. All been a bit frantic.
That murder case in the marina is all over the news. Look after yourself.

She hesitated for a moment. It lifted her spirits to know

he was concerned. It added to the sense of hope she felt for the future. Then she replied.

Thanks for the message. Appreciate it.

Aled ate his favourite cereal while Caren drank a mug of tea. She'd have something to eat after the postmortem. She piled the dishes into the bowl in the sink and turned to her son. She straightened the collar of his polo shirt and brushed an imaginary fleck of dust from the sweater he wore that had the name of the school embroidered on the left-hand side. He looked so grown-up in his uniform, although his shoes were getting a little small for him. And they looked scuffed. She wondered if all mothers had this problem with children.

Aled asked if she was going to pick him up from school. She wanted to reply with a certainty he could never doubt. But things were never that easy.

'It'll be me or Mamgu,' Caren said. At least she had had breakfast with her son that morning. They left the house, and she dropped him off at school and made her way to headquarters.

The team was already at their desks in the Incident Room when she arrived. Huw had chosen a pinstripe suit with a dark navy shirt and tie of a similar colour that seemed to blend into the background. Rhys Davies and Alice Sharp both looked refreshed from a decent night's sleep. Rhys was the youngest and when she dealt with him, it reminded her she had been his age once. He had to learn from his mistakes.

Caren had matched one of her pairs of dark trousers with a discreet pink blouse. There was a specific reason when she needed to power dress – press conferences and meetings with the chief constable, which were few and far between, or other senior officers fell into that category.

'Good morning.' Caren stood by the board.

'Boss,' the three officers said, almost in unison.

'Huw and I are going to the post-mortem, then the marina. I want both of you' – she nodded at Rhys and Alice – 'down there by lunchtime so that we can talk to the house-to-house team and staff at the Hope and Anchor. In the meantime, get cracking with following up on Rachel Scott's social media.'

Caren could tell by looking at Rhys that he was eager to contribute to their preliminary briefing. 'A man has contacted the helpline. He thinks he was the person seen running through the marina on the night Emily was killed.'

'So where the hell has he been?' Alice said. 'Does he live in a cave?'

'He was very apologetic but said that he'd been working in London when the original story about Emily broke in the press.'

'Plan to see him in the mobile incident room in the marina later,' Caren said.

Rhys nodded. Caren glanced at Huw, who stood, and they left.

'I've been thinking about what you said yesterday about the drugs they found at Rachel's place,' Huw said as they reached Caren's car. 'Maybe whoever broke in was trying to implicate Rachel in drug dealing by deflecting us from the right course in the inquiry.'

Caren had become quite accustomed to Huw's dogged, thorough application to police work. Clearly the investigation hadn't been far from his mind. And that pleased her, as did his ability to often think differently from her. It made them a good team.

'Let's hope the CSIs can recover some fragments of evidence linking us to somebody who broke into her place. But if you're right and nothing was stolen, then why break in? Unless, of course, she had a wad of cash, just like Emily? Or it was to plant the drugs.'

Caren drove out of headquarters and made her way to the mortuary, a journey she was now accustomed to making. Nigel Langmore, the pathologist, dressed in scrubs, was waiting for Caren and Huw in reception.

'Good morning. Any more developments since I saw you

yesterday?'

'Rachel Scott's bedsit was trashed. But we do not know what the intruder was looking for,' Caren said.

'Let's get cracking then.'

Langmore led them through into the mortuary where an assistant wheeled in Rachel Scott on a trolley. All the implements needed had been carefully laid out, together with the stainless steel receptacles that would hold the body parts during the procedure.

The pathologist dictated an introduction with Rachel's full name and date of birth. Then he began an examination of the feet and legs before moving up the body to the arms and shoulders. Rachel's breasts were flattened against her chest and her genitalia had been shaved, but neither was the subject of any comment by Nigel Langmore. He'd undertake a more detailed intimate examination in due course to identify if there had been any sexual assault, but there was no suggestion from the crime scene that had been the case.

Caren was pleased he turned to the wound on Rachel's skull prior to making the usual 'Y' incision to remove the vital body organs from the chest and abdomen.

'At least we have a murder weapon, or what we believe to be it.' Langmore reached over for the winch handle in its plastic evidence pouch on one of the trolleys by his side. 'I made a detailed analysis of the head, the part that goes into the winch itself. There are bearings on the inside of the handle that operated the winch.' He leaned over and began making an examination of the wounds. His measurements were precise and his dictation quite specific. Once he had completed the task, he checked the details against the winch handle. 'I've got one more test to actually undertake, but from a preliminary examination, it seems that the injuries are consistent with this being the murder weapon.'

Then he positioned the winch handle within the plastic evidence pouch carefully against one wound on Rachel's head. It didn't take more than a few seconds and when he straightened, he announced, 'No doubt in my mind that the winch handle caused the catastrophic trauma that led to a massive extradural haemorrhage and depressed skull fracture, leading to her death.'

Langmore replaced the winch handle on one of the trolleys by his side. He reached for a scalpel and, carving the 'Y' incision, he looked over at Caren. 'Will you be staying for the main course?' A weak smile played over his face.

Caren had seen enough.

'Thanks, Nigel, but we've got a killer to catch and you've confirmed what I needed to know.'

Before she turned for the door, Caren saw Langmore's first slice through the body with a scalpel. Then he announced, 'I'll send you my report in due course.'

Caren stood outside the mortuary for a few moments, taking in the fresh air. The smell of frying bacon wafted over from a mobile canteen.

'I'm dying for something to eat,' Caren said.

'Did you really mean that, boss?' Huw gave her a look that suggested she hadn't realised the irony in her comment.

Caren ignored him. She was hungry and they had a lot of work to do.

Chapter 33

Rhys got started on the work Detective Inspector Waits had allocated as soon as Caren and Huw had left the Incident Room. He wanted to make his mark, be certain that he was contributing effectively to the team. Emily Hughes had seemed quite ordinary when they had first began building a picture of her. He hadn't expected a student at the University to have been moving in the social circles that included the sailing club at the Swansea Marina. Although he had been impressed she had volunteered at the homeless shelter.

Alice had made some sarky comment when they had first learned about her volunteering. But she was forever the cynic and Rhys wasn't going to indulge his colleague even though she was more experienced.

He wasted little time and began with Rachel Scott's Facebook page. She had over 500 friends, and he wondered how many of them kept in touch with her regularly. He didn't have nearly as many on his own account. He had friends that boasted about the number of friends they had on their Facebook, and he often thought it was a substitute for actually knowing people well. But her account with Instagram had hundreds of posts.

There were dozens of photographs of Rachel in various holiday locations in Europe. He began with the most recent, where she had visited a resort in Ibiza. She had numerous friends tagged, but he didn't recognise the names of Donna or Liz that the inspector and Huw had mentioned when they'd arrived back from the crime scene yesterday.

Photographs from a second holiday had been taken in a similar hotel in Rhodes. He found dozens of images of her with friends drinking from large, tall glasses with different coloured fruits and paper umbrellas.

Another trip had been to a resort in Tenerife. Rhys had been to the island with his parents years ago, so he googled the details of the hotel and discovered it was a five-star destination. He wondered how a person who worked at a shop in Swansea and as a part-time model could afford such luxury.

Rachel certainly enjoyed taking photographs, both selfies and of her friends, which she then posted on her social media account. Rhys hated when people took photographs of their meals and posted them on Facebook or Instagram. He just didn't see the point, but Rachel was an expert at it.

Besides her trips overseas for holidays, there were images of events linked to the sailing club at the marina and also to sailing clubs further afield, in Cardiff and Somerset. A few of the pictures featured Emily, but Rhys could not find a likeness to Johann Ackland, nor his wife, nor Mark Tremain. He wondered how they all fitted together. The drugs discovered at Rachel's bedsit certainly suggested she was involved with supplying. It wouldn't come as a surprise that the wealthy sailing set would use cocaine. How many times had he heard that it was the middle-class drug of choice?

Alice had been complaining about the work she was doing to identify the sort of winch handle used to assault Rachel Scott. During the morning Rhys had helped her to establish the exact make and model of the handle and whether it could be used for any yacht or whether there had to be a specific fitting.

He got back to his desk and settled down to finalising the interrogation of Rachel's Instagram account. It amazed him she was such a frequent visitor, posting regularly. The boss wanted them in the marina by lunchtime, which meant he had to get cracking.

Alice didn't want to admit that Rhys was a good detective, but the help he had given her that morning to identify the make of the winch handle had saved a lot of time. She had found the manufacturer and, after emailing a query, someone from the technical department had spoken to her on the telephone. Their conversation was brief and Alice realised it would not be particularly helpful. The manufacturers of deck hardware used varying material, some alloys and others heavier. Alice checked the weight of the one that had been used to kill Rachel and discovered that it was an older version.

Some manufacturers even offered pockets that could be screwed conveniently onto an upright section of the yacht where their handles could be stored. And that raised the possibility that anybody walking past a yacht could just jump on board, steal a handle and nobody would be the wiser where it had gone.

Then she turned to the CCTV footage that they had been sent by the sailing club and the marina office. There were other cameras, and she'd need to speak to the owners of the commercial premises to request any recordings. She had more than enough footage to take all of her time that morning.

The first was from the sailing club. Scrolling through she started the footage at eight pm. She had done this so many times it became second nature to her just to play it at an enhanced speed, clicking only to check whether activity or people recorded seemed relevant. She played the footage for both cameras until after eleven-thirty pm.

Donna and Liz had confirmed Rachel had left the Hope and Anchor a little after ten-thirty, so watching for an hour afterwards seem sensible. She had to pause the footage on a couple of occasions, only when she spotted activity, but they were couples walking from the sailing club, the marina and presumably their yachts.

She started watching the footage from the two cameras on the marina building at the same time. It was a little before ten when she noticed two figures skirting along one side of the marina office. It troubled her that they seemed to make an effort to conceal themselves from the cameras, so she stopped the footage to get a clearer view. After some adjustments and playing and replaying the footage, she was convinced she had seen Mrs Harriet Ackland and Mark Tremain. She made a note of the time of the specific footage and made a mental note to share all the details with the boss.

As a break from viewing the footage, she pursued another line of inquiry that had been bubbling in the back of her mind. The boss had wanted to find an address for Kate Evans, who they knew was Sammy Evans' daughter. It had been made quite clear that Alice wasn't to contact Sammy Evans under any circumstances. She didn't want him to know that his daughter was potentially implicated in a murder inquiry.

And speaking to retired officers that she knew would only alert Sammy Evans. Although she didn't share Caren's reluctance. If talking to Kate Evans was a priority, then Alice reckoned it would be much easier just to call Sammy and ask him where his daughter lived. But she wasn't going to risk a warning and possible disciplinary proceedings for stepping out of line. There was a retired detective sergeant she knew from years ago who hated Sammy Evans. He'd be the last person to warn him about the inquiry. But it was a long shot and even if he didn't know where Kate lived, the officer might have some background information.

A couple of telephone calls later Alice preened herself. She looked over at Rhys. 'You won't believe this. I've been promised an address for Kate Evans.'

'Bloody hell.'

'My contact is going to call me back later. Once I have the details, I'll tell the boss.'

'We'd better get down to the marina to interview the bar staff.' Rhys got to his feet.

Chapter 34

Caren and Huw arrived at the mobile incident room in the marina just as the sergeant in charge of the house-to-house enquiries was finishing a briefing. The officers streamed out, and some exchanged a greeting with Huw and Caren.

Caren stepped inside and when the sergeant saw her he beckoned her over to the board, which had a plan of the marina pinned to it.

'Are you making progress, Sergeant?' Caren said.

'We've spoken to a lot of the homeowners previously. Some of them are getting tired of seeing us again. And the cafés and some of the commercial outlets are frustrated their businesses are being disrupted.'

'Murder has a habit of being inconvenient,' Caren said.

The sergeant nodded stoically.

Caren continued: 'An individual seen running through the marina the night Emily was killed is going to turn up for an interview. If he arrives and no one from my team is here, contact me. He isn't allowed to leave until we've spoken to him.'

The sergeant nodded.

'Yes, ma'am.'

Walking over to the Hope and Anchor, Caren and Huw noticed rubberneckers gathered at one end of the marina behind the fluttering crime scene perimeter tape. It amazed Caren how people thought that something dramatic was likely to happen at a crime scene. Was there a voyeuristic streak in everybody? Caren thought. There had been enough coverage on the television and local news to satisfy most people's curiosity.

Huw was ahead of her and he pushed open the door. The place had the warm, welcoming feel of a popular bistro pub, as the name above the door on the outside suggested. Customers were lining up to order drinks, others ordering an early lunch.

She didn't have to wait too long after introducing herself

to a member of the bar staff for the manager to appear. He was a serious-looking man in his thirties with heavy stubble and black well-groomed hair hanging over the top of his spectacles as though he wanted to shield his eyes from prying stares.

'Two officers on my team will be here to interview all of your staff. I'm sorry for the inconvenience, but it won't take long – I'm sure your customers will understand if you explain that it's part of the murder inquiry.'

The manager opened his mouth slightly as though he were about to say something but clearly thought better of it and kept silent.

Caren thanked the manager and she and Huw walked back into the bar. She took a moment to walk around the establishment. A specials menu had been added in chalk to a board near the bar. The place seemed clean and friendly and Caren could imagine the marina users and sailors enjoying downtime in the place.

'Why did Rachel Scott come here last Sunday?' Huw stood by her side.

'Maybe they like the place.'

'I can imagine there would be places with more nightlife in the city.'

'Let's talk to the marina manager.'

Once they had left the Hope and Anchor, they made their way over towards the marina building. In the first-floor operations office, Caren flashed a warrant card at a young woman in her twenties, long dank hair and oversized glasses over a heavily made-up face.

'We want to speak to Captain Maynard.'

'I'll see if he's available.' The girl sounded far too self-important.

'This is part of the inquiry into the latest murder in the marina. I'm not going to wait. Tell the manager we need to see him now.'

They stood over the girl sitting by her desk as she picked

up the phone and they listened to her explanation that the police wanted to speak to him.

Caren didn't have to wait too long until the door behind them opened heavily and crashed against the wall behind it.

Maynard looked well beyond retirement age, and badly needed to lose weight, judging from the size of the paunch stretching his white shirt, which had 'Marina Manager' sewn onto the pocket on the left-hand side.

Caren didn't bother with her warrant card. 'Captain Maynard?'

'How can I help?'

'We need to speak to you about the murder of Rachel Scott.'

Maynard gave her a world-weary look, as though he were tired of explaining himself. 'You'd better follow me then.'

He led them down a corridor to the office that he used. He pointed at two visitor chairs and they sat down.

'My team will send you the footage from the CCTV cameras we operate later today.'

'Did you know Rachel Scott?' Caren said

'No, of course not.'

'Her body was found in a building used as part of the marina complex. Do you have access to it?'

'I know the building you mean. It's owned by the council, and I suppose you could say that it's part of the marina complex.'

'Who has access to that building?'

'It's pretty derelict. The marina leased it out to a local company some time ago. They used it for storage, I believe. I don't think it's good for anything else.'

'What local company was that?'

'It's the chandlery business McCarthys.'

Caren and Huw exchanged a look. Was it a coincidence Mark Tremain's employers had access to that storage building?

'And who is your contact at McCarthys?'

Maynard gave Caren a name she didn't recognise.

After leaving the Captain's office, Caren read the time and realised they didn't have much time until Rhys and Alice were due to meet them at the mobile incident room. So she picked up her pace, Huw following.

'It might be coincidence, boss,' Huw said.

'I don't believe in them,' Caren said.

McCarthys chandlery business had a sprawling location in the marina. There were workshops and a retail outlet linked to the business. And a yard where smaller boats and yachts were hauled up out of the marina for winter storage and antifouling. Caren made her way through the racks of sailing jackets and clothes of various weights and colours.

'You should see the cost of some of these, boss,' Huw said, stopping briefly to read a label.

'You know what they say, if you have to ask the price, you can't afford it,' Caren replied.

By a sales counter, she flashed her warrant card at a youngster manning the till 'I want to speak to the boss.'

He gave Caren a frightened look and picked up the telephone. She heard a nervous voice explain that the police wanted a word.

Moments later, they were joined by a woman in her forties with well managed curly blonde hair, immaculate make-up and an expensive gym membership, from her slim build.

'What's this about?'

'I'm in charge of the investigations into the murders of Emily Hughes and Rachel Scott.'

'Terribly sad.' There was no emotion in the voice. It was said as a simple statement of fact.

'I understand that the old building where Rachel's body was found was leased to your company at one time.'

'That's right, but we gave it up. It wasn't that secure, and it was very damp. So we had a new dry container added to our yard.'

'I'd like details of who would have had access to that old storage building.'

'I can't see how that is relevant. We surrendered the keys a long time ago.'

'But who would have had access?'

'All the lads in the chandlery workshop, I guess, and anyone who knew where to find the key. But I can only stress again that the key was returned to the marina when we gave up the unit.'

'We'll need a list of your employees working in the workshop who would have known about the storage unit and might have had access.' Huw added: 'So that we can eliminate them from our inquiry.'

Caren had seen the look of worry and concern on the woman's face only slightly disappear with Huw's reassurance about the reason they needed the details.

The woman disappeared for a few minutes and returned with a printed sheet she handed over to Huw. As they had waited, Caren had walked around the store. She had spotted various winch handles being offered for sale.

She rejoined Huw at the counter, having opened her mobile phone to show an image of the winch handle used to kill Rachel Scott. She showed the image to the manager as Huw was thanking her for the list of staff.

'Do you recognise this winch handle? Is it something you sell here?'

Both the woman and the assistant shook their heads. 'It's not a make we stock.'

As Caren walked back to the mobile incident room, Huw was scanning the list of McCarthys employees.

'Mark Tremain is on this list, boss,' Huw said.

'Excellent. Let's see what Rhys and Alice have to say.'

When they reached the mobile incident room, a thin man was deep in conversation with the sergeant Caren had spoken to earlier. He turned to her when she entered and, in a loud voice, questioned her. 'Are you in charge? I spoke to somebody about that public appeal.'

'I'm Detective Inspector Waits and I'm in charge of the investigation. We have footage of a man running through the marina from the evening Emily Hughes was murdered. Was that you?'

Before he could answer, Rhys and Alice walked in.

'Yes, that was me. I'm not in any trouble, am I?'

'What were you doing running through the marina?'

'I was meeting my girlfriend at that pub. I was late. Nothing wrong with that, is there?'

'We'll need your full details.' Caren sounded dismissive.

Rhys pulled the man to one side and jotted down his full name address and mobile number. Caren had already commandeered the small room at the end of the mobile incident room. Huw and Alice joined her, as did Rhys moments later.

'How did you get on this morning at the post-mortem?' Alice said.

'As expected, the pathologist confirmed the winch handle we recovered at the scene was the murder weapon.'

'We've watched the footage from the marina buildings that have been sent to us so far,' Rhys said. 'We spotted Mrs Ackland as well as Mark Tremain lurking around the marina.'

'And I hope to have an address for Kate Evans later, boss.'

Caren gave Alice a wary look but knew she had to rely on her being discreet. They couldn't afford Kate Evans being tipped off by her father. One of the uniformed officers that Caren had seen earlier rapped his knuckles on the door that hadn't been closed properly. Caren waved him in.

'I just thought you should know, ma'am. We've spoken to two of the members of staff at the Hope and Anchor and both remember seeing Mark Tremain and Kate Evans the evening Rachel Scott was killed.'

'Thanks,' Caren said. She turned to Rhys and Alice. 'Get back and finish all those interviews. I want all the details about what they can remember about Tremain.'

'What do you want to do now, boss?' Huw said.

Caren paused. 'Let's see what Mark Tremain has to say.'

Chapter 35

'Tell me about Sammy Evans.' Caren sat back in the chair at the desk in the mobile incident room and gave Huw a serious, determined look. 'If his daughter is implicated, then we need to second-guess how she might react.'

Caren knew it was more than that. Her predecessor's reputation and presence in the team she had inherited in Western Division had been unwelcome, as though she were being unfairly compared to him. Now she felt it was an opportune moment to consign Sammy Evans to history, or at least to a happy retirement.

'I never really knew him that well.'

'What was he like?'

'He could be demanding and difficult and then charming and complimentary.'

'Did he ever mention his family?'

'Hardly ever. I could count on one finger how many times we socialised as a team in all the time that I worked with him.'

'Did he ever talk about his daughter?'

'No. And I found that surprising. But perhaps he just wanted to keep his private life exactly that. It's difficult mixing home and work. You must find it tough, boss.' Huw sounded conciliatory.

'Why does everybody mention him in hushed tones as though he had some superpower?'

'He wasn't the easiest to get on with. He had a reputation years ago for being tough and uncompromising. He spent time in the anti-corruption unit.'

'Really.' Doing a stint in the internal department that policed their fellow officers could help an officer's career, but it could also make other officers wary of working with that officer when they returned to front line policing.

'He never talked about it, of course.'

'Did you ever see him break protocols or engage in any illegal actions?'

Huw shook his head unconvincingly. 'He could badger a witness or a suspect and often I found he had an overbearing approach, which I didn't think helped.'

'Did you ever suspect that his daughter was in trouble with the police?'

'No, never.'

'Did you ever suspect that he was protecting her?'

'Like I said, boss, I don't remember him talking about her specifically.'

'Did you ever find that the senior officers were protective of Sammy Evans?'

'What do you mean?'

'Did they ever turn a blind eye to what he was doing or his tactics or methods?'

'I saw nothing like that whilst I was working for him, but Alice might give you a better answer.'

Was she fretting unnecessarily about Sammy Evans and his impact on her? After all, he had retired and the three officers on his team reported to her now.

It played on her mind that she might have been oversharing with Huw. Would he think she was worrying unnecessarily about how Sammy Evans' reputation could affect her career? She hated the prospect that something might come out of the woodwork, a case he had handled badly misfiring on her team, the senior officers blaming her vicariously somehow.

'The impression I got from talking with other officers that knew DI Evans, boss,' Huw added, 'was that he had stayed too long in the job. His retirement was overdue.'

Caren nodded as she got to her feet. 'Let's visit Mark Tremain.' From her brief conversation with the woman in McCarthys she knew he had taken the day off.

She retraced the steps to her car and Huw found the previous entry in the satnav for Mark Tremain's address. It didn't take long for the satnav to give them directions, and they left the marina. Soon they were pulling into the small yard in front of Mark Tremain's home.

It surprised her that there was a BMW 3 Series parked outside. It had recently been washed by the way the paintwork glistened and from the puddles on the ground.

'That's a nice car,' Huw said before they left their vehicle.

'I wonder how he bought that?' Caren said, before adding: 'I think we should ask him.'

Tremain gave them a world-weary look when he opened the door.

'What the hell do you want?' Then the realisation spread all over his face. 'Of course, you think I have something to do with the murder of Rachel Scott?'

Either he was an effective actor who had rehearsed the initial response, knowing they'd appear on his doorstep or he was telling the truth. Caren couldn't decide which it was.

'We need to speak to you.'

It wasn't a question, and she didn't imply that Tremain had any choice in the matter.

He pushed the door open wide so that they could enter. He made an exaggerated theatrical flourish, inviting them in.

The neatness and order inside the house surprised Caren. They went through to a kitchen at the rear of the property. The work surfaces were clean and clutter free. An expensive coffee machine stood in one corner and a full wine fridge had pride of place under the counter.

'I'm in charge of the murder investigations into the deaths of Emily Hughes and Rachel Scott,' Caren said after they had sat down by the dining table in tall upright chairs. 'We recovered CCTV footage from the evening that Rachel was killed and we've been able to identify that you were in the marina that evening. What were you doing in the marina on Sunday evening?'

Mark was wearing a well-pressed polo shirt and chinos that were definitely not from a high street chain. Rays of sunshine caught the gold bezel of his expensive wristwatch, which he surreptitiously covered with his shirt cuff.

'I don't believe this, I really don't believe this. I don't have to account for my movements.'

'She was found in a workshop that had once been used by McCarthys – your employers. Do you know where I mean?'

'Of course I bloody do. It's been disused for a long time.'

'How well did you know Rachel?'

Mark shrugged. 'She was friends with Emily. They went out together.'

'Did you socialise with her too?'

'Yes, but not for a long time.'

Caren paused and Huw picked up the questioning. 'Is that your car outside?'

'Yes, why do you ask? What's that got to do with you, anyway?'

'Is this your place?' Huw looked around the well-appointed kitchen.

'It's in my brother's name. He owns it.'

'When did he buy it? Has he owned it for a long time?'

'Nothing to do with you.' Mark sounded defensive.

Caren made a mental note that one of the first things they needed to do back at headquarters would be to requisition a search of the records at the land registry. It would give them confirmation of when the property had changed hands and who was now the registered proprietor.

Huw continued: 'Are you aware of several burglaries that have taken place in the marina area? And there have also been thefts from boats.'

'Yeah, I've heard about them. And you think because of my previous convictions you can pin the burglaries on me. You must be mad.'

Caren picked up the questioning. 'Your financial position isn't particularly positive. And you've paid a lot of cash into your account. How did you come by that money?'

Tremain rolled his eyes as though he were tired of the

questioning.

'I've told you it's none of your business.'

'The cash deposits you've made into your account follow shortly after the various burglaries that are being investigated. Where did you get the money?'

'I don't have to tell you. I don't have to tell you anything.'

Caren returned to his movements on Sunday evening. 'Where were you Sunday evening after ten pm?'

Mark abruptly stood up and jabbed a finger at Caren. 'You can fuck off and leave me alone.'

Chapter 36

Caren drove back to headquarters, her thoughts playing with the possibility she might be able to go back home to see Aled for tea before returning for a final session in the Incident Room. She dismissed the idea as being impractical. It would be too disruptive for her son and she wanted to hear from Rhys Davies and Alice Sharp as soon as possible. So she called her mum on the hands-free of the vehicle and explained that she wasn't likely to get back home until much later.

Tomorrow was the tenth day of the inquiry, but it felt much longer. She wanted to be a good detective and a good mother, but she knew that very often they collided. She couldn't avoid Huw listening to her conversation. His description of the secretive Sammy Evans and the way his team knew little about his personal life wasn't something she wanted to emulate. Although she was in charge of the team, she wanted to feel that she was bonding with all of the officers under her command.

'It must be difficult for you, boss,' Huw said. 'Having to juggle childcare with your job.'

It pleased her that Huw sounded genuinely sympathetic. It was the sort of empathy she had grown to expect from him since joining Western Division.

'My parents are very supportive, and they look after Aled a lot.'

The traffic on the M4 was light and Caren was doing a steady sixty-five miles an hour in the outside lane.

'I don't mean to pry, boss,' Huw said. 'But is everything finished now with your late husband's estate?'

'At least the inquest is out of the way.' Caren wasn't going to take the step of discussing Miss Hale and the intricacies of Alun's infidelity with Huw. It was a step too far. But she wanted to feel her sergeant didn't feel excluded. 'I'll be able to push on with the sale of the smallholding in North Wales. I can buy somewhere of my own.'

'I'm sure that'll be a big relief.'

'The boiler in the place I'm renting makes these very odd noises as though it's on the verge of exploding.'

Huw chuckled. 'I don't suppose the landlord has much interest in keeping the place up to date. How much land did you have with your smallholding?'

'Alun and I started an alpaca farm years ago but it never worked out. I was busy with my job, and he never seemed to have the commitment for it.'

'My family on my mother's side come from farmers in Monmouthshire. She often talks about the farm where she grew up as a child,' Huw said.

They reached the Pont Abraham roundabout at the end of the M4 and Caren slowed so she could negotiate her way onto the A40 for the final part of their journey to headquarters.

'You can over romanticise farming life and become too sentimental. It's hard work,' Caren said. Sharing with Huw about her past and learning about his family made her feel they were growing closer, which pleased her.

When they got to the Incident Room Caren's focus returned to the investigation.

'You make coffee,' Caren said to Huw. 'I'm going to talk to Aled.'

Aled had become quite accustomed to brief WhatsApp video conversations with his mother. He showed her a new toy his Mamgu had bought him from one of the supermarkets in the town. The blue toy car was an addition to his substantial collection. When Caren asked about school, he launched into a detailed account of what he had done with Ieuan. Then she spoke to her mum, telling her she wouldn't be too late back.

Once the conversation had finished, she heard activity in the Incident Room as Rhys Davies and Alice Sharp returned. Caren spotted the coffee Huw had made for her, and she helped herself to one of the biscuits he had piled onto a plate. Not Huw's usual favourite chocolate digestives this time, but she enjoyed the sugar hit nevertheless.

She stood and walked over to the board, leaving her

coffee on a desk.

'We spoke to Mark Tremain this afternoon. And something about his background doesn't fit. He has a BMW in the drive and the house is well maintained and comfortable. He told us the house is "in his brother's name".'

'That's an odd way of putting it,' Alice said. 'It probably means Mark has laundered all his money through his brother who bought the house.'

Caren noticed Huw nodding slowly.

'I agree,' Caren said. 'I want a search done of the land registry to establish who actually owns the property. If it is his brother, we'll need to speak to him.'

'If Mark Tremain and his brother have been laundering money, isn't that a matter for the economic crime unit?' Rhys said.

Caren didn't reply directly, allowing her mind to be directed towards the detailed analysis of any motive Mark Tremain may have had to kill Emily and Rachel. 'We know Mark Tremain has got previous convictions for handling stolen goods. He works in the marina and would be well accustomed to knowing when the yacht owners wouldn't be at home.'

Huw picked up the thread Caren was developing. 'He's the one responsible for the burglaries or he's sharing his information with Gerard Rankin or one of the other organised crime groups. Somehow Emily and Rachel get wind of what he's doing, and they decide they want a slice of the pie by blackmailing him.'

'And that's not a recipe for a long and happy life,' Alice added.

'Or they were helping him?' Rhys said.

Caren shook her head. 'That doesn't make sense. But we know he was angry when Emily dumped him and his DNA was on her clothes.'

'And the regular cash deposits into his bank account suggest he's linked to the burglaries.'

'We also have evidence he's linked to Gerard Rankin.'

'Do we have enough to arrest him and bring him in for questioning?' Huw said.

Caren didn't reply but scanned the board again looking at all the faces in turn, trying to build a picture in her mind of how all the threads connected together. 'How did you get on taking statements from the staff at the Hope and Anchor?' She turned to look at Rhys and then at Alice.

Alice took the initiative. 'No breakthrough, boss. But we discovered there was a function at the sailing club on the night Rachel was killed. We've spoken to several people who confirmed Mr and Mrs Ackland were there. We also know from CCTV footage that Mark Tremain was in the marina the evening Rachel was killed.'

'And he admitted knowing about the workshop,' Caren said. 'It looks as though the door had been forced but we're still waiting for the CSI report. But he refused to tell us where he was at the time of Rachel's death.'

Caren still hadn't heard from the CSI team that investigated Rachel Scott's flat. Deciding to arrest Mark Tremain on suspicion of murder until they had all the available evidence wasn't going to be sensible.

Alice's mobile rang and, after seeing the caller's identity, said she needed to take the call. It was short and Alice scribbled in her notebook. 'I've got Kate Evans' address.' She sounded pleased with herself.

'Good work,' Caren said.

'And I didn't get it from anyone who might tip off her father.'

Caren nodded, pleased that Alice had found the details without going against orders. She got back to reviewing progress. 'I've applied to the land registry for details of the ownership of the house where Mark lives. It's suspicious and I want to know what the truth is. First thing in the morning I want you, Alice and Rhys, tracking Kate Evans down and talking to her.'

Alice and Rhys nodded.
'Tomorrow we've got a lot to do.'

Chapter 37

'You knew Sammy Evans for a long time,' Rhys said to Alice as they drove out of headquarters the following morning, hoping she would take it is a question. Of the officers on their current team, she was the one that had worked with him the longest. Rhys had always been intimidated by the detective inspector who he had never heard compliment anybody for doing a good job. He had thought Sammy Evans was a bit of a dinosaur. The first few months Rhys had worked on his team he had belittled him and taken every occasion to poke fun at the young constable.

Working with Detective Inspector Caren Waits was a much better experience. He had begun to enjoy his job, and he wanted that to continue.

'He was a good cop, stubborn, down-to-earth and he got results.' Alice sounded as though she wasn't going to debate the matter any further.

'Did he ever mention his daughter?' Rhys said.

'He never talked about family. He was old-fashioned and kept his private life at home. He rewarded the loyalty of officers by sharing his best single malt.' Alice gave Rhys a heavy don't-ask-me-any- more glance.

'Okay, I get the message. It might have helped to know something about his daughter and her family.'

'I'm not going to start reminiscing about her father with her if that's what you think. She is an important witness in this inquiry, and we need to treat her as such.'

Rhys was driving and followed the instructions on the sat nav for the address in Morriston.

'I just hope your contact has got the address right,' Rhys said.

'Don't worry about that, just drive,' Alice snapped.

It surprised Rhys his fellow detective constable had become so sensitive to his questions about their former boss. Talking to Kate Evans would inevitably mean her father would get to know what was happening. He might decide to call the boss or even Superintendent Brooks, so Rhys thought it was perfectly reasonable to get a little background. Wasn't that what detective work was about?

He drove down the street of terraced houses searching for number eight. All the exteriors had been built from dressed stone, although the original windows and doors had been replaced by UPVC versions nearly all in the standard white colour. A sign attached to a lamppost indicated that parking was for residents only, or one hour only for non-residents with no return within two.

They pulled up outside number eight. It had been recently painted, by the pristine glistening white paint on the door surrounds and bricks that formed the upper reveal to the windows.

Alice took the lead and rang the doorbell.

A woman in her thirties, thin T-shirt under a man's flannel shirt, wearing a pair of tight-fitting jeans appeared at the door. Rhys was convinced she could tell they were police officers.

Alice flashed her warrant card at the woman and Rhys did the same. 'Kate Evans?'

'Yes, what do you want?'

'May we come in?'

Kate ignored the warrant cards they produced. She looked reluctant to start with and briefly glanced along the pavement on the opposite side of the street as though she were checking for nosy neighbours. Then she left the door open and beckoned for Alice and Rhys to follow her.

A strong smell of stale cannabis smoke hung in the air. It was so difficult to get rid of the smell if it was being smoked regularly. And most users simply got used to the odour, not realising the impact it had on visitors. Kate Evans didn't seem perturbed by a visit from two police officers. She led them through into a room at the rear of the property. There were two low sofas and a coffee table under the window looking out over a small yard. She waved a hand at one of the sofas for Alice and Rhys, and she sat down opposite them.

'We are investigating two murders in Swansea Marina,' Alice said.

Rhys was watching her carefully for any reaction.

'Is that why you're here?'

'Did you know Emily Hughes or Rachel Scott?'

'Yeah, I knew them both. It's terrible what happened.'

Rhys had the distinct impression she had rehearsed the answers, knowing her name would come up within the inquiry.

'Your name has been connected with parties Emily Hughes and Rachel Scott attended where drugs were used. I'm not here to investigate any drug offences. My priority is the murder inquiry.'

Kate looked down at the floor at a spot she seemed to be focusing on intently for a few seconds.

'Yeah, I know.'

'Do you have a drug problem?' Alice asked bluntly.

'I'm not—'

Alice softened her tone, clearly hoping to elicit Kate's trust. 'I'm not here to investigate a drug offence. But I want you to tell me the truth.'

'A social worker looks after me and I've been in rehab too.'

'But have you fallen off the wagon?'

'I get invited to parties and…'

Kate's eyes bulged as though she was terrified of sharing any more.

'The temptation is too much?'

'It's not what you think.' Her voice trembled.

'All we're interested in is finding out if you know anything that might help our murder inquiry.' Alice cocked her head to one side and gave Kate a warm look.

'I'm doing my best. I really am, but sometimes…'

Alice nodded sympathetically now.

'Did you succumb at these parties?'

Kate mumbled. ''Spose.'

'Who is responsible for supplying the drugs to the parties at the marina you attended?'

'I'm not getting anyone into trouble.'

Alice gave Rhys a leave-this-to-me look. He could sense Alice was making progress with Kate.

'I'm looking for someone who murdered Emily and Rachel. They were your friends.' Alice sounded a little more strident now as though it was Kate's duty to cooperate. 'And we believe you might have information that could help.'

Kate paused and looked first at Alice and then at Rhys as though she was working up the courage to reply.

'Was there more than one person who supplied the drugs?'

Kate blinked nervously.

'Who did you believe was the supplier?'

Kate gave a half-hearted shrug.

'If you don't know a name then do you know anything about them? Are they local?'

Now she nodded. 'There's this smooth guy who works at the University.'

Rhys immediately found his mobile and scrolled through the images, stopping when he found one of Johann Ackland. 'Can you describe him?' Rhys said.

They listened to Kate Evans describing one of their main persons of interest in the inquiry. Then he pushed over his phone with an image of Ackland on the screen. 'Is this the man?'

'Yeah, that's him.'

'Was he a regular supplier?' Alice said.

'Definitely, and he told everybody he had a good supply of coke and cannabis. But if you repeat that I'll deny I ever said it.'

'Are you aware of the burglaries from various properties in the marina as well as thefts from some of the yachts?'

'Everybody knows about those.'

'What do you mean?'

'Just that. If you think I had anything to do with that you can leave now.'

'Do you know who was involved?'

She nodded and paused before applying. 'I don't know who was behind it. But Mark Tremain boasted about his connections with some gang or other.'

'We've spoken to Tremain.'

'He'll probably deny any involvement. But he was splashing money around all the time. Just like Emily and Rachel.'

'Do you know who was behind the gangs Mark Tremain mentioned?'

Kate got up and walked over to the kitchen sink. She turned and leaned against the worktop folding her arms together and pulled them close to her body. 'If anybody gets to hear I spoke to you I could be in the shit.'

'What do you know, Kate?'

She paused for a few seconds shaking her head and chewing a lip.

'Is it true you're Sammy Evans' daughter?'

'Yeah, how did you know?'

'Witnesses have told us you've been flaunting the fact he is a former police officer and that he'd be able to protect you and your friends.'

Kate didn't reply.

'I'm sure your dad would want you to help. So who do we need to speak to?'

'You need to speak to a man called Billy "Tartan" Jones.'

'Where can we find him. We've had enough difficulty tracking you down.'

'That's easy enough. He is in Swansea jail.'

Chapter 38

The Incident Room was eerily quiet when Caren arrived. Rhys Davies and Alice Sharp were en route to speak to Kate Evans. Her mind felt a little easier now that she knew more about Sammy Evans' background. His reputation had cast an unwelcome shadow over the start of her career with Western Division. Now she knew he was probably a rather lonely, disaffected individual. After all, how many people never talk about their family at work? Had working in the anti-corruption department affected him?

Consigning his memory and its impact on her to a small, controllable part of her mind was a positive. She walked over to the board and looked at the images and all the notes and memoranda relating to the various players on it.

By later that day they'd have clarity, she was certain, and one of the things she needed to prepare that morning was a detailed memorandum for Superintendent Brooks.

One of the first things she found in her inbox was the result of a search of the records kept by HM Land Registry, the government body that had details of landownership. The name Jonathan Tremain with an address in the Gower Peninsula, a few miles west of Swansea, appeared as the owner of the house where Mark Tremain lived. Money-laundering regulations should have made it impossible for Jonathan Tremain to buy a house without explaining where he had got the money. She needed to allocate officers to speak to Jonathan Tremain, but in the meantime she did a search against his name, including a request for full financial details.

Huw arrived and she called out a greeting which he reciprocated. Moments later, he appeared in the doorway to her office. 'I've had the result from the land registry and it confirms that Jonathan Tremain owns the house where Mark lives.'

'If he can't account for how he got the money to buy the place he could be in big trouble,' Huw said. 'Have you requested his financials?'

Caren nodded.

'Have you heard anything from Rhys and Alice yet?'

Caren read the time on the monitor on her desk. 'It's too early.'

Caren hadn't seen Susan Howard at the school run that morning, so she hadn't had the chance to ask her about the reports from Rachel Scott's flat nor the crime scene at the workshop where her body was found. So she scooped up the handset of the telephone on her desk and called the CSI department.

'She's on her way to speak to you now, Detective Inspector,' the young voice replied.

Caren didn't have to wait long until she heard the door to the Incident Room open and Susan greeting Huw. Caren made her way out and joined them. Susan and Caren sat at empty desks. The CSI manager looked up at the board

'Is it all making perfect sense?' Susan said.

'I hope your visit is a sign you've got something positive to contribute to the inquiry.' Huw sounded too formal.

'It's always lovely to see you, Susan,' Caren said.

Susan smiled at her friend. 'We've been working on Rachel Scott's mobile. There were lots of WhatsApp messages between her and her friends. Hundreds in fact – not friends, messages I mean. Although she did have a lot of friends and it's taken us quite a while to work through and see if there was anything of relevance. We came across an exchange between Rachel and two other people, one of which was Emily Hughes and the other we believe is Johann Ackland. He is referred to simply as JA in their exchange, but we've cross-referenced the mobile number to his.'

'Really, is there anything significant about the messages?'

'You need to go through them, but we haven't been able to find anything we think is important. It's pretty banal stuff about social events but the exchange of messages isn't particularly lengthy. It stopped a couple of months ago.'

Caren looked over at the image of Emily Hughes on the board. They hadn't recovered her mobile. It had been assumed her killer had thrown it into the marina or destroyed it. There was no way of being able to recover WhatsApp messages without the handset.

'Did you find any messages between her and Emily Hughes only?'

'Quite a lot. They were good friends, and you'll need to go through to establish if there's anything of relevance to your inquiry. And there was a WhatsApp group that included a Kate Evans. I understand she's a person of interest in your inquiry. As with so many of these WhatsApp messages there are codes and slang that only the participants would know or understand.'

'Something for Rhys and Alice to do when they're back,' Huw said.

Caren nodded. 'Anything to report about Rachel Scott's crime scene?'

Susan walked over to the board and pointed to a collection of photographs of the workshop. 'We still haven't finalised our work. We've recovered fingerprints and some partial prints but we've still got a lot to do.'

'The place had been used as workshops for the chandlery and the marina for such a long time that any fingerprints recovered probably belong to their staff,' Huw said.

'Anything on the winch handle?' Caren said.

'No, nothing.'

'And what about the investigators working on Rachel's flat?'

'I'll get the team down in Swansea to send you the details. They've been a bit slow finalising their work. But there was nothing of any interest. Some fingerprints and all the clothes have been removed for detailed examination. It could take days, maybe even weeks, to go through everything.'

'Why the break-in?' Caren stood up and walked over to

the board. At the opposite end to the photographs of the workshop was a set of photographs of Rachel's bedsit. 'Somebody was looking for something.'

'Maybe it was Mark Tremain looking for the money he had given Rachel for her silence, as he had done with Emily,' Huw said

'But why hadn't he taken Emily's money?' Caren said.

'Maybe he didn't have the opportunity.'

'And what would taking the money achieve anyway?' Caren wasn't expecting a response. 'I think there's more to it. Whoever broke into her place was looking for something. Something incriminating.'

'It's impossible to know what that could be, boss,' Huw said.

'It's a loose end and I don't like that.'

Caren's mobile rang on the desk. She noticed it was Alice's number. She answered the call, explaining, before Alice said anything that she was going to put her on loudspeaker, telling her that Susan Howard was present.

'We've just finished speaking to Kate Evans,' Alice said. 'She confirms being at parties in the marina. And she's a regular user. She mentioned having a social worker and being in rehab, but from the look of her I don't think there's much chance of her quitting successfully. She was surprised that we knew Sammy Evans was her father. My guess is she was just namedropping when she was high. She did mention that Johann Ackland boasted about being able to supply drugs. However, she won't give evidence.'

'Damm,' Caren said, 'that's no bloody good.'

'I don't think she's in a good place and her evidence wouldn't be reliable. And she mentioned that Mark Tremain bragged about his connections to organised crime. But once we pressed her she got a bit cagey. Told us that she could be in the shit if what she told us got out. But she was able to confirm she had seen Rachel and Emily throwing money around. But she gave us the name of someone connected with the gangs. His name is Billy Tartan Jones.'

'Did you get an address?'

'That's the thing. He is in Swansea nick.'

'We'll just have to pay him a visit. Right after we've spoken to Johann Ackland.'

Chapter 39

Once Susan Howard had left the Incident Room, Caren turned her attention to the exchange of WhatsApp messages between Johann Ackland and Emily Hughes and Rachel Scott. But before that she emailed a request to the appropriate authorities at Swansea jail requesting a visit with one of their prisoners.

Then she turned her attention to Kate Evans' information that Johann Ackland had supplied drugs to the various parties she had attended. Was it sufficient to arrest him on at least a charge of suspicion of possession with intent to supply?

'It could be that Johann Ackland was being blackmailed by Emily Hughes and Rachel Scott.' Huw's tone was challenging, as though he wanted to convince himself.

'And maybe they got greedy and were looking for a bigger slice of the action.'

Huw nodded. 'They'd become too much of a risk for Johann Ackland and he decides to dispose of both women.'

'I think we need to interview him under caution.'

Caren spent time working through the messages Johann Ackland had exchanged with Emily Hughes and Rachel Scott.

The first question that came to her mind was why on earth did he have a group with both women? As he was having a relationship with Emily it would be natural for him to be communicating with her, but why Rachel? The inquiry would need to search for patterns. Who was communicating with who, and why?

Caren had decided she would look at the actual context of the messages, whereas Huw would focus on their dates and how they fitted into the relevant dates of the inquiry and, in particular, with various burglaries.

'Are you sure you want to check the dates of the burglaries against his WhatsApp messages?' Now Huw struck a sceptical tone as he stood in the doorway to Caren's office.

'If we're building a case against Ackland or Tremain we need to look at everything.'

'But there's nothing to suggest Ackland could be

implicated in any of these burglaries.'

'Keep an open mind. We need to build a complete picture of everything.'

Huw didn't look convinced as he returned to his desk.

Caren got down to the work she needed to complete. She found messages from Emily and Rachel about meetings with Ackland.

Same time usual place xx – Emily to Ackland

His reply: *Of course see you there*

Caren jotted down the dates and times of all the similar exchanges between Ackland and the two women. When she finished, she yelled at Huw. 'I've sent you an email. Check the dates against the list of the burglaries we know about.'

Whilst Huw got that work done Caren continued.

She found that Rachel Scott and Mark Tremain were friends. She didn't have time to go through each message in turn, resolving that it would be a task Rhys and Alice could do, so she emailed them instructions.

Huw stood at the door to her room moments later. 'All the dates of messages you sent took place no more than a month after the burglaries had taken place.'

'Interesting.' Caren didn't like coincidences. It made her feel uneasy. It was something she had to explain.

'If Ackland was in on the burglaries these messages might demonstrate his involvement.'

Caren stood up. 'Let's go and speak to Johann Ackland. And hopefully by the time we've finished I'll have confirmation of our visit to Swansea nick.'

Huw followed Caren out of the Incident Room and down to her car. Driving to Swansea, Caren dictated an outline of the interview plan with Johann Ackland to Huw, who made notes. Occasionally he made suggestions, and she welcomed his input. The journey passed quickly enough and after parking Caren introduced herself to a different receptionist at the department where Ackland taught. 'We need to see Johann Ackland.'

The woman in her fifties with pronounced creases on her forehead wore a permanent scowl. She called Ackland, and once Caren knew he was in the building she marched over to his office.

Johann Ackland was wearing a suit that morning with a casual but expensive-looking button-down shirt and a thin elegant tie with red and orange stripes. He waved a hand at the visitor chairs, as though he was expecting students for a tutorial.

'We need to interview you under caution, Dr Ackland,' Caren said.

Ackland didn't move. He looked at both officers as though they had spoken some foreign language.

'I have tutorials and a lecture today.'

'They'll have to wait. I do hope you won't be difficult about this.'

'This is madness.'

'We'll tell the staff to cancel your tutorials and lecture.'

Ackland got to his feet and after picking up his mobile from his desk he put it into his jacket pocket. 'We'll take your mobile for now,' Caren said.

'This is intolerable.'

Huw escorted Johann Ackland out of his room and they left the building, although Caren made a brief detour to reception to inform the surprised receptionist that she needed to contact Ackland's students. She said nothing in reply, but her mouth opened like a fish gasping for water, as though she wanted to say something but the words wouldn't form.

Huw had spoken to the custody sergeant at Swansea Central police station to ensure an interview room would be made available. This time it was the full modern digital version with a camera to record the questioning and every facial grimace and reaction from Johann Ackland.

Once all the formalities have been completed and Johann Ackland had been booked into the custody suite he was escorted to the interview room. The duty solicitor called to advise Johann Ackland was a fierce looking woman with an ill-fitting suit and chunky hands. Her engagement ring and wedding band seem to be squeezing the life out of the finger of her left hand.

'I don't think we've met,' Frances Metcalfe said, looking over at Caren.

'Detective Inspector Waits,' Caren announced simply. Lawyers were never her favourite people, and she knew nothing of Mrs Metcalfe.

Once everyone around the room had been introduced for the purposes of identification Caren began.

'As part of our investigation into the deaths of Emily Hughes and Rachel Scott it has come to our attention you had an intimate relationship with Emily. Is that correct?'

'We've been through this already.' Ackland sounded frustrated.

'Please answer the question.'

'Yes, I had.'

'And what was your relationship with Rachel Scott?'

'I didn't have one.'

'But do you know who I mean? Rachel was a friend of Emily's.'

'Of course, I know who you mean. I wasn't in a relationship with her.'

'Would you describe her as a friend?'

'How would you define a friend?'

'I'll ask the questions, Dr Ackland.'

Ackland hesitated for a moment. He gave the solicitor a brief glance. She didn't respond.

'When we spoke to you before, Dr Ackland, you were very reluctant to confirm you had an intimate relationship with Emily Hughes. I want to be clear for the purposes of this interview whether you were friends with Rachel Scott.'

'Yes, I'd met her a couple of times socially.'

Caren pushed across the table towards him and Frances Metcalfe a photograph of the winch handle used to kill Rachel

Scott. 'Have you seen this before?'

Ackland peered down at the image. 'It's a winch handle.'

'Is it yours?'

'Don't be absurd. There are dozens of these around the marina in all sorts of different yachts. They're very common.'

'Do you have this brand on your yacht?'

'No, of course not. And I'll give you permission to search my yacht, but it'll be a complete wild goose chase.' He fumbled into the pocket of his jacket and deposited a set of small keys on the table with a theatrical thump.

'I want to ask you about your financial circumstances. I understand you have been making payments on your credit card by cash. And that some of these payments have been substantial. How did you come by that money?'

'None of your damned business.'

'It is my business when it's associated with a murder inquiry.'

'Don't be ridiculous.'

'We recently interviewed a person who has confirmed you were a regular provider of drugs for a social circle who attended various parties in Swansea Marina. Is that true?'

Ackland folded his arms together and scowled at Caren.

'Have you ever used drugs recreationally?'

'I have no intention of incriminating myself.'

Caren looked over at Huw who rolled his eyes in exasperation before he continued the questioning.

'Your wife seemed surprised when we told her you were having a relationship with Emily Hughes. But it seems to be part of a pattern of behaviour, as you had similarly ill-advised relationships with students at the Mid-Somerset University.'

'That's a downright lie!' Ackland exploded, straightening himself in his chair.

Caren was pleased that Huw had been able to get some sort of reaction.

'And we've examined your academic qualifications. Not

everything is as it seems, is it, Dr Ackland?'

Ackland didn't reply, just shook his head slowly.

'As I recall, you called it tittle-tattle we should ignore.'

Ackland looked down at his feet.

'But you have a status in life I'm sure you want to protect. And when Emily Hughes and Rachel Scott learned of your professional indiscretions they threatened to expose you to the University authorities. And you couldn't have either woman spreading rumours about you, so you decided to kill them both.'

'Emily and Rachel wouldn't know the first thing about my professional career. This is completely preposterous. Of course I didn't kill either of them.'

Caren continued the questioning. 'But you were in the marina on the night Rachel Scott was killed?'

'I was in a function at the sailing club if you must know. There were probably a hundred who could confirm I was there.'

'Do you know about the workshop where Rachel's body was found?'

'This is absurd. Of course I do. But I've never been in it. And I don't know who owns it.'

'One more thing, Dr Ackland.' Caren paused and kept her eye contact directly with Ackland. 'Why were you in a WhatsApp group with Emily and Rachel?'

'Oh, for goodness' sake. I'm in lots of WhatsApp groups. It means nothing.'

Caren looked over at Huw, signalling she thought the interview was at an end.

'I assume you'll be releasing my client as soon as this interview is over,' Metcalfe said.

'We'll arrange for a couple of officers to visit the yacht you have in the marina. Once I've spoken to them, we can authorise his release.'

Caren finished the interview, got up, followed quickly by Huw, and left.

Chapter 40

Before leaving the custody suite Caren had instructed Rhys and Alice to collect the keys to Ackland's yacht and search it. Then they walked to the canteen where Huw fetched coffees. Caren stared at the odd yellow colour which was completely unlike the crema of an espresso.

An email reached her mobile confirming an appointment at Swansea jail for later that afternoon. At least the prison authorities had reacted quickly to her urgent request to visit Billy Tartan Jones.

'Let's go and find a decent coffee.' Caren pushed the coffee to one side. They had time for lunch and a proper coffee.

She had read about an Italian café in the centre of Swansea that went back several generations. Googling the name was easy enough and the result gave them directions.

'I've heard about this place,' Huw said.

'Somewhere new for you and Christopher to try.'

Huw nodded as he tapped the postcode into the satnav. It gave them the directions and he announced that there was a car park nearby. It only took them a few minutes to drive from the police station into the city, where Caren parked.

They walked over to the Kardomah Café as Huw gave Caren a running commentary on what he had discovered. 'It first opened in 1905 and relocated to this spot in 1957. Dylan Thomas and some of his mates were regulars in the 1930s. There's a lot of history to the place.'

Caren pushed open the door and looked down into the café. Tables and chairs seem to be unchanged from 1957 as did the décor, which included net curtains.

Lunchtime customers were leaving, and it was easy enough to get a table where they ordered panini and an Americano each. Huw shared with her a potted history of the Italian families that had moved into the South Wales Valleys over the years.

'What did you make of Ackland, boss?'

'If he was being blackmailed by Emily Hughes and Rachel Scott, where was he getting money from to pay them?'

'He certainly wasn't taking it out of any bank account. And from the little we know of Mrs Ackland's finances she probably had enough to give him without blinking.'

'So, it suggests he was getting money from somewhere else?'

Huw nodded.

A waitress bought the paninis and coffee. After her first mouthful Caren nodded her approval at Huw. 'It's good.'

'The coffee's a bit strong.'

'Not everything is perfect, Huw.' Caren sipped her coffee, realising he was right.

'Once we get down to establishing exactly how Emily got that money and why Rachel's flat was ransacked we'll be nearer to finding the reason for both their deaths.'

After they finished their meal, Caren paid and after returning to the car she drove down to the prison, not far from the marina. Huw had visited before, so he knew where to park, which saved Caren searching for a public parking space. The Victorian jails built in the middle of towns up and down the country hadn't been designed for the twenty-first century, with car parking for visitors.

She held her warrant card ready after entering the first reception area. A woman with a severe haircut and a dark, uncompromising stare glared at her and then at her warrant card as if it were a fake before she nodded her head towards the door. Moments later it opened and two officers stood there, chains dangling from their belt loops.

'This way please,' the taller announced.

They led Caren and Huw through into another lobby area where they had to deposit their mobiles and all personal belongings in a tray as if they were about to go through airport security. Several substantial barred doors had to be unlocked and then relocked after Caren and Huw had passed through. None of the officers who escorted them said a word. Small talk was definitely off the agenda.

Caren heard her presence being announced as a legal visit as she was pointed into a large room with a Perspex window. She sat down at the wooden table screwed to the floor. They didn't have to wait too long until a third officer escorted in a tall thin man with a long narrow face and tattoos over his forearms. Caren wasn't certain what to expect, but the name Billy Tartan Jones conjured up a larger, stocky image in her mind.

'What the hell do you want?' The accent left nobody in doubt at all that Billy was from Glasgow.

'I'm Detective Inspector Caren Waits, and this is my colleague Detective Sergeant Huw Margam. We're in charge of inquiries into two murders which are likely linked.'

Billy threw his hands up in the air. 'And why the hell do you want to talk to me.'

'I understand you're connected with Gerard Rankin and some of his associates in Swansea.'

'And who's telling you that?' Billy managed a deeply patronising tone.

'And your name has come up as somebody who might be able to help us in relation to burglaries in the marina and thefts from yachts.'

'Sorry, love. I cannae help.'

'Do you know a Mark Tremain?'

Billy's attitude changed. His body language softened. 'What's in it for me?'

'You would be cooperating with my inquiry.'

'Me cooperate? With the cops?' He scoffed at the idea of it.

'But you know what, Billy? Two young women have been brutally murdered. One had her head nearly cut off and the other had her skull caved in by a winch handle.' Caren pulled out the photograph of the murder weapon in its evidence pouch and pushed it over at Billy. 'I could show you photographs of Emily Hughes' severed neck if you like. Do you have kids, Billy?'

Caren knew the answer. He had two daughters back in Glasgow. He hadn't seen them for at least three years.

Billy stared at the image and shook his head slowly.

'So, what can you tell me? Is Mark Tremain involved with the burglaries?'

Billy grinned at Caren, revelling in her discomfort. He knew she needed information. It was the only negotiating tool he had.

He stood up. 'Tremain is involved right enough but I'm not telling youse any more. I want to go back to Scotland. You get me a transferred tae Barlinnie and I'll tell you what I know.' Then he turned and waved a hand at the officer standing in the corridor on the other side of the Perspex.

Seconds later he was out of the door, leaving Caren to mull over his demands.

'Let's get back to headquarters,' Caren said.

Chapter 41

Susan Howard was standing beside the board in the Incident Room when Caren returned. Her clothes smelled musty and the tangy odour of decay from inside Swansea jail had permeated into her nostrils. She'd already decided to stand under the shower when she got home and let the hot water work its magic on her skin. All the clothes she had worn would be piled into the washing machine and given a hot wash.

'I understand you had the pleasure of a visit to HMP Swansea,' Susan said.

'I hate going to prisons. I can never get the sound of chains with keys out of my head. Then there's the banging as doors are closed. I can never understand the different alarms. And sometimes there's a two-tone bleeping sound that can be really annoying. It's all very depressing, and I wonder how much rehabilitation actually takes place.'

Susan raised a hand to stop Caren. 'Enough. I'm not planning a visit any time soon.'

'What time is it?' Caren didn't want a response. It was more a statement that she had lost track of time.

'You should be getting home soon.'

Huw entered the Incident Room moments later with two mugs. 'I didn't know you were here, Susan, would you like something to drink?'

Susan shook her head. 'I need to get going. I wanted to tell you that the results for the partial fingerprint samples we took from the workshop are a match to those for Mark Tremain.'

Caren put down her coffee mug and looked over at Mark Tremain's image.

Huw walked over to the board. 'That's the second piece of forensic evidence that links Mark Tremain to both murders.' They had the DNA evidence from Emily Hughes' clothes and now the partial fingerprint.

'Thanks, Susan. That's good news. It gives us enough to

justify arresting Mark Tremain and executing a full search of his property.'

Despite the clear evidence linking Mark Tremain to both murders, an element of doubt swam around in her mind. She couldn't put her finger on exactly what it was.

Susan Howard chided Caren, saying she should get home. 'You need a good night's sleep.'

It reminded Caren how dirty she felt from her visit to the prison. The last thing she wanted was to stay in the Incident Room the way she felt.

The telephone rang on her desk in her room and she traipsed through to answer it. The fresh, clean smell of her room provided by the office plants lifted her spirits.

'DI Waits.' Caren hoped her voice didn't sound too tired.

'She recognised the name of the constable who introduced himself as one of the team that had called at Jonathan Tremain's house – Mark Tremain's brother.

'It looks like he's done a runner,' the officer said.

'What do you mean?'

'There was nobody home and the back door was unlocked. There were dishes all over the kitchen sink. I spoke to a neighbour who told me he saw Jonathan Tremain piling an overnight bag into his car and driving away at high speed.'

'Did the neighbour have any idea where he might have been going?'

'He had no idea. He went over to Jonathan Tremain's place to give him a parcel that had been left by the postman. Tremain practically knocked him over as he was leaving.'

'Thanks, Constable, send me the details in a report.'

Caren finished the call and sat at her desk, looking at the unfinished coffee. She called her mother, telling her she'd be back very soon. Then she walked out to the Incident Room and exchanged greetings with Rhys and Alice who had arrived.

'We went down to the marina, boss,' Rhys said. 'And we used the key Ackland had given you to access his yacht.'

'It's quite a fancy setup,' Alice said. 'There are enough bunks for four guests. We found a load of champagne and prosecco bottles, so he doesn't skimp on entertaining.'

'And what about the winch handle?' Caren got enough impatience to her voice to make both officers realised she wanted to hear about progress.

'There are two brand new-looking winch handles in specific pockets screwed to the side of the wheelhouse so they could be accessed easily by the crew. We didn't find any that corresponded with the make and model used to kill Rachel,' Rhys said.

'But he could have bought the winch handle used to kill Rachel recently,' Huw said.

Caren nodded. The mere fact that he didn't have a matching pair in the yacht didn't mean that Johann Ackland was innocent of her murder.

'We could ask around all the chandleries locally and see if they recall selling the offending winch handle to Ackland,' Huw said.

'But he might have bought it online,' Rhys added.

'We'll need to go through all his financial records,' Caren said. 'In the meantime I've spoken to an officer who went to see Jonathan Tremain at his address, but apparently he's done a runner. And his neighbour has no idea where he was going.'

'Maybe he's going on holiday,' Alice said.

Sometimes Caren tired of the snide comments Alice Sharp could make. Perhaps she was trying to be light but it didn't work. 'Well, I think it's downright suspicious that he has left in such circumstances the day after we spoke to his brother.'

'What do you want me to do about it, boss?' Rhys said.

'Nothing,' Caren sounded irritable. 'There's nothing we can do about it. He's hardly a suspect. I'm going to arrange a meeting with Superintendent Brooks first thing in the morning. I want everyone prepared to arrest Mark Tremain.

In the meantime, go over everything, all the statements, and establish exactly what we know and what evidence we've got against Mark Tremain.'

Once Caren was back in her room she called Superintendent Brooks' office and arranged to see her superior officer first thing in the morning. Then she turned her attention to the details she'd need to use to persuade him to agree that Mark Tremain needed to be arrested for the murder of Emily Hughes and Rachel Scott. She welcomed the opportunity it would give them to complete a full-scale search of his property. Every murderer left a trace, it was only a matter of finding that scrap of evidence in Tremain's personal possession that would be the final building block in the case against him. For the next couple of hours she directed the attention of her team to the priorities needed to focus, laser-like, on the specific timeframe and evidence implicating Mark Tremain.

It was later than she had hoped by the time she left headquarters and drove home. She felt fatigued as though every part of her body had been battered. Aled was fast asleep when she arrived home and her mum looked at her with an expression of sympathy and concern.

'You're working too hard.'

What could she say? This was the life she had chosen, being a detective and a mum. She thanked her mum profusely and, once she had left, went upstairs to her son's bedroom and sat for a few minutes after adjusting his duvet, looking at him sleeping.

Later a glass of Pinot Grigio only made her exhaustion worse as it mellowed every part of her body. After some scrambled eggs and toast she got to the bathroom, hoping there'd be hot water. Standing in the shower, she let the hot water cascade over her, soothing her body and bringing a sense of calm to her mind. She didn't remember going to sleep that night.

Chapter 42

Superintendent Brooks pinched his lips together before frowning as he listened intently to Caren explaining everything they knew about Mark Tremain and the evidence against him. He had scribbled some notes on a notepad on his desk. At one stage frustration showed when he drew lines through some of the notes he had made.

The other person present was Nicola Jones, one of the Crown prosecution lawyers that Caren had met on another of the cases she had conducted. She was a woman about the same age as Caren, but she wore a cropped jacket with a simple white blouse and a dark mini skirt. The elegant appearance was matched by immaculately shaped eyebrows coloured in with a dark pencil.

'Everything suggests you have more than enough evidence to justify an arrest,' Nicola said.

Brooks still looked troubled and the creases on his forehead didn't abate. 'How much are you relying on this Billy Tartan Jones?' Brooks went on. 'I really don't like relying on evidence from prisoners.'

'I've requested details of his current status, sir. Then we can establish whether he would be a candidate for transfer back to the Scottish prison system.'

Brooks nodded. Both women looked over at him.

'You know what the prison estate is like. They are overcrowded and they move prisoners around from one jail to another without even thinking about their families.'

'Yes, sir,' Caren said.

'The briefing you have prepared is very thorough, Caren,' Nicola said. 'And your team have done a lot of work.' She looked over at the superintendent. 'I think you can authorise the arrest of Mark Tremain, Derek.'

At the start of Caren's career it had taken her some time to become accustomed to civilians calling her superior officers by their first names. The hierarchy she was part of demanded formal respect between ranks.

Brooks nodded. 'I agree, arrest him as soon as you can.'

Caren walked back to the Incident Room with more vigour than she had done leaving it. Despite the fact she believed there was enough evidence to arrest Mark Tremain it was always welcome to have her decisions confirmed by a senior officer and a CPS lawyer.

All the team assembled around the desks turned to look at her as she entered. 'We're authorised to move ahead with his arrest. Let's plan exactly how we do it.'

Caren looked over at the board. 'Rhys, you're with me. We'll go over to his property while, Huw and Alice, you go down to the chandlery. Once we know he's not at the chandlery he's probably at home. We'll get a full search team on standby. I want his property taken apart.'

Huw and Alice left the Incident Room and Caren retreated to her office. Once she was satisfied the search team was on standby, she emailed them with the address.

Planning the arrest of a suspect inevitably meant the rest of her day was going to be involved in the mechanics of getting Mark Tremain back to headquarters, coordinating the search of his property and completing the interview. Her mum had looked after Aled regularly since the inquiry had begun so she hoped Susan, or her husband, could collect Aled from school that afternoon.

'Of course, that's not a problem.' Susan didn't ask for more of an explanation other than Caren confirming she was likely to be late finishing.

'I'm going to call Mum and tell her what's happening.'

'I've got your mum's number too. I can coordinate with her later on. Look after yourself, Caren.'

'Thanks.'

After a brief conversation with her mum explaining the arrangements for childcare, Caren returned her attention to the priorities that morning. She ran through her usual mental list for a pre-arrest protocol. They'd need to make certain they had the usual stab jackets with functioning body cams. She wasn't going to take any chances that things might get ugly.

Then she left her office and nodded at Rhys to join her. They walked down to a pool vehicle and a quick examination of the contents of the boot confirmed to Caren that all the right equipment was in place.

Rhys tapped the postcode into the satnav and they set off in the direction of Mark Tremain's property. Half an hour or so later, they pulled up in a layby where she called Huw.

'We've just finished at the chandlery, boss. And there's no sign of him.'

'Thanks, get over here.'

Caren finished the call and looked over at Rhys. There was an edge of worry on the young constable's face. She remembered her own trepidation on the first occasions when she been part of the team arresting a suspect in a murder inquiry.

She drove off towards the property where Mark Tremain lived. She knew from studying the map and from her previous visit that the lane from his home led onto a narrow road. She parked not far from the junction between the lane and the narrow road, satisfied that she could see anybody leaving or approaching from the road she was on. Huw messaged with regular updates, and she knew he was only a few minutes away. In her mirror she saw a Western Division minibus pulling up. A message reached her mobile confirming the search team was ready whenever she gave the order.

She felt her pulse pounding in her neck. Arresting a suspect who had a history of violence, and whom they believed was responsible for two murders was challenging. She wasn't going to take any risks when she had Aled to look after. These were the sorts of occasions when she challenged herself about whether she really did want to be at the sharp end of policing.

It was a few minutes later when Huw pulled up behind her. They exchanged messages and once they were good to go she led the small convoy down the lane to Mark Tremain's house. His car was still there, the curtains were open. It looked as though he was home. They parked a little distance from the BMW 3 Series and got out.

'The staff at the chandlery haven't seen him for a couple of days,' Huw said.

'Well his car is still here so he probably hasn't gone very far.' Caren nodded at the house. 'Let's go.'

Caren led the way down towards the front door. When she reached it she realised it was ajar. She pushed it open with her foot and called out. 'Mark Tremain, police.'

Nobody replied.

Rhys was to her right looking in through a ground floor window and Alice was to her left doing the same. They both shook their heads at her when she looked at each. Huw had ventured around the corner towards a garage. She entered the house and called Tremain's name again. There was no response. Rhys was behind her.

'Place feels empty,' Rhys said.

'Let's take a look around.'

Slowly they walked around the ground floor They looked out from the kitchen window and noticed Alice in the garden. The lawns and shrubbery and sandstone patio looked well maintained.

Before they had a chance of visiting the first floor Huw called out from the front door. 'Something you should see, boss.'

Caren retraced the steps to the front door with Rhys behind her. Huw led Caren over to a garage; its up-and-over door had been forced open. Inside were benches laden with computers and televisions and bottles of champagne.

'What the hell is this?' Caren said.

Huw didn't have time to reply as a little way into the shrubbery and trees at the rear of the property she heard a single gunshot. Instinctively she made for the garage door with Huw by her side. Rhys and Alice had ducked down onto their knees. A second shot, this time much nearer, had them all hurling themselves to the ground. It sounded close, as though someone had aimed at them. Dirt and sand caught in Caren's mouth and from the pain in her hand she must have caught something as she fell. She moved her prone body to one side and saw blood oozing from her right palm.

She found her mobile. Calling for support from armed officers was her only option.

Chapter 43

Caren looked over at Huw and Alice and Rhys, who all confirmed they were unharmed. She let out a long breath of relief. None of her team had been injured. A message bleeped on her mobile confirming an armed response vehicle was en route. Alice and Rhys were kneeling by the corner of the house and Huw was near the garage entrance.

'Did you see anyone?' Caren said.

All of her team shook their heads. They dared not move. They weren't wearing bullet-proof vests and if someone was out there with a gun Caren wasn't going to risk any injury or even the lives of her officers.

'An ARV is on its way.'

All the team nodded their understanding. Caren took stock of her position. She was comforted by the fact the shots appeared to have come from the trees at the rear of the property. It worried her that the shooter might traverse to the front of the house for a clear shot. They needed to get under cover quickly.

She motioned for Rhys and Alice to get into the house. At least then they'd be out of sight. They nodded their understanding and, crouched over, they moved towards the front door and into the house. Caren then motioned for Huw to join her as they crawled into the garage. It took no more than a few seconds for her to pull herself towards the up-and-over door, where Huw joined her. The door would only half close and Caren sensed the danger they faced filling her mind as her heartbeat raced.

'Where the bloody hell is the ARV?' Caren said as she angrily called operational support.

'I don't have an ETA, ma'am,' said the voice at the other end.

'Tell them it's bloody urgent. There's someone taking shots at my team.'

'I understand—'

'Well tell them not to delay.' Caren finished the call

abruptly.

'Who the hell was shooting at us?' Huw said. 'And why only two shots?'

'Maybe the shooter was trying to scare us, I'd guess.' Caren's pulse was gradually returning to normal.

Huw looked at Caren's bleeding hand. 'You've not been hit have you, boss?'

Caren shook her head. 'No, just a scratch. No harm done.'

'You'll need a tetanus jab.'

'There's a first-aid kit in the car.'

Huw got to his feet and sidled up towards the window of the garage. He peered out carefully, but it was obvious he couldn't see anything or anyone. 'The shots came from those trees behind the house.'

Caren heard the ARV before she saw it as its siren increased in intensity until it pulled into the lane down to Tremain's house. She moved to the garage door and yanked it fully open. A marked police vehicle pulled in behind the ARV. Two authorised firearms officers emerged from the first vehicle, each holding Heckler and Koch G36 rifles. At least they weren't taking any chances.

Two further officers emerged from the marked police vehicle behind them and immediately removed similar weapons from the rear of the armed response vehicle.

The first AFO ran up to her. 'Detective Inspector Waits?'

'Yes, and this is Detective Sergeant Huw Margam. Two other officers of my team are in the house.'

'Has anyone been hurt, ma'am?' The officer looked down at her hand.

'No, nobody is hurt. I scratched my hand when I fell. We were here to make an arrest as part of our murder inquiries. The house appeared to be deserted but when we came outside there were two gunshots from the trees.'

'We'll do a full sweep and search the trees nearby. Do you know if your suspect has any experience with handguns and rifles?'

'He has previous convictions for violence, but nothing related to handguns.'

Huw added, 'But we believe he might be connected to an organised crime group.'

'How long since the last shots?'

'A few minutes,' Caren said.

'The shooter has probably legged it, but don't take any chances. We'll do what we can, ma'am, but searching for a suspect in those trees is going to be difficult. I suggest you leave this to us and get yourself cleaned up.'

Caren nodded. 'I've got a search team waiting to go over the property.' Caren jerked her head at the house.

'Just as long as they don't get in our way.'

The AFO didn't wait for a response and yelled at his colleagues. They darted past the garage and down into the trees, shouting a warning as they did so. Caren and Huw sprinted over to the safety of the house. Alice and Rhys emerged from the house and once the cut on Caren's hand had been properly bandaged, she gave the search team instructions.

'I want this place taken apart.' Caren knew her anger was clouding her judgement. 'I mean the usual full search. And don't venture outside and be careful.'

Caren looked over at the officers on her team. 'I want everyone back at headquarters.'

Huw insisted that he detour to the emergency department at Morriston Hospital on the way back to headquarters. He sweet-talked the reception staff and Caren was seen within five minutes of arrival. After a tetanus injection she was told to keep an eye on the wound every couple of days.

Ambulances were backed up outside the entrance to the emergency department as Caren left, feeling guilty she had been able to jump the queue. News reports on the television regularly had patients complaining about the long delays in emergency departments.

When they joined the M4 Caren could feel the tiredness brought on by adrenaline draining away and she struggled to keep awake.

Huw nudged her when he had parked at headquarters. 'We've arrived, boss.'

Caren shook the torpor from her body and stepped out of the car, stretching as she did so. They walked through the headquarters building towards the Incident Room where they joined the two detective constables on her team. Alice offered to make coffee and when she returned Caren gratefully finished the first mug quickly, pleased with the invigorating effect of the caffeine.

'The search team have called, boss,' Alice said. 'They reckon Tremain had been there this morning. The kettle was warm and dishes had been left in the kitchen bowl.'

'It could be the shooter was after Tremain,' Rhys said.

'Who the hell would want to kill him?' Huw said.

'When we're dealing with somebody like Mark Tremain and the likes of the gangs he's associating with, we can't take any chances,' Alice said 'We've issued an alert for all officers to be on the lookout for him. Do you want us to issue a public appeal so that nobody decides to play the vigilante?'

Caren nodded. 'Top priority, Alice – speak to public relations. And I want our intelligence interrogated for details of anyone in the area who might have access to guns. Talk to all the gun clubs – find out if Tremain or anyone associated with the inquiry is a member.'

Caren's mobile rang as Rhys and Alice got to work. It was a member of the reception team. 'Detective Inspector Waits, we've got a Jonathan Tremain in reception to see you.'

Chapter 44

'What the hell is this about my brother?' Jonathan Tremain paced around one of the conference rooms in reception.

'Do sit down, Mr Tremain,' Caren said.

Jonathan glanced warily at the bandage on Caren's hand. 'And you've had officers calling at my property in Gower. They've spoken to that dreadful busybody neighbour I've got.'

Caren took the initiative and sat on a chair by the table. Before doing likewise, Huw pointed at one of the chairs nearest to Jonathan. 'Can I get you a tea or coffee or something?' Huw said.

Jonathan shook his head and sat down.

'Can we start with background? Are you Mark Tremain's brother?'

Jonathan looked warily at Caren and Huw.

'I'm not trying to catch you out, Mr Tremain.'

'Yes, Mark's a couple of years younger than me.'

'I'm the senior investigating officer in the murder inquiries of Emily Hughes and Rachel Scott. They were both killed in the Swansea Marina. Both were connected in some way to your brother. He remains an active suspect in our inquiry, and we'd like to talk to him. Do you have any idea where he might be?'

'What the hell do you mean? He's at home, of course.'

Caren exchanged a glance with Huw that suggested Jonathan didn't know exactly what had been happening at his brother's home that morning.

'We've been there this morning and Mark wasn't there. Does your brother have any experience of firearms?'

Jonathan chortled. 'Don't be absurd.'

'Is he a member of a gun club to the best of your knowledge?'

'No, of course not, why do you ask?'

'We visited the property where your brother lives this morning with the intention of arresting him and shots were fired. Your brother wasn't there and we urgently need to trace him.'

'Shots! Was anyone hurt?'

'No, thankfully. Do you have any idea where he might be?'

'No, I don't. Perhaps he's gone to stay with friends – God, that sounds like a cliché. I have no idea where he is.'

'Mark told us that the property he lives in is owned by you. Can you confirm that?'

'Of course I bloody can. I sold a couple of properties that have done very well for me in the Hampshire area a few years ago and I moved here. I've made a number of profitable property investments. Mark has been renting the house after he moved to the area.'

'We were told by officers who spoke to your next-door neighbour you seemed to be in a hurry to leave yesterday.'

'My pregnant wife, Detective Inspector, was visiting her mother in Cardiff and she was rushed to hospital. There was an overnight bag prepared for her which I took with me. I've got a good mind to tell that neighbour of mine to keep his nose out of other people's business.'

'How is your wife, Jonathan?' Caren deflated the man's anger with a simple question of concern.

His body language relaxed back into his chair. 'Thank you for asking. A false alarm I'm pleased to say.'

'I do hope you might be able to help us with our inquiry, however. Can you think of anywhere where Mark might have gone?'

Jonathan shook his head. 'I really don't know.'

'The garage at your brother's place was full of televisions and computers and several hundred bottles of champagne. You have any idea how he came by them?'

The shock was evident on Jonathan's face. 'No, of course not.'

'Have you noticed anything odd in your brother's behaviour recently?'

'What do you mean odd?'

'Anything out of the ordinary. Something you might have thought was a little out of character or unusual.'

Jonathan shook his head. 'Nothing I can think of. We don't see each other that often. Our worlds are quite different. I run a computer security company, that's where I've made money. Mark was more interested in boats and engines. I suppose you know he had a run-in with the police years ago in Southampton.'

Caren nodded.

Huw picked up the thread Caren had developed. 'How often do you see your brother?'

'It depends. We have no fixed arrangements.'

'Did you always see him at the property where he was living? Or did he visit you in your home? Or did you see him elsewhere?'

Caren knew it was the final question that really interested Huw.

'We had lunch a couple of times in some of the restaurants and pubs in the marina near where he worked.'

'Did you ever meet any of his friends?'

'No, I can't say I did. But I did see him arguing with a man once. He was smartly dressed and they were having words when I arrived for lunch.'

Huw was already scrolling through the images on his mobile. Caren guessed he was looking for the image of Johann Ackland. The detective sergeant pushed his handset over the desk at Jonathan, who nodded confirmation. 'Yes, that was the man. And they were both very angry'

'And did Mark ever mention his girlfriends?'

Jonathan frowned again. 'He was never very good with girls. He never mentioned anybody in particular.'

'Do you have a mobile number for your brother?'

Caren jotted down the number in her notebook, but it was the same as the one she already had for him.

Caren got to her feet and nodded to Huw that she thought

the interview was over. 'If you think of anything else that might be helpful at all please get in contact with us, Jonathan. And if Mark contacts you, please tell him we need to speak to him urgently.'

They saw Jonathan Tremain to the main entrance and watched as he left the building.

'What did you make of that, boss?' Huw said as they walked back to the Incident Room.

'I think it was genuine enough. I think he was telling us the truth.'

Huw nodded his agreement.

She pushed open the door to the Incident Room and Rhys and Alice looked over at her.

'We've done a search of the gun clubs in the local areas,' Alice said. 'There's no mention of Mark Tremain being a member of any of the clubs and he hasn't got a licence.'

'But we did find,' Rhys added, 'that the Acklands are members of a firearms club.'

Caren reached the board and examined the faces of Mr and Mrs Ackland, wondering if either had fired at them in Tremain's place and, if so, what could possibly have been the motive. 'Have the firearms officers reported back?'

Alice and Rhys shook their heads. Caren found her mobile and walked over to her office, knowing she had some priority calls to make. She called the officer in charge of the firearms team.

'We've just completed a scan of the woodland behind the house and we haven't been able to find anybody. There are a lot of worried neighbours.'

'I'll get a house-to-house team in place.'

Caren finished the call then embarked on another round of speaking to officers to arrange a house-to-house team to reassure the homeowners near Mark Tremain's home. She called the search team supervisor who told her they still hadn't finished at his property. He promised to send her a full inventory of all the items in the garage by the morning. 'I bet it's all been stolen.'

She got back to the Incident Room, intent on directing further activity and stood by the board, looking over at her team.

'The use of a gun in this case is a serious development and we need to get on top of it before somebody is seriously hurt or killed.'

Caren didn't have time to give further instructions for her team as Superintendent Brooks bustled in.

Chapter 45

All the officers around the tables scrambled to their feet, acknowledging their superior officer with a simple 'sir'. Brooks nodded towards the door into Caren's office. She led him over and once she was at her desk he closed the door carefully.

'First of all, Caren,' Brooks said as they sat down, 'how are you?' He looked at her bandaged hand. 'The health and well-being of my officers is the utmost priority.'

'It was just a scratch. There was a lot of blood but it was patched up by the emergency department.'

'Is there any sign of Mark Tremain?'

'The firearms officers have completed a search of the woodland behind his home and there was no sign of anybody.'

Brooks didn't reply immediately. 'So we have no way of knowing if he was the gunman or a possible victim.'

Caren had been focusing on the threats to her and the team. As they believed Tremain had been in the house a little while before they had arrived, he must have left for a reason.

'That's right, sir.'

'But we need to find him. The press release needs to make clear we believe Mark Tremain is armed and dangerous and should not be approached under any circumstances by members of the public.'

'We've spoken to his brother this afternoon and he has no idea where Mark might have gone.'

'Did he have anything useful to say?'

'He'd seen Mark Tremain arguing with Johann Ackland, but we knew they had history and had been seen arguing before.'

'Could it be that Johann Ackland was trying to kill Tremain for some reason?'

'Ackland does have a licence and he is a member of a firearms club.'

Brooks nodded his head. Anything involving a firearm was certain to change the nature and complexity of an inquiry.

'I don't want any risks taken with you or any member of your team.'

'Thank you, sir.'

'I've also spoken with the prison authorities at Swansea jail about Billy Jones. Apparently, he's been a model prisoner. He is pining for his family back in Scotland and is likely to be granted parole next year. If you contact the prison, they'd be sympathetic to expediting his transfer.'

'Thank you, sir. I'll make arrangements to see him again. He wouldn't tell us any more until his transfer was approved.'

Brooks got to his feet. 'We need to find and arrest Mark Tremain. And let me know as soon as you have the result from the search of his home. Let's hope that all the items recovered can be linked to burglaries and thefts from the marina and yachts.'

Caren left her room with the superintendent, who stopped to talk to the officers on her team. She admired the way that he was able to sound empathetic and complimented their work. Caren had experienced other officers of a similar rank who didn't have that skill.

She turned to look at the photograph of Mark Tremain's home on the board. Did someone want him dead? Or was she the intended victim?

Then she looked over at Rhys and Alice. 'For the rest of the afternoon I want you trawling through Mark Tremain's social media accounts and speaking to all his work colleagues. We need to find out where he's gone. People can't just disappear.'

'Do we have details about the weapon used to shoot at us?' Alice sounded worried.

'The firearms officers haven't been able to find anything. Recovering a cartridge in the trees behind his house would be like finding a needle in a haystack.'

'Mark Tremain strikes me as an unpredictable, difficult character. He might have panicked and decided he was going to do everything to evade arrest once we arrived. He must have known the game was up once we found all the kit in his garage,' Alice added.

Once Caren was back in her office she called Susan Howard's home and her husband Dafydd answered. 'Aled's just fine, we're going to have tea in a minute. He is watching television with Ieuan. Do you want to speak to him?'

Caren decided not to interrupt Aled. She found the number and the contact name that Superintendent Brooks had given her for the prison service at Swansea jail. Tracking him down eventually led her to an administration officer who sounded uninterested and ignorant of Billy Tartan Jones' existence. Caren explained carefully she had been told by her senior officer she was the person to contact.

'I remember him. He's the Scottish prisoner. Give me a minute.'

Caren didn't keep track of the time, but it certainly felt far longer than sixty seconds.

'I've found the details now. What do you want to know?'

'Billy Tartan Jones has got information relevant to a murder inquiry I'm conducting. He is holding us to ransom by suggesting he'll share more details once he is transferred to Barlinnie jail in Scotland. Apparently, he's from Glasgow.'

'Scottish prisoners are always the same, complaining like mad about our system here. It's ten times worse up there.'

'He's going to be near family.'

'I think my supervisor has reviewed this file. Transferring prisoners is never easy. There is a cost involved, Detective Inspector. As you know, the prison service is cash-strapped at the best of times.'

Caren could feel her hackles rising. In her mind she counted to ten knowing she needed this person's cooperation. 'Has a decision been made to transfer Billy Jones?'

She heard breathing and then paper being shuffled about. 'I hope this helps and yes, a decision has been made in principle that he is going to be transferred to Barlinnie.'

Relief filled her mind she could tell Billy Tartan Jones

she had been able to facilitate his transfer when in reality it was already in the pipeline. She only had to ask the administration officer one more thing. 'I need to be able to communicate that decision to the prisoner by tomorrow when I visit him.'

There was a sharp intake of breath from the other end of the telephone. 'I'll see what I can do.'

'This is a murder inquiry, and lives may well be at stake.' Caren sounded utterly serious.

'Of course, Detective Inspector. I'll get it done now.' She couldn't hide the annoyance in her voice that this was causing him inconvenience.

'Thank you. You've been most helpful.'

Caren sat back in her chair after she made a second call to the Swansea jail requesting another legal visit the following morning. At least now she'd have some good news for Billy Tartan Jones who she hoped in turn would give them the evidence they needed.

In the Incident Room Rhys Davies and Alice Sharp and Huw Margam were poring over their screens.

'I've spoken with some of Mark Tremain's work colleagues,' Rhys said. 'And they haven't seen him for a couple of days. And none of them have any idea where he might be.'

Alice nodded. 'I spoke to one person who thought that he had some friends up the Swansea Valley.'

'Show me.' Caren was still ignorant about the exact geography of the area.

Alice pulled up a map of the area she was referring to, which ran from Morriston to Pontardawe and on to Ystalyfera.

'Do they have any names or contact details for his friends?'

'No, boss.'

'Then focus on social media for people linked to him who live in that area. If Mark Tremain is out there with a firearm he needs to be stopped. Unless he's going to be living in a cave somebody will see him.'

Tiredness overwhelmed Caren when she returned to her room. She gathered the papers on her desk together. She could justify leaving the Incident Room early because of the injury to her hand although it was only partially true. She wanted to see Aled more than anything.

After telling her team to report any significant discoveries to her, she left headquarters. She drove home, her mind full of conflicting emotions: she had left the inquiry because of wanting to spend time with her son. She kept telling herself that family was the priority and that after the events that morning, being with him was more important than anything.

Her mum was alarmed to see the bandage on her hand and fussed over Caren. She listened in wide-eyed silence at the events that had led to her injury. Caren tried to play it down as much as she could, that it was only a scratch, but she could tell from her mother's face she was appalled. 'You've got to be careful. You've got Aled to look after.'

'I know, Mum. I was never in any danger.' Caren's reassurance didn't seem to work. Her voice must have revealed to her mum how unsettled and rattled she really felt.

Aled didn't pay the bandage on his mother's hand much attention and seemed happy with the explanation she offered about falling and scratching herself.

Ann gave the pile of papers Caren had deposited on the table in the kitchen a wary look. Caren nodded gratefully when her mother offered to defrost a ready meal from the freezer. She ate it quickly and then helped her mum give Aled a bath. After her mum left, Caren read to her son in bed. It had the desired effect of settling her mind, banishing into a distant corner the risks she had faced that day.

Once he was asleep Caren filled a glass with a generous slug of Pinot Grigio and sat by the kitchen table, notebook open, ready to refresh her mind in the safety of her own home about the progress of the inquiry.

Chapter 46

Caren couldn't recall dreaming the night before. She felt rested, although the implied recriminations from her mum about the risks she was running as a detective still played on her thoughts as she drove into work.

Revisiting her notes and memoranda to Superintendent Brooks the previous evening was the quickest way for her to review everything to date. She had been looking for something they had missed. She wasn't certain what that was, and her mind turned to the possibility that Billy Tartan Jones wasn't going to be as helpful as she had first hoped.

When she arrived at the Incident Room Rhys Davies was the first to ask how she was. Caren had cleaned and dressed the wound that morning, substituting the bandage from the hospital with a large sticking plaster. It created the impression things weren't as bad as they had been yesterday.

'Much better, thanks. I slept well.'

The other officers on her team seemed to physically relax, pleased with the update on her health.

'Have you been able to track down any of Tremain's friends in the Swansea Valley?' Caren asked.

Huw took the lead. 'We've got three people on Facebook we believe he knows well.'

'It's pretty dangerous though, if they know he's armed,' Caren said. 'After all, they might be assisting a fugitive.'

She turned her back to the team and faced the board. The summaries she had provided to Superintendent Brooks came back to her mind. She was looking for a thread that needed to be followed up. She scanned the photographs on the board from the original crime scene to an image of Rachel Scott lying in the workshop. Her gaze then examined the details of the scene at Rachel's flat.

'Have we had any more information about the CSI report into the break-in at Rachel's flat?'

She heard a chair being moved and Huw joined her. 'Nothing, boss. What's on your mind?'

'Why did someone break into her property?'

'They must have been looking for something.' Huw stated the obvious.

'But we still haven't been able to work out what that was.'

'It could be something or nothing. It could have been one of the other tenants in the building.'

Caren read the time. Her thoughts were coalescing around that unanswered question – was the burglar looking for something specific?

'Did we find anything on her mobile?'

'Some photographs but nothing to help us,' Alice piped up, 'and not as many as I expected.'

'I think we visit her sister on the way to Swansea jail. She might know something.'

Caren left headquarters with Huw in the passenger seat, tracking down the address for Rachel's sister. Caren was more convinced than ever that the deaths of both women were connected. Mark Tremain must now realise he was being considered seriously as a suspect for him to have gone to the trouble of evading arrest in such a dramatic fashion. She was convinced Rachel and Emily knew something about Tremain's links with the organised crime groups responsible for the burglaries and thefts around the marina. How else could they account for the money stashed in Emily's bedsit? But even so, a grain of doubt persisted in her mind. She knew from her time as a detective in Northern Division of the Wales Police Service that it paid dividends to listen to that inner voice. She hoped it would only be a matter of time until Mark Tremain would be apprehended. She looked forward to interrogating him.

'I've got the address where they live, boss.' Huw tapped the details into the satnav and the screen began to populate with the route.

Once Caren's mobile had been linked up to the hands-free system of the vehicle, she called Alice.

'You told me earlier that there weren't as many photographs as you expected. What did you mean by that?'

'Just that, boss. She used Instagram but not Facebook. Apparently, that's for older people. But she did use a lot of Snapchat.'

'Thanks.'

Snapchat had featured in one of Caren's previous cases and usually the photographs were removed once they had been shared. A user could store them to memory, but she knew Rachel's phone had been examined and nothing of significance had been discovered.

Jane Scott looked surprised to see Caren and Huw when she opened the door to her flat in a neighbourhood not far from her parents' home.

'Has anything happened?' Jane sounded worried. 'Have you caught the person who killed Rachel?'

'No, we haven't. May we come in? We'd like to ask you some questions,' Caren said.

'Yes, of course.'

Jane showed them through into a sitting room where two other girls of a similar age were watching morning television and drinking from colourful mugs, a plate of doughnuts on the table in front of them. They paused the television when Jane explained she needed some privacy. The room smelled clean but the furniture was old and battered, the sort Caren expected to see at a tenanted property in the middle of a city.

'What can I do to help?'

'We still haven't been able to determine exactly why anyone would want to break into Rachel's flat. Are you aware if any of her possessions are missing?'

Jane frowned in worry. 'I don't think so. She had an old TV which was still in the flat when I went there with an officer to check. The place was a mess and I couldn't really tell if all her furniture was there. I know she had some expensive clothes she valued but they were still there.'

'Did she have any personal papers? Bank statements or

letters?'

'Who gets those these days?'

Caren nodded. 'We know Rachel used a lot of WhatsApp, but did she use any of the other apps?'

Jane nodded. 'She would post images to her Instagram account quite often, but she preferred using Snapchat. And she had been experimenting with videos on TikTok. She wanted to build a following on that platform.'

'Do you use Snapchat?'

Jane nodded.

The recollection from a previous inquiry surfaced in Caren's mind and she thought about the way Snapchat deleted images. 'Did you ever store any of the Snapchat images to your Memories account?'

'Yes, sometimes. And come to think of it I've got some of the images Rachel sent me.'

'I'd like to see them,' Caren said.

Jane reached for her mobile and scrolled. Caren looked over at Huw who gave her a puzzled look as though he was unaware of the intricacies of Snapchat accounts.

It took a few moments for Jane to find the right page on the app and when it was on the screen she pushed it over at Caren. 'I got into a habit of storing Snapchat images on my Memories. I wasn't using a lot of the app and it was a good way to keep track of Rachel and some of my friends.'

Caren scrolled through the images. There were dozens of Rachel with various friends including Chloe and the other two girls from the house Emily shared. Others featured Emily and also some of the staff at St Hubert's. Caren's pulse spiked when she spotted the image of Mark Tremain sitting with Emily and Rachel in the bar of the Hope and Anchor. But it was the subsequent photograph, still inside the pub, that caught her attention. She recognised the two men deep in conversation. One was Johann Ackland and the other was Gerard Rankin; she recognised him from the mugshot on the board in the Incident Room.

She showed the image on the screen to Huw and his face darkened.

'We'll need copies of all these photographs,' Caren said measuring every word.

Chapter 47

Caren sat with Huw in their car outside Jane Scott's home for a few moments. 'What did you make of that?' Huw said.

'It looks as though the photograph was taken surreptitiously without either man being aware of what Rachel was doing.' Caren's mind was focusing on what needed to be done now that Johann Ackland was definitively connected to Gerard Rankin. She read the time on the dashboard clock, knowing she didn't want to be late for her visit to Billy Tartan Jones. 'We need to get down to Swansea jail. In the meantime, I want Rhys or Alice contacting the regional crime unit dealing with OCGs. Gerard Rankin was supposed to be sunning himself in the south of Spain.'

'On it, boss.'

Caren drove off, her mind full of the implications of seeing Johann Ackland and Gerard Rankin. Talking to Ackland again was urgent. But seeing the image of Rankin with him had given Caren goosebumps. Could Rankin be implicated in the murders of both women? If so, the team dealing with organised crime had to be notified. Her inquiry might be dragged into something far more complex, which she dreaded.

She shook off the possibility they'd never apprehend Emily's or Rachel's killer or killers. The satnav told them the journey to the car park they had used on their previous visit to Swansea jail would take them twenty minutes, and eighteen minutes later she parked.

They sat in reception, waiting for the administration officer Caren had spoken to before. Her mind was full of the possibility that Johann Ackland was now their principal person of interest. She wanted more than anything to discuss with Huw everything going on in her mind, but there were other visitors present. So she whispered, 'It could be that Ackland was feeding information about the owners of flats and yachts to Gerard Rankin and his OCG.'

Huw nodded. 'And Emily and Rachel find out and decide

to blackmail him. He divis up the money he's been getting from the OCG between them. But when they get too greedy, he decides…'

'It makes perfect sense… But we still need to speak to Mark Tremain. I want to be able to interview him under caution in due course and hear exactly what he has to say. And I want to know why he decided to take a shot at us?'

'It might not have been him.'

Caren didn't have time to respond as a woman entered reception and walked over towards them. She introduced herself as the administrative officer Caren had spoken to and without ceremony handed her an envelope. 'That's the transfer authorisation for Billy Jones you want. I hope it works.' She turned on her heel and was about to leave when Caren said, 'You're coming with us. I want you to be able to tell him yourself. He might think it's a fake coming from me.'

The woman turned to face Caren her eyes fierce with annoyance she was being inconvenienced.

Caren motioned to the prison officers that she wanted to be escorted through to speak to Billy Tartan Jones. The door from the reception area where they had been sitting had no handle or lock on Caren's side but it swung open and two officers stood there. They were tall and burly and swarthy with the standard key chains hanging from their belt loops. Wordlessly they motioned for Caren and the other two to enter.

Once they were through the standard security checks, they were led through a series of doors that needed to be opened and then relocked behind them. Caren hadn't heard of anyone escaping from these old-fashioned jails since she had been a police officer.

They were led to the same room as on their first visit. The administration officer stood alongside Caren and Huw looking angry and frustrated. 'I've never had to do this before.'

Caren ignored her. They didn't have to wait too long for

Billy Tartan Jones to be led into the room. He recognised Caren and Huw but looked puzzled at the other person present.

'You again,' Billy said.

'Sit down,' Caren nodded to a chair by the table in front of her. Huw joined her, sitting on one of the chairs next to her.

Billy fixed her with a hard glare. 'I've got nothing else to say.'

Caren pushed over the envelope she had been given. She had already scanned the contents as they had walked through the various locked sections of the prison. Its language was unequivocal confirming that within twenty-eight days William Frederick Jones was going to be transferred to Barlinnie jail in Scotland. She just prayed he wasn't illiterate like so many of his fellow prisoners.

He read the details. 'How do I know this isn't a fake?'

Caren introduced the administration officer.

After she confirmed her status within the prison system, she named Billy's probation officer. Then she added, 'And your prison number is PZ8702 and your full name is William Frederick Jones. But everybody knows you as Tartan.'

Caren was pleased when she saw the realisation on Billy's face the piece of paper in his hand was genuine. He tugged it back into the envelope and relaxed back into his chair. Caren nodded at the admin officer, signalling she could leave them.

'It wasn't easy,' Caren said. 'I've done everything possible to get you transferred to a Scottish jail. Now I need you to do your part and tell me exactly what you know.'

Billy smiled. 'Barlinnie, eh…. That's fucking good going.'

Caren wasn't going to ruin the effect by telling him that his transfer was going to take place regardless of what he had to tell her. It seemed a shame to spoil the effect.

'I'm investigating two murders in Swansea Marina. The victims are two young women, one of whom had a substantial amount of cash and the other was her friend. Our assumption is they had probably become aware of somebody associated with the burglaries and thefts in and around the marina and had decided a little blackmail might be quite handy.'

Billy chortled. 'A wee spot of blackmail, you say. No' the best plan for a long and happy life.'

'So, what do you know about the organised crime group involved with the burglaries and thefts. I want you to give me names and details, something I can go on. Is Gerard Rankin involved?'

'Gerard? He's in Spain.' The smirk on Billy's face told Caren he was lying.

'We know he's in the UK. Lying to me is not going to help, Billy, I can always ask the prison authorities to reconsider that transfer authority.'

He shook his head, knowing that that wasn't going to happen.

'Gerard is no' yer man.'

'Then who are we looking for?'

'I don't know. I don't fucking know.'

Caren let out a short breath of annoyance. She glanced over at Huw, and she could tell from his face he shared her anger, if they were being played by Billy.

'All I've got is a nickname. The person you need to speak to was known as Skywalker.'

It startled Caren when she realised its significance. She felt an overwhelming urge to fist-pump but settled for looking at Huw. She could see in his eyes that he had realised the significance of what they had been told.

Huw seized the initiative. 'Do you mean like Luke Skywalker from the Star Wars films?'

Billy shrugged. 'Suppose.'

'Is there anything else you can tell us?'

Billy beamed. 'He was in hock for buying drugs but got out of his league. He was an idiot thinking he could swim with sharks.'

Caren nodded at Huw and he understood she meant their conversation with Billy was at an end. She jerked a hand at the prison officer standing in the corridor outside the room. Moments later Billy was escorted out.

Caren and Huw bustled out. Huw announced as he scrolled on his mobile: 'On it, boss. Give me a minute.'

Chapter 48

Caren and Huw trotted out of Swansea jail, jogged over the road, weaving in between cars slowing at lights as they returned to their vehicle. Caren wasted little time and crunched the car into first gear and accelerated hard towards the M4.

She glanced over at Huw who was still staring at the screen of his mobile.

She was certain they had the answer now and that the name 'Skywalker' had been the key to everything. 'Well?' Caren said, impatience in her voice.

'I've found it, boss,' Huw said. He held up his mobile its handset displaying the image of a yacht. 'Johann Ackland's yacht is called the Millenium Falcon.'

'Yes,' Caren thumped the steering wheel with her palm. She couldn't help herself – even though she was more or less certain about the name she had to see it on the side of the yacht for confirmation.

'I can't believe he called his yacht the *Millennium Falcon*,' Huw said

'We know Ackland's full of himself. But letting an organised crime group use the nickname Skywalker is a whole new level.'

'Are we going to arrest him?'

'Of course we bloody are.' At the same time, she had to brake hard for a road traffic signal that changed from green to red with little warning. She drummed her fingers on the steering wheel. 'I want to know where Mark Tremain is. And we need to plan the arrest of Johann Ackland. Once we're back at HQ we go through everything again. I'll need to talk to Superintendent Brooks and the CPS lawyer.'

After parking, Caren and Huw detoured to the staff canteen at headquarters. She needed sustenance and once they got back to the Incident Room, she left the packs of sandwiches and chocolate bars on the table much to the puzzlement of Rhys Davies and Alice Sharp.

'We'll bring you up to date in a minute, but I've got a couple of calls to make,' Caren said, heading for her room. She heard Huw asking Rhys and Alice for their choice of drinks as she closed the door to the Incident Room.

Her first call was to her mum. She explained she might be very late that evening. Her mum knew better than to ask for an explanation. 'Aled can stay with us. He can have a sleepover. And Caren' – Ann added in measured tones – 'be careful.'

Sometimes her mum could be too fussy – after all, Caren wasn't going to take any risks.

'Of course, I'll contact you later.'

The second telephone call was to Superintendent Brooks' secretary requesting an urgent meeting with him that afternoon.

'He's supposed to be at a planning meeting. Is it urgent?'

'I wouldn't ask unless it was, and please get that CPS lawyer to attend, the one who was present at our last meeting.' After slamming the phone down Caren realised she had been unnecessarily rude with Brooks' secretary. Sometimes civilians couldn't see the big picture.

She left her office after finishing the calls. Rhys and Alice had begun eating a sandwich each and Huw stared at the board. She walked over, turning to face her team.

'We've recovered a photograph from Rachel's sister this morning that shows Johann Ackland with Gerard Rankin.'

Alice whistled under her breath. 'So he's back in Swansea?'

'We turn our focus to Johann Ackland. And have we had any word about the search for Mark Tremain?'

Rhys and Alice shook their heads.

'And the evidence from Billy Tartan Jones in Swansea jail implicated a person with the nickname Skywalker.'

'Doesn't Johann Ackland have a yacht called the *Millennium Falcon*?' Rhys has a note of incredulity in his voice.

'Exactly,' Huw said.

'And the source told us this Skywalker was in hock to an organised crime group for drugs. He was paying off his debts with information they could use for the burglaries.'

'That makes sense,' Alice nodded. 'Can we trust that information? You know what these prisoners are like, they will say anything to give themselves an advantage.'

'We work on the basis the information is reliable until we've been able to prove otherwise.'

Caren looked back at the board and pointed towards the face of Johann Ackland. 'We know that he was associated with Emily, and he had been in the company of Rachel. If Emily and Rachel got wind of what he was doing, they could quite easily have decided to blackmail him. And Emily may have found out about his dodgy curriculum vitae. It's the only explanation we've come up with so far for all that money being present in Emily's flat.'

'They get greedy and ask for more and more money. So Johann Ackland decides that paying them off has to stop.'

'And he lied to us about where he had been on the night Emily was killed,' Huw said.

'I don't like it when people lie to us,' Caren said. 'And we didn't pay enough attention when Emily's brother told us he'd seen her out with him arguing.'

'And Tom had seen Ackland giving her money.'

'If he's got a heavy drug problem and he can't afford to pay off his supplier it would be easy enough for him to pay his debts by giving them information. And being involved with the sailing club would mean he'd have lots of information and addresses.'

Rhys continued: 'The background checks we did against him show he had a lot of debts so he must have been in difficulty paying off drug debts. And he probably couldn't ever go to Mrs Ackland and ask for a sub.'

Alice chuckled.

'I'm seeing the superintendent and a CPS lawyer later.

We need to authorise an arrest. Good work everyone.'

Caren sat by a desk and ate her chicken and salad sandwich as the conversation turned towards the fine detail of everything that justified the arrest of Johann Ackland. It didn't take long for Huw to have a detailed memo prepared which he emailed to Caren. She finished the chocolate bar and her coffee, a sense filling her mind that it could well be the only meal she'd have that day.

Now the only outstanding issue was where an earth had Mark Tremain gone and what had he to tell them? She got up and left the Incident Room for the bathroom, where she doused her face with warm water before pulling a comb through her hair. She stared at herself, knowing this was the part of the job she loved. Justifying all the hard work her team had undertaken to her superior officer and then setting off to arrest the culprit.

She returned to the Incident Room, where all the team were on their feet. Rhys was on the telephone the other two looking over at him intently. Caren could sense the tension.

'Mark Tremain has been spotted in the Swansea Valley,' Rhys said.

'What are you waiting for? Rhys and Alice, get up there,' Caren said.

Chapter 49

Rhys Davies and Alice Sharp left the Incident Room with detailed instructions to keep in regular contact with Caren. They were meeting a team including an armed response vehicle with two officers, as well as another marked police vehicle. Caren had given them clear instructions that no chances were to be taken under any circumstances.

One of the AFOs would be the operational firearms commander but the overall officer in charge would be a strategic firearms commander. Caren never envied the task of these officers who often had to make split-second decisions about discharging their weapons.

Moments after both her detective constables left, the door to the Incident Room burst open and Superintendent Brooks and Nicola Jones the Crown prosecution lawyer marched in. Brooks was wearing his full uniform. When he reached the board and stood, he clenched his jaw. He stared at the various photographs and details. The CPS lawyer Caren had met previously stood by his side.

Caren had anticipated speaking to Brooks in his office, around the conference table. So having him appear in the Incident Room, which was her domain as the senior investigating officer, caught her off guard.

'I hear you have requested the deployment of an ARV.' Brooks stared over at Caren. Although it wasn't a question he expected an answer to.

'There's been a sighting of Mark Tremain in the Swansea Valley, in Clydach. A member of the public saw him entering a shop to buy food.'

Brooks nodded his confirmation.

Caren continued: 'I wasn't going to take any chances, sir. If Mark Tremain was the person who discharged the firearm near his home, then we can't afford to take the risk he would use a firearm again.'

'And what if he wasn't the person who shot at you near his home?' Nicola said.

Typical lawyer, Caren thought, always looking at every conceivable angle.

'We have to make every operational decision based on the information at the time,' Caren replied, with as much vagueness as she believed she could get away with. 'The reason I wanted to see you, sir, is we now believe Johann Ackland is a suspect we need to arrest and speak to.'

'Please explain.' Brooks frowned.

Caren took a step towards the board, pleased now that Brooks and the lawyer were in the Incident Room. 'We have evidence a person with a nickname Skywalker was linked to the organised crime group connected to the burglaries. We've made the link between that nickname and Johann Ackland's yacht – the *Millennium Falcon*. It's from the Star Wars films.'

'Yes, I know,' Brooks said. 'Harrison Ford and all that.'

'And we've recovered an image of Johann Ackland meeting Gerard Rankin.'

Brooks looked startled. He gave Caren a double take. 'Gerard Rankin. Where was the photograph taken?'

'Inside the Hope and Anchor by Rachel Scott, surreptitiously. She sent it to her sister on Snapchat. The sister routinely saved her photographs from Rachel on her mobile. Otherwise, the image would have been lost.'

'Gerard Rankin.' Brooks repeated.

'Is he somebody we should be interested in, Derek?' Nicola said.

'Damned right we should. But if all we've got is a picture of them together in a pub it's hardly evidence to incriminate Gerard Rankin.'

'I'll go through the other evidence that implicates Johann Ackland, sir,' Caren said.

'Of course, carry on.'

Caren outlined all the evidence accumulated that suggested Johann Ackland had the opportunity and motive to kill both women. Occasionally Superintendent Brooks interrupted, asked a question for clarification. Nicola stared at

Caren intently, following every detail of her explanation.

'I don't like the reliance on evidence from a prisoner. They can be notoriously dishonest,' Nicola said.

Brooks didn't say anything for a moment, he just stared at the board. Caren was convinced he was looking at the image of Johann Ackland. Then she spotted him moving his gaze towards Mrs Ackland and then at Mark Tremain.

'Why the hell would he let the nickname Skywalker be used?'

Neither Caren or Huw nor the Crown prosecution lawyer responded.

Brooks continued: 'I just hope you're right about his motive.'

Establishing motive wasn't a prerequisite to arresting a suspect. All they needed was evidence. There were very few motiveless murders and Caren guessed that Superintendent Brooks was challenging her to justify her decision to arrest Johann Ackland.

'He's lied repeatedly to us and his academic achievement and status are clearly suspect. He has his career and lifestyle to protect.'

'Does the evidence build a motive?' Brooks said.

Caren wasn't certain if the superintendent was really challenging her.

'I think so, sir. We found evidence that Emily had a substantial sum of cash in her possession. She must have got it from somewhere.'

'But they were in a relationship of sorts,' Brooks said.

Nicola responded: 'I think you've got more than enough to justify his arrest.'

Superintendent Brooks continued to stare at the board. Although Caren was the senior investigating officer, she wanted the final decision in this case about arresting Johann Ackland to be made by Superintendent Brooks and a prosecuting lawyer.

Caren could hear her pulse beating. She wanted to say

something, anything that would convince Superintendent Brooks and eliminate that lingering doubt in his mind. But she kept silent: she had said enough.

Eventually Superintendent Brooks turned to her and Huw.

'Arrest the bastard.'

Chapter 50

Rhys Davies hammered the vehicle in the outside lane of the M4 motorway eastbound, lights flashing. Traffic quickly filtered into the nearside lane. His entire focus was on making certain he drove safely. He paid little attention to Alice sitting in the passenger seat scrolling through her phone.

'I got the details of those three contacts that we believe he might have known,' Alice said.

Rhys mumbled an acknowledgement. Two articulated lorries ahead of him were hampering his progress and he flashed his headlights, encouraging them to move out of the way, but they lumbered on until a space appeared on the middle and inside lanes. 'They shouldn't be in the outside lane.' Rhys sounded annoyed.

As soon as he passed junction 46 he knew he needed to slow to leave the motorway at the following junction. He didn't switch off the flashing lights as he indicated left off the motorway for the slip road that would take him through the village of Ynystawe and then on to Clydach.

He spotted the two marked police vehicles parked ahead and he pulled up. He exchanged a message with the first vehicle that they were to follow him towards the address they had been given. The radio communication from the other two vehicles crackled as each confirmed their understanding. Rhys led the way where Mark Tremain had been spotted entering the convenience store. He parked, as did the other two cars.

'Let's go and see what these shop assistants have got to tell us,' Rhys said.

Alice followed Rhys as he entered the store, interrupting a customer being served at the till. He held aloft his warrant card. 'Police. We need to speak to Margaret Price,' Rhys said, mentioning the name of the witness who had called.

The customer at the counter seems surprised, but the store assistant jerked her head towards the back of the shop. 'She's with the manager.'

Rhys nodded his understanding and threaded his way through shelves laden with tins and the usual dried food. The door was beside a series of freezer compartments full of ready-made pizzas and instant meals. Rhys pulled open the door and found the manager's office easily enough. A woman in her fifties sat at a desk, with a man of a similar age. They both looked up, startled at Rhys and Alice appearing unannounced. They relaxed once they had caught sight of both warrant cards.

'Are you Margaret Price?'

The woman nodded.

'I'm Detective Constable Davies and this is DC Alice Sharp. What can you tell me about Mark Tremain?'

'It was him. I recognised the name from the photographs on the television and on Facebook. He looked wild.'

'Did he say anything?'

She shook her head. 'He bought some bread and milk and cheese.'

Alice had an image of Mark Tremain on her mobile which she pushed towards Margaret Price. 'Is this the man you saw?'

Margaret nodded again.

'Did you see where he went?' Alice said.

'He was only in the shop for a few minutes. He left dead quick and ran over to a blue car on the opposite side of the road.'

'Was he driving?'

She shook her head.

'Did you see the number plate?'

Another shake. 'The place was full of customers.'

'What sort of car was it?'

'It was small and a bit old. But I'm useless with makes and models.'

Rhys shared a glance with Alice that said they needed to leave and return to their vehicle. On the pavement outside the store, they shared the information with the other officers.

Then Rhys added: 'We visit each of his known contacts in turn. The first lives in Pontardawe and the second in Ystalyfera and the final is in Ystradgynlais.'

'And we will do a search with the DVLA for any vehicles registered in their names,' Alice added.

The other four officers nodded their understanding. They took the road out of Clydach and drove as fast as was safely possible, passing the terraces and detached properties of Trebanos. They had to slow as they negotiated their way through the centre of Pontardawe, one of the small towns that had grown from the coal industry that had once dominated the area.

Alice gave directions and announced once they were near to the first address that none of the contacts had a small blue car registered in their names. The DVLA, the government body responsible for vehicles in the United Kingdom, had been pressurised to provide her with the details quickly.

'Somebody else is helping him,' Rhys said.

He indicated left off the main road running through the town northwards and pulled up abruptly outside the semi-detached house Alice had pointed to as their first destination.

The white UPVC windows and front door sparkled as though they had been recently cleaned, and a new dry stone wall had been built along the front boundary with the pavement. The garden to the side of the property stepped down in a series of terraces. This was often the case with properties in the South Wales Valleys built upon a steep bank. One of the officers from the armed response vehicle made certain Rhys and Alice pulled on their bullet-proof vests.

Then they hurried down the path to the front door whilst two of the other officers made their way to the rear of the property down the carefully constructed steps. Rhys hammered a fist on the door and he could hear the officers at the rear. Alice had stood back and Rhys saw her on the pavement gesturing at one of the neighbours. The man came over to her and they had a brief exchange of words. Rhys then stepped to his right and peered into the lounge of the property. It looked empty apart from the normal furniture and television.

Alice called over: 'There's nobody there – apparently he is on holiday and the neighbours haven't seen anybody staying recently.'

The two other officers emerged from the rear of the property joined Rhys. 'Place is empty and there's no garden shed or outbuilding that might be used.'

'Okay, let's go to the next property,' Rhys said.

The screeching of car tyres filled the air as three police vehicles managed five point turns on the narrow street. The satnav told Rhys his journey should have taken eleven minutes to the property in Ystalyfera, but they managed it in eight. This time they had to run up steps set back into the hillside, that reached the front door of the property looking down over the valley.

The woman who opened the door looked terrified at Rhys and Alice.

Rhys identified himself and Alice, pushing forward their warrant cards. 'We're looking for a Mark Tremain and we understand a Richard Jones lives here. He is friends with Mark Tremain, and we need to speak to both men urgently.'

'I don't know who you mean. We've just moved into this house three months ago. I don't know anybody called Tremain or Richard Jones.'

Two of the uniformed officers who had run into gardens at the rear of the property returned shaking their heads and Rhys and Alice.

'Thank you for your time,' Rhys said.

He waved for all the officers to return to their vehicles.

The journey to the final address should have taken six minutes but Rhys managed it in five and they drew up outside the semi-detached property, its front yard covered with a mixture of slate waste and gravel. Weeds and grass tufts struggled for life. A white van was tucked into the narrow drive leading up to the front door at the side of the property. There didn't seem to be a rear access.

Rhys and Alice got out of their car as the armed response vehicle parked on the pavement in front of them. They both walked up the drive and knocked on the door. There was the sound of furniture being moved and activity inside. Rhys couldn't see over the tall fence to his right but he heard the sound of running footsteps on the other side and then a car engine being started. Rhys ran back towards the pavement and seconds later a blue Fiesta emerged from a side street.

He yelled over at the armed response team. 'It's him.'

Rhys and Alice got back to their car seconds later, as the armed response vehicle pulled off its lights flashing and sirens blaring. Then they set off in pursuit. The blue car headed north and the armed response vehicle tried to keep up, despite the obstruction caused by householders' cars lining the street. The Fiesta hurtled along at a breakneck speed and Rhys lost track of it for a few seconds until he saw it slowing at a roundabout after it had ignored a red light at a pedestrian crossing. The armed response vehicle had done the same and they powered ahead northwards. Once they were clear of the residential area there was a longish straight stretch of road as the Fiesta hurtled ahead, the ARV keeping a safe distance behind.

'He hasn't got a hope of escaping,' Rhys said.

'He's busy going northbound heading for the main road over towards Glyn Neath. I'll call it in and get uniformed vehicles to assist with stopping him,' Alice said.

Rhys listened to Alice's one-sided conversation. Within seconds they were at a stretch of the road lined with thick shrubbery and mature trees. It had given the driver of the blue Ford Fiesta the opportunity to push the car and it had disappeared from view. Rhys accelerated and caught sight of the ARV lights flashing and sirens blaring in the distance. Rhys did the same and caught up with the ARV so that he was a safe distance behind the vehicle.

'There are two small roundabouts up ahead so he'll have

to slow down,' Rhys said after consulting the sat nav.

The road dipped and then they came to the first roundabout. The ARV was braking hard, and Rhys had to do the same. The blue Fiesta cornered tightly but the driver misjudged the position of the raised part of the kerb in the middle of the road. He clipped it with his offside wheels. The Fiesta tipped over onto its side and skidded on its passenger side, the momentum enough to propel it over the road, colliding with the pavement on the opposite side. It landed on its roof in a small section of grass verge.

Rhys parked in the middle of the road as did the officers of the ARV. All the officers left their vehicles. The authorised firearms officers removed weapons from their vehicle with practised ease. The two officers from the marked police car sprinted in different directions toward the traffic slowing for the roundabout yelling a warning for them to stop. Rhys joined Alice as they crouched behind the rear of their car peering over as the AFOs approached the Fiesta. A warning shout was called, but Rhys didn't hear any reply and spotted no movement either. Both AFOs circled the vehicle, carefully taking time to make certain there was no imminent danger. Once they were satisfied it was safe they waved at Rhys and Alice to join them.

Chapter 51

Caren almost knew her way to the building where Johann Ackland had his office at the University. But she still got Huw to punch the postcode into the sat nav, although she'd rely on his directions as well. She didn't bother keeping a check on the speed limits as she sped down the M4 before taking a right into the city. During the journey Huw had spoken regularly with Alice, getting updates on their progress tracking Mark Tremain. An armed response vehicle manned by two authorised firearms officers joined them as they covered the final part of the route. Knowing the Acklands were gun owners meant she had to be careful. By the time Caren and Huw pulled up at the University office building Rhys and Alice still had nothing to report. After parking, the AFOs motioned for her and Huw to join them. One of the officers found bullet-proof vests in the boot of the armed response vehicle which Caren and Huw dragged on.

Caren made directly for the desk of the administrative support staff. Both authorised firearms officers followed her, weapons at the ready, earning their group incredulous glances. But this time she didn't bother introducing herself or flashing a warrant card. 'We want to speak to Dr Ackland.'

Caren knew that he was in the building as she had called in advance to check he was there.

'I am sorry, but he's not here.'

'He was here earlier. We called to check.'

'Well, he's not here now.'

'Do you know where he's gone?'

'No, of course not. He probably decided to work from home as he didn't have any tutorials or lectures today.'

'Thanks,'

Caren and Huw left the building.

'I don't like it, boss,' Huw said.

'It could be he is just working from home, like that woman said.'

Caren saw the scepticism on Huw's face. They returned

to their vehicle as Caren yelled instructions for the ARV to follow them. Caren didn't bother with the satnav. Huw recalled the route and his knowledge of the area meant she'd rely on his directions.

They parked by the pavement outside Johann Ackland's home.

They walked up to the front door. It troubled Caren that there weren't any vehicles parked on the drive. Both AFOs stood alongside her.

'It looks as though there isn't anyone home,' Caren said.

She used an old-fashioned knocker attached to the middle of the door and the sound of it colliding with the wood echoed through the house. There was no movement or a greeting from anyone inside.

'Where has he gone?' Huw said.

'Let's check around the back.' Caren jerked her head at the AFOs.

Both officers left the porch area and jogged round towards the rear of the property. Caren and Huw did the same peering through the windows into the house, but there was no sign of anyone. The rear garden was surprisingly small with a neat pergola and patio area on which there was a covered hot tub at one end.

The armed officers joined Caren and Huw. 'Nothing, ma'am.' The older man said.

They stood for a moment looking up at the substantial property. 'He might well have made an excuse about working from home so that he could be on his yacht. Maybe he's persuaded some other young student she's the only one for him,' Caren said.

Huw nodded. 'I agree, boss.'

Caren turned to the AFOs. 'I need you down in the marina.'

Both nodded their understanding. Back in her car Caren fumbled for her mobile.

Huw gave her directions for the marina. Caren got

frustrated when traffic delayed her. The BMW with the armed officers was close behind them. It gave Huw an opportunity of calling Rhys and Alice again. They confirmed that the address of the second person they had as a possible friend of Mark Tremain had proved to be a dead end. They were heading for the third address. 'Just be careful,' Huw said.

It wasn't long until they reached the marina where they parked. The AFOs left their vehicle and joined Caren and Huw.

They sprinted down towards the marina. As Caren did so she recalled there were CCTV cameras covering the entrance to the pontoons. When she reached the ramp down onto the pontoons she called the marina building. The duty manager confirmed he had seen Johann Ackland running in the marina towards the entrance for the pontoons earlier.

The gate down to the pontoon buzzed open as Caren demanded to know where exactly they could find the *Millennium Falcon*. Once she had the directions she finished the call. They ran down the connecting ramp from the side of the marina to the pontoons. The AFOs led the way until she was able to establish where exactly Ackland's yacht had been moored.

'Stay back, ma'am,' the senior of the AFOs said as they cautiously ventured forward, weapons drawn.

Caren dropped back with Huw. The AFOs covered the distance towards Ackland's yacht in measured, careful steps taking time to make certain they weren't challenged.

Movement in one of the yachts nearby startled Caren, but the AFOs ahead of her motioned wordlessly for the startled yacht owner, who stared in amazement at the armed officers, to stay well hidden. Ackland's vessel was at the end of one section of the pontoon. It was easy enough to spot, its name on the transom.

Both AFOs signalled for silence and dropped to their knees scanning and checking the surroundings. Quickly the AFOs sprang into action and with each covering the other they approached the vessel. Caren tried to draw nearer but she was ushered back by an angry look from the senior AFO.

Caren spotted the canopy over the cockpit flapping open. The first AFO hauled himself up over the safety rail, quickly followed by his colleague. The second AFO reached out a hand for Caren. Once they were into the cockpit, one of the AFOs yanked the flapping section of the awning to one side, weapon at the ready. He stepped into the cockpit proper where the yacht captain would helm.

He called out. 'Johann Ackland?'

There was no acknowledgement nor reply in return.

Caren followed him, her heart pounding. She took a few steps down into the galley and main salon. It didn't look as though anybody had been there. And definitely not Ackland brandishing a weapon. Then she ventured further into the bow guessing there'd be a cabin.

She stopped in her tracks and gasped. On the floor was the body of Johann Ackland. A bullet wound to the head had made certain he'd never be sailing again. Caren yelled at Huw who appeared at her side seconds later.

'Bloody hell, that's a mess right enough.'

'Find out whether Rhys and Alice have caught Tremain yet and get a CSI team down here.'

Caren thanked the AFOs, who agreed to wait for the CSI team. She took one further look around the yacht, familiarising herself with the scene. She couldn't help but think Mark Tremain had been the culprit. She made a mental note to make certain she warned the CSI team she and Huw and both AFOs had no idea it was a crime scene before they arrived.

'I haven't been able to get hold of Rhys and Alice yet. My call went to voicemail,' Huw said.

'Let's go and talk to the marina manager.'

'The CSI team are en route boss and uniformed officers are accompanying them.'

Caren clambered off the yacht followed by Huw. They

marched back along the pontoons up to the exit gate where she jogged over to the marina building and took the stairs to the first floor two at a time. A startled marina manager soon complied with her request to see all the footage from that morning of people arriving at the pontoon. He played it at a fast speed and Caren spotted Johann Ackland approaching the gate.

'Is there any other way someone could access the pontoons?'

'If you come up on a yacht or boat you can.'

'Send me all of that footage now.' Caren left her business card on the manager's desk. She stood outside the building for a moment as Huw took a call.

'The CSI team will be here in five,' Huw said.

'Good. Let's get back to headquarters.'

Chapter 52

Caren paced around the Incident Room. She kept coming back and standing before the board. Alice and Rhys were on their way back, but she knew from their update that Mark Tremain was unconscious and being rushed to Morriston Hospital after the car accident. Nobody was going to be talking to him any time soon.

'We've missed something,' Caren said.

Huw – standing by the board – didn't reply.

'We need to look at everything again once Rhys and Alice are back.'

Her mobile rang before Huw had an opportunity to contribute. She snatched it off the table where she had left it. 'Yes!' She knew she sounded irritable.

She paused for a moment when she heard Susan Howard's voice. 'It's me, Caren. We're down in Swansea Marina.'

'Oh, I'm sorry if I sounded rude.'

'No problem. I thought I should tell you we found a piece of yellow fabric caught on a hook in the yacht. But we didn't find any similar item of clothing on the yacht.'

'So do you think the killer left it?'

'Probably, it was near the galley.'

'Any signs of a struggle?'

'No, that was odd. Perhaps the killer surprised Ackland. I'll let you have a full report.'

Caren finished the call as the door to the Incident Room opened and Rhys Davies and Alice Sharp walked in. Rhys was the first to regale Caren and Huw with the details of exactly what had happened and how the car accident involving Mark Tremain had seemed like something out of a movie. But Tremain wasn't a stunt driver who could pull himself clear of the carnage. It had taken a specialist fire engine crew to cut him out of the vehicle and the attending paramedics believed he may have broken several bones.

'We need to work out exactly where Tremain was today,'

Caren said. 'Johann Ackland was seen alive walking down onto the pontoons at 12.15 pm.'

'That's about the time Tremain was in a convenience store,' Rhys said.

'Damn it. That means he can't have been the person to have killed Johann Ackland.' Annoyance was clear in her voice.

She turned to look over at the board. Rhys launched into an enthusiastic assessment of exactly what had happened, but she wasn't listening to him. She turned and raised a hand telling him to stop. 'I need coffee, extra strong, now. As well as something to eat.'

'Yes, boss.' Rhys scurried out of the Incident Room to the kitchen.

'Who the hell would benefit from Ackland's death?' Caren said.

'Gerard Rankin?' Alice said. 'I think we should arrest the toerag and find out exactly where he was this afternoon. He is the sort of person who could quite easily have access to handguns.'

'Access to handguns?' Caren said. Repeating rather loudly what Alice had said silenced the other officers on her team. Something had sparked in her mind. 'We know Johann Ackland was a member of a gun club.'

'And his wife,' Huw said.

'Mrs Ackland,' Caren announced with more formality than she had intended. 'So, she is familiar with using a gun. Call the secretary of the gun club where she's a member. I want to find out if she is a regular.'

Alice got straight to work. Caren returned to her office, knowing she had to review statements and details as the name of Mrs Ackland dominated her mind. Rhys returned with coffees, and he brought a mug into Caren's room.

'Thanks, Rhys.'

But something from Susan's comments resurfaced in her mind. Where had she seen yellow fabric in the inquiry? Once she had focused, she knew exactly what needed to be done. She called Susan.

'I need to check that yellow fabric you recovered against the polo shirts worn by the staff at McCarthys where Tremain works.'

'I'll get an investigator onto it right away.'

Caren thanked Susan. Then she heard Alice on the telephone getting more and more irate. After she had finished her drink and eaten half of the sandwich she marched back into the Incident Room.

'Mrs Ackland is a regular at the firing range, apparently. She has a licence for a firearm which is stored securely in her home,' Alice said.

Caren walked over to the board and tapped the image of Mrs Ackland. 'What if she was the source of the information to the organised crime groups about properties in the marina. After all, she is the membership secretary of the sailing club.' Caren turned back to look at her team, all of whom were looking puzzled. 'She realises her husband has a heavy drug problem and is in hock to the likes of Gerard Rankin. So in order to get him off the hook she provides useful information to the OCGs.'

Huw continued: 'But Emily and Rachel get in the way by blackmailing Johann. I thought there was something odd about her reaction to us telling her about his relationship with Emily.'

Caren nodded. 'And they decide between them that Emily and Rachel needed to be disposed of. But Johann Ackland is completely unaware that his wife believes he is now disposable.'

Rhys nodded his head vigorously. 'I did some digging into Mrs Ackland's background. She comes from a really posh family. She made a point of telling us that her father had been Commodore of the Cowes sailing club. I checked out the details and it's one of the most prestigious sailing clubs in the country. There's a waiting list for membership which means you have to wait for somebody to die.'

'Dead man's shoes,' Huw said. 'And that's hardly the sort of family that would want to be involved with somebody with a drug habit who was unfaithful to their daughter.'

'So you think a motive for killing her husband would have been to protect her reputation?' Alice sounded sceptical. 'Divorcing him would have been much easier.'

'It's more than that. She'd be angry and humiliated and hurt by his philandering.' Caren looked over at the board again. 'Rhys and Alice, I want both of you checking on Mark Tremain's health. As soon as he has recovered consciousness I want to speak to him. In the meantime, get all the footage from the marina showing boats and yachts coming into the marina basin. We can pinpoint when Johann Ackland went down to his yacht, but I want to find out if there is any way we can establish if Mrs Ackland got onto the pontoons without accessing them from the locked gate.'

'Yes, boss.'

'And we need to find out where Mrs Ackland is. I think we need to interview her under caution after we've arrested her for murder.'

'I think I know exactly where she'll be, boss.' Huw said.

Chapter 53

'She'll be at a bakery event at the Bella Cucina.'

'How do you know?' Caren said.

An animated expression filled Huw's face. 'There's a bakery demonstration there today. I know Harriet Ackland is a regular at these events. Christopher will be there too.'

'Call them now and find out,' Caren raised her voice.

Huw nodded and found his mobile.

Caren and Rhys and Alice listened intently to Huw's part of the conversation. He sounded casual as he asked to speak to one of the staff by name.

'*Ciao*,' Huw sounded an informal tone. 'Has Marco's bakery demonstration started yet?'

He nodded at the reply.

'I just wanted to check that Christopher had arrived.'

The person on the other end obviously offered to contact Huw's partner.

'No, no need to interrupt him but I was wondering too if Harriet Ackland was there. It's her birthday this weekend and I wanted to leave her a present when I call for coffee later.'

Huw nodded again and then he finished the call. '*Ciao*.'

Huw turned to Caren. 'She's there all right. The demo has just started.'

'Excellent. Good work, Huw,' Caren said. 'I want a detailed map of the surrounding area printed off and on the board by the time I come back from seeing Superintendent Brooks. And I need two authorised firearms officers to accompany us.'

And with that, Caren left the Incident Room and paced through to the senior management suite. She stood in the reception area outside of the super's office despite encouraging glances from Brooks' secretary for her to sit. When she was eventually invited in, she stood again, outlining in brisk, articulate terms why the arrest of Mrs Harriet Ackland was a priority.

'Jesus, Caren. If you're right, she's a maniac. But I still

want someone from your team talking to Mark Tremain as soon as he has regained consciousness.'

'Of course, sir,' Caren said.

He nodded for her to leave his room, and she walked, and then almost trotted, back to the Incident Room. Rhys was pinning to the board a map of the suburb of Swansea showing the location of the café and the various streets surrounding it.

'I don't want to take any chances with this woman.' Caren pointed at the café's location on the map.

'Yes, boss.' Huw sounded focused.

'Rhys and Alice, you'll escort the customers out of the café. And the AFOs will accompany us when we arrest her.' Caren turned to Huw. 'I want two police vehicles to block off any means of escape from the café itself.'

'What do we do about the other people attending the demonstration?' Huw said.

'She's not going to do anything stupid with other people present.'

'Let's hope not,' Huw said.

Caren clocked the worry in his voice. He'd be concerned about Christopher, his partner. But was Harriet Ackland the sort of killer to take a gun with her into a bakery event at an Italian café? This wasn't like a scene from *The Sopranos*. It was a suburb of Swansea.

It took Caren half an hour to coordinate all the support officers she needed. She had to shout and cajole but eventually two marked vehicles had been allocated and arrangements made for two AFOs to meet her outside Bella Cucina.

Caren gave instructions for Huw to drive down into the middle of Swansea whilst she coordinated with the two marked police vehicles that would join them to assist with the arrest. She had a printed large-scale copy of the map on her lap, showing the location of the café. She radioed instructions to the other police vehicles of where she wanted them to park.

Huw parked a little distance away from the café. Caren's heart was beating loudly in her chest and she sensed her mouth drying.

'When they have these sorts of events, they do a demonstration for an hour or so and then the participants have an opportunity to practice making similar breads or pastries or cakes. Then everyone sits in the café sampling what's been made.'

Caren nodded. She pointed over at the first police vehicle to park a little distance ahead and she glanced in the rear-view mirror at the second pulling up behind her. Each knew exactly what they had to do after Caren and Huw had gone into the café. A third vehicle with the AFOs parked behind her.

Both authorised firearms officers marched over to Caren and Huw once they were standing on the pavement. Caren ignored the shocked looks from shoppers nearby.

'All ready, ma'am,' one of the AFOs said.

Caren tipped her head towards the café.

'She's inside.' Then she showed both officers a photograph of Harriet Ackland.

'Do we know if she's armed?'

'No way of knowing – we're assuming she's not but we're taking no chances.'

The AFOs nodded their agreement. Caren and Huw had already pulled on bullet-proof vests under their police hi-viz jackets. Moments later Rhys and Alice joined them.

Protecting herself and Huw and the lives of others was paramount.

And more than anything she wanted to be able to go home to Aled that evening.

They walked over and Caren pushed open the door and Huw recognised one of the members of staff, who smiled at him quizzically. 'Are you coming for the bakery event?'

Huw shook his head. 'I'm Detective Sergeant Margam, and we'll need everyone in the café to leave with these two officers.' He pointed at Rhys and Alice. Caren stood for a moment as the place emptied, her heart pounding so fast it was stealing her breath. Both AFOs led the way through into the kitchen where a man in bakery whites was demonstrating how proper sourdough should be proved and folded. He carried on the instructions for the dozen or so people around the stainless steel-topped work area. Christopher was one of the first to look up and frowned as he saw Huw and Caren. It soon changed into a deep worry.

Caren had already told Huw to have his handcuffs at the ready to avoid any wrong move by Mrs Ackland. Harriet Ackland gazed in stunned disbelief as both authorised firearms officers went up to her.

A woman by her side dropped a large piece of dough and her elbow caught two proving baskets, which fell to the floor. Another woman caught her breath and stood speechless and wide-eyed in shock. The man running the course piped up: 'What the hell is going on?'

Caren ignored him and walked up to Harriet Ackland, satisfied the AFOs knew they had everything under control. 'Mrs Harriet Ackland?'

Harriet turned and gave Caren her best cold, dark, death stare.

'I'm arresting you on suspicion of the murder of your husband Johann Ackland. You do not have to say anything. But it may harm your defence if you do not mention when questioned something you later rely on in court. Anything you do say may be given in evidence.'

There were gasps of surprise around the room as Huw fastened her arms behind her back with handcuffs.

Chapter 54

Caren looked through the one-way glass at Harriet Ackland sitting in the interview room. By her side sat Ifan Llywelyn. He had been a detective before retraining so that he could advise suspects in interviews. Caren found him determined to defend his clients' interests but he was also fair and even-handed.

Despite having spent a night in the cells at headquarters, Harriet looked composed. Caren wondered what on earth was going through her mind. She had attended the bakery event yesterday in her best casual clothes, including a pair of shoes with not insignificant heels. Her hair had recently been cut and Caren recalled her delicate and expensive perfume.

Caren continued to stare as Huw entered the small room.

'Do you think she will cough?' Huw said, referring to the jargon officers used for a suspect confessing to a crime.

Caren nodded towards Harriet. 'She looks so serene and completely in control.'

'Rhys and Alice have been able to take a statement from Mark Tremain this morning,' Huw said. 'He doesn't have a gun and didn't shoot at us when we were at his property. He had arrived moments before us and he reckons someone had just burgled his home. He admits doing a runner because he thought we were going to arrest him for murder.'

'Did they believe him?'

'He admitted to handling stolen property but categorically denied being involved with the burglaries at the marina.'

Caren's mobile rang and she saw it was Susan's number. 'I haven't much time. I'm about to interview Mrs Ackland.'

'Something you should know. We matched the piece of fabric in Ackland's yacht to the polo shirts worn by McCarthys' employees.'

Caren didn't immediately reply. She looked over at Harriet again who seem to be staring at her directly in the eye. 'Thanks Susan. I think I know someone who can explain the fabric.'

Caren turned to Huw. 'Let's go and see what she's got to say.'

Caren had spent most of the previous evening preparing with Huw and the rest of the team a plan for her interview that morning. She wasn't about to rush questioning Harriet Ackland who wasn't going anywhere for some time. They had more than enough evidence to justify her continued custody for a couple of days. And that gave them enough time to do a complete search of her home. Caren hadn't been able to sleep well, as was often the case when she had to prepare for an interview. The tactics and the strategy could play over and over in her mind. Aled had stayed with his Mamgu. She had got to sleep the night before about one o'clock in the morning after a glass of wine and watching two episodes of *New Amsterdam*, the Netflix medical drama. She always preferred watching a crime drama if she could, but last night had decided that if she did, she'd probably be awake all night.

She had woken early and was at the Incident Room before seven thirty. It was always the same before an interview in a major inquiry. She couldn't afford to make mistakes. She had to get it right. When she read her emails she wanted to fist-pump when new pieces of the puzzle had been discovered. She had smiled to herself at the prospect of challenging Harriet Ackland.

She and Huw left the observation room and walked into the interview room itself. She exchanged greetings with Ifan Llywelyn and once Huw had set up the recording equipment and the formalities out of the way, Caren looked over at Harriet.

'I understand you are the membership secretary of the sailing club at the Swansea Marina. Does that give you access to the records of members and their home addresses?'

'Yes, of course, I take my responsibility very seriously.'

'And I understand your family are keen sailors too.'

Playing to the woman's ingrained snobbery seemed to be

working. 'My parents have been members of the Cowes Yacht Club for years. My father was Commodore of the Cowes Yacht Club some years ago and he is a most experienced sailor.'

'Would you say you value the contribution you make to the club?'

'Where exactly are we going with this line of questioning, Detective Inspector?' Ifan said.

Caren gave him a thin smile. 'Background, you know what it's like, I'm sure.'

Caren continued: 'There have been a series of burglaries in apartments in the marina and from properties owned by members of the sailing club who live in the Cardiff area. There have also been thefts from yachts. We believe they are all linked.'

Caren waited for Harriet to react, but she chose to stare over at Caren, her eyes disinterested.

'We've built a picture of the burglaries and there's a clear pattern. They all take place at times when the properties were empty. And, in the case of the properties in Cardiff, when the owners were likely to be sailing here in Swansea. We believe you and your husband made that information available to members of an organised crime group.'

'Don't be absurd.'

'Tell me about your relationship with Johann?'

'We were happily married.'

Caren took a moment – was this woman serious? 'Is that despite your husband's repeated infidelities with students both at the Mid-Somerset University and here in Swansea.'

'They meant nothing to him.' She spat out the reply.

'And isn't it true that your husband had a major drug problem. We have evidence he was a regular user of cocaine and when he attended parties he also supplied others.'

'That's ridiculous.' Harriet managed genuine conviction in her voice.

'And Rachel Scott and Emily Hughes became aware your

husband owed money to an organised crime group for drugs. And he was able to repay them by providing information about property owners in the marina and beyond. And we believe you are implicated in that too.'

'I don't know what you're talking about.' She looked over at Ifan for moral support. He gave her a brief, non-committal nod.

'We discovered a large amount of cash held by Emily Hughes and we've been able to establish there was no way she could have come by that money legally. Is it true she and Rachel blackmailed your husband?'

Harriet shook her head out of disbelief and exasperation. There was a glimmer of pity in her face too.

Caren reached into the papers on the table and pushed over the photograph of Johann Ackland and Gerard Rankin. 'Do you know this person with your husband?'

'No, I do not.'

'His name is Gerard Rankin. And he has links with organised crime groups in the Swansea area. Why do you think your husband was talking to him?'

'Perhaps they were discussing sailing.'

Caren sat back, pleased that Harriet had now decided to contribute absurdity to her replies. She was treating the interview process with contempt and that meant she was guilty as hell.

'We found the photograph linked to Rachel's social media accounts. We believe that she took the photograph and used it as part of blackmailing Johann. He broke into her flat didn't he? Did you encourage him to do so?'

'Don't be mad.'

'We know he broke into her flat because we found his fingerprints there. He must have been looking for a laptop or tablet or a USB stick. Emily and Rachel had become a nuisance and you wanted to get rid of them. We believe you were responsible for the murder of both girls.'

Caren saw the shocked reaction on Harriet's face, just as

she had expected. It seemed genuine and it confirmed for Caren that Harriet was either a talented actress or wasn't responsible for the murder of both girls. So she decided to push.

'You see all the evidence we have suggests you are protecting your status in life, including your place as an officer of the sailing club. But your husband's behaviour must have been humiliating for you. How did that make you feel?'

Harriet narrowed her eyes.

'It must have been embarrassing having the staff at the University talking about you behind your back.'

Harriet kept her eye contact direct. But there was a darkness in her face.

Caren pulled from the file the image of Emily's bloodied neck and that of Rachel Scott's battered skull. 'This is your handiwork. You garrotted Emily Hughes and assaulted Rachel with a winch handle.'

'I don't need to respond to this. I thought you already had a suspect. Mark Tremain. He was always arguing with my husband. They fell out about Emily. And I'm sure that Mark has been on the yacht.'

'Do you think Mark Tremain killed your husband?'

'I think that's very possible. You should be concentrating on treating him as a suspect.'

Caren passed a photograph of the piece of fabric recovered from Ackland's yacht across the table. 'We recovered this piece of fabric from your yacht. Do you recognise it?'

'No, of course not.'

'Can you explain how it could have been caught on a hook on your yacht?'

'I can only assume it came from whoever killed my husband.'

'The fabric matches the polo shirts worn by staff at McCarthys, the chandlers in the marina.'

'Well, there you are then – it must have been Tremain

who killed Johann.'

'The problem is, Harriet,' Huw said, 'Mark couldn't have been responsible because at the time Johann was on the yacht Mark was being pursued by officers up the Swansea Valley.'

Harriet's eyes narrowed as she glared at Huw.

'And there was no sign of a struggle on the yacht. It was as though your husband wasn't taken by surprise.'

Harriet clenched her jaw, and she stared at Huw but said nothing.

Caren continued: 'We believe you were responsible for leaving part of Mark's polo shirt in the yacht after you stole it from his property. And you did that to have something to conveniently implicate Mark Tremain.'

Harriet snorted in disbelief.

'When we called to speak to Mark Tremain you were in the trees, and it was you who fired twice at us. You were trying to deflect blame onto the criminals you and your husband were involved with, weren't you?'

A discreet nod to Huw was the signal for him to show her a piece of evidence they had uncovered just before starting the interview.

'And there's a full search team at your home at the moment. They have already discovered a handgun, carefully hidden in the attic, that preliminary ballistics analysis has confirmed was the weapon used to kill your husband. Where did you get it?'

Harriet blinked quickly. Caren could see the dawning realisation on this woman's face that everything she had planned so carefully was unravelling.

'I suspect it was given to your husband by the organised crime group you were mixed up with. Is that correct?'

Huw added, 'And we shall be combing through all the CCTV footage near the marina and making an appeal for eye-witnesses who may have seen you on the pontoons before your husband was killed.'

Caren spotted a nerve twitching on Harriet's face. She

continued the questioning.

'So you decided that the final part of the jigsaw would be to lure your husband to the yacht. Where you killed him hoping to blame Mark Tremain who was a suspect because of the public appeal we had already circulated.'

'We believe you killed your husband in order to protect your reputation, your lifestyle. And out of pure revenge for Johann cheating on you so publicly. You're a cold-blooded murderer.'

Harriet clenched both hands together on the table in front of her.

'You murdered two innocent girls in cold blood and then your husband, hoping to pin the blame on Mark Tremain.'

Harriet began to tap the table with her clenched fingers.

She shook her head again.

'He was weak,' Harriet hissed. 'He got himself caught up with those two witches. I had nothing to do with killing them. He did that. Because he was weak and he didn't see any other way out. They were going to destroy him and his career. He would have ruined everything.

'And you're right – I hated the sniggering behind my back and whispered giggling about me and Johann. I could imagine the comments – *poor old Harriet, how long will she put up with him? Nobody else would put up with him.*'

She paused, but Caren sensed she had more to add.

'His cocaine and cannabis habits were the start. He said so himself. It was like a massive spider's web. Once he was involved there was no way out. And when he told me about those criminals, he sounded so pathetic and weak it repelled me. I don't know what he was thinking.'

She brought her clenched fist down onto the table. 'He made me so mad. I hated him for it.'

Harriet Ackland folded her arms together, drew them tight to her chest and said nothing further.

Chapter 55

After the intense interview, which had required careful and deliberate planning, overwhelming relief filled Caren's mind. She left the custody suite after making certain Harriet Ackland had been locked behind bars. Once tried and sentenced, the prison service would be looking after her for a substantial amount of time. Although she'd be sentenced to life imprisonment, the minimum tariff – the time she'd spend behind bars – would be set by the trial judge. The families of victims often complained that life imprisonment didn't mean that, and Caren found it easy to sympathise. Did it mean justice hadn't been served? She wasn't certain she knew the answer.

Superintendent Brooks was waiting for her in the Incident Room with the rest of the team when she arrived after finishing Harriet Ackland's questioning.

He beamed when she shared how Harriet had finally admitted her guilt in killing her husband.

'Bloody good result, well done.' Brooks looked at Huw and Rhys and Alice sitting at their desks. 'Good job.'

Superintendent Brooks left and Caren flopped into one of the chairs by a spare desk.

She looked over at Rhys and Alice. 'You'd better give me the latest on Mark Tremain. We'll interview him after lunch.'

'He's fit enough to interview,' Rhys said. 'But it'll have to be in the hospital.'

'Good,' Caren said.

'I'll fetch some sandwiches,' Alice said, scrambling to her feet.

Caren nodded. 'Once you're back we'll prepare. In the meantime, I'm going to talk to my mum.' Caren walked over to her room and called her mum on WhatsApp. She used the video function and, with Harriet Ackland safely locked up and Tremain in a hospital bed, she had more than enough time.

It had been late when she had returned the previous

evening after Harriet Ackland's arrest. Aled was already in bed and fast asleep. Her brief conversation with her mum had been perfunctory and the first thing she did was to apologise if she had been rude and sharp the previous evening.

'Don't worry, I understand the pressure you're under. I'm just glad things have finished,' Ann said.

'How is Aled?'

'He's fine. We'll take him for a walk in the park and buy him an ice cream this afternoon.'

'Thanks, mum. I'll be home at a reasonable time later.'

After she finished, she heard the sound of conversation and packages being deposited on the desks drifting through from the Incident Room. She joined her team. She took a chicken salad sandwich with a pack of plain crisps and sat in one of the chairs.

'We gave everyone at Bella Cucina a hell of a fright yesterday,' Huw said. 'Christopher went back to the restaurant this morning for a coffee and that's all the customers were talking about. I think they quite enjoyed being involved.'

'Did they carry on with the bakery lesson once we'd arrested Harriet?' Caren said.

Huw chuckled and then shook his head. 'Everybody had a stiff drink.'

'They'll be talking about it for years.'

The chicken in the sandwich was rubbery and the lettuce limp and browning at the edges. But it was the sort of nourishment Caren needed to see her through to the end of an interview with Mark Tremain.

She listened to the team sharing their plans for the following day, a Sunday. Rhys was going to be spending it with his family. His mother had arranged for her brother and his family to come over for a lunch which meant an enormous meal around the kitchen table that would last for hours. Caren knew from other comments Rhys had made in the past that lunch for the farming community was always at midday sharp.

Alice had promised herself a visit to an out-of-town shopping centre with her husband. It made Caren realise that she hadn't had some proper retail therapy for a long time.

'Have you got anything planned for tomorrow, boss?' Huw said.

Caren shook her head. 'I'm not going to think about work. I'm going to spend time with Aled, and then get an early night.' She knew it sounded boring. But spending time with her son was more precious than anything. Next week they would face the task of putting all the paperwork together for the Crown prosecution lawyers. There would be questions to answer, clarification sought and action plans undertaken. It often felt there was more work after the final interviews.

She finished her sandwich and quaffed the remains of a soft drink before curling the skin of a banana she had eaten and depositing it on the tray Alice had used to deliver their lunch. She turned to Huw. 'Let's get going.'

Caren drove and listened to Huw as he reminded her about the standard protocols for interviewing a suspect in hospital. Then he summarised the questions they needed to ask him. 'Do you think he'll cooperate?' Huw said.

'We'll just have to wait and see.'

Luckily Caren found a parking slot at the hospital easily and she walked over to the entrance with Huw. She had the name of the ward on her mobile and a lift took them to the second floor. They navigated their way to the right ward and pushed open the door. Caren spotted a bored looking uniformed officer sitting on a chair at the end of a corridor. They joined him after she had introduced herself to a nurse.

She flashed her warrant card at the constable who jumped to his feet. 'Ma'am.'

When she walked into the room a look of resignation spread over Mark Tremain's face.

It was late in the afternoon when Caren and Huw returned

to the Incident Room. The palpable tension from the previous week had dissipated. The place felt calm as Caren and Huw walked over towards the desks occupied by Rhys Davies and Alice Sharp. They both gazed up from their computers, acknowledging the presence of Caren and Huw.

Caren stood by the board. 'Thankfully, he cooperated.' She turned to look at the images looking down at her and the team. Soon enough everything would be removed from the board and boxed away. 'He was going to dispose of all the stolen items in the garage.'

'Apparently all the champagne bottles were on route to Romania,' Huw added.

Rhys nodded. 'Shoplifting to order is quite a problem.'

Caren continued: 'He confirmed that he had a connection with an organised crime group who had been responsible for all the burglaries in the marina and the thefts from the yachts. He was just beginning the process of disposing of the stolen items through people he knew. Which means that we've got enough to charge him with handling stolen goods. He's going down for a long stretch.'

'Did he implicate anybody involved with the OCG?' Alice said.

Caren shook her head. 'All he said was that he was contacted anonymously by someone using a burner phone asking if he could dispose of items. And the stuff he had was only a tiny proportion of the items stolen. It looks as though the OCG was hedging their bets about how to dispose of everything that had been nicked. They had delivered the items to him and he had to wait for them to contact him again.'

'Do you believe him, boss?' Rhys said.

'No, of course not.'

'So there's nothing we can do about the burglaries?' Alice said.

'We report everything to Detective Inspector Jenkins. He and his team can decide how they want to proceed.'

'Did Tremain mention Gerard Rankin?'

Caren shook her head. 'When I asked him, he completely clammed up.'

'Just as well,' Rhys said. 'We learned this morning that Rankin is back in Spain.'

'And Tremain did confirm that he'd already left the house when he realised we were arriving. Harriet Ackland must have assumed we'd link the shooting to an organised crime group trying to get rid of Mark Tremain.'

Caren paused. It had tied up all the loose ends.

'Do you reckon she didn't kill Emily Hughes and Rachel Scott?' Huw said.

Caren didn't immediately reply. She sat down again at one of the desks. They couldn't prove she had and the fact she was blaming her husband for those two deaths would seem convenient, even if implausible.

'She's admitted to one murder. She's going down for a long stretch.' Caren knew she hadn't answered the question. 'If we could prove she killed both girls it might make a difference to the minimum term she'd serve in prison.'

'We might struggle to prove she had the strength to garrotte Emily.'

Caren nodded her agreement.

Did that mean justice had been served for both girls? The families would be informed that the Wales Police Service believed the person who killed their daughters had himself been killed. But she guessed a grain of doubt would always remain. Would the families of Emily and Rachel feel satisfied that the truth had really been established? The system was imperfect, Caren knew that, and trying to explain it to the families of murder victims was often painful. She and her team had done the best they could and a killer was going to be behind bars for a long time.

Caren read the time. 'We've done enough for today.' She got up, walked over to her room, found her coat and followed her team out of headquarters.

Chapter 56

During the following week Caren had been able to take Aled to school every morning and collect him at the end of the afternoon. She loved the normality of the daily routine and only once did Aled ask if his Mamgu would be collecting him at the end of the day. Knowing that a new inquiry would derail this regular domesticity filled her with a mixture of excited anticipation and alarm.

She loved being a detective and enjoyed all the pressures and challenges her job involved. But she also knew it was difficult keeping a regular nine-to-five routine which had an impact on her young son and their family life. More than anything she wanted to make Aled proud of her.

She had arranged with David Hemsby that they would go out the following Saturday and spend a day at the National Botanic Garden. She had been there before with Aled and David and now she felt her son would be comfortable meeting David where he had seen him before. It had been a warm summer's day, and she had enjoyed every second in his company and she could tell he felt the same. When Aled had first met David she sensed her young son had found it difficult to relate to him. He had been uncharacteristically overexcited and energetic but now he was his normal self, enjoying his time with his mum and David. She wondered what went through her young son's mind about her relationship with David and whether he ever thought about Alun, his father.

She resolved it would be a conversation she needed to have with him. But she didn't have the first idea of how to start it. Perhaps she would ask her mum for some advice or better still talk to Susan Howard. She had become a friend Caren relied on and who knew Aled well.

Over a meal at a bistro pub on the outskirts of Carmarthen she could sense the warmth in David Hemsby's face and the hunger in his eyes too. Since they had first met she had avoided making a commitment of intimacy to him. Her excuse had been that Aled was far too young for someone to replace his father. Or was it simply that she was making an excuse for not making a commitment to David Hemsby? He was clearly smitten with her and she could see how he could be the right man for her.

She had never anticipated her life panning out this way. She didn't have a strategy. Restarting her life as a single person with a man showing an interest in her and then dating had never occurred to her while she was married. As she looked over at David Hemsby she was reminded that the coroner's inquest into Alun's death was over. That part of her life was at an end. She had to move on and be positive for the future. But she was going to take things carefully, she wasn't going to do anything to threaten her son's happiness. But she knew she didn't want to live the rest of her life on her own and her son's happiness also meant she needed to be content.

They returned to Caren's home at the end of the evening. She wasn't going to invite David to stay the night, not yet anyway. He smiled broadly when she offered coffee and as she pottered around in the kitchen, he and Aled played with the substantial toy car collection in the living room.

As the kettle boiled, she picked up an email on her mobile from the estate agents in North Wales.

Dear Caren, we've had a viewing this afternoon from a couple who are looking for a smallholding exactly like yours. They're cash buyers and have made an offer for the full asking price. I'm sure you'll be pleased with this. They have asked whether you'd agree to take the property off the market whilst the sale to them is proceeding. Please call me as soon as you can. Best wishes, Robert James estate agents.

Caren took a moment to read the email a second and third time. Realising it was far too late to contact the agent she tapped out a reply.

'Good news. And I agree that the house can be taken off the market whilst the sale proceeds. I'll tell my solicitors accordingly.'

It was what she had been hoping for, praying for. The smallholding in North Wales was empty. It could be sold immediately and first thing on Monday morning she'd call the solicitors and ask how long it would take.

Now she really could move on with the rest of her life and her new career. Her mind filled with the prospect of buying a house and making a home for Aled and herself.

David appeared in the door to the kitchen and looked over at her clutching her mobile.

'Good news?' He smiled.

Caren nodded. 'Excellent news.' She beamed back at him.

Printed in Dunstable, United Kingdom